ROSIE CHAMBERS loves writing uplifting, feel-good stories set in sun-filled locations around the world. Her stories are filled with fun, friendship and foodie treats, which Rosie hopes will bring a smile to her readers' faces. She's always in the market for quirky stationery and is never happier than with a pen in one hand and a cup of tea in the other. You can follow her on Twitter @RosieCbooks

Also by Rosie Chambers

A Year of Chasing Love

Katie's Cornish Kitchen

ROSIE CHAMBERS

ONE PLACE. MANY STORIES

This novel is entirely a work of fiction. The names, characters and incidents portrayed in it are the work of the author's imagination. Any resemblance to actual persons, living or dead, events or localities is entirely coincidental.

HQ
An imprint of HarperCollins*Publishers* Ltd
1 London Bridge Street
London SE1 9GF

This edition 2020

First published in Great Britain by
HQ, an imprint of HarperCollins*Publishers* Ltd 2020

ISBN: 978-0-00-836478-6

MIX
Paper from
responsible sources
FSC™ C007454

This book is produced from independently certified FSC™ paper
to ensure responsible forest management.

For more information visit: www.harpercollins.co.uk/green

Printed and bound in Great Britain by
CPI Group (UK) Ltd, Melksham, SN12 6TR

To Ben, with love

Chapter 1

Katie removed the carefully wrapped package from her beach bag and tucked it into the battered leather satchel that hung on Maya's peg alongside her pristine apron. Her time in Bali was at an end, and whilst her stay on the Indonesian 'Island of the Gods' had been a million miles away from the romantic Parisian honeymoon she'd been dreaming of for the last twelve months, it had been the perfect escape from her misery-strewn life in London after Dominic had dropped his bombshell.

She would have preferred to melt away into the sunset, but she couldn't leave without saying goodbye to the person who had done so much to ease her heartache and help her get back on track. With a final glance around the empty kitchen-cum-class-room housed in a wooden shed at the back of Agatha's Beachside Café, Katie spun on her sparkly flip-flops and made her way to the veranda overlooking the Indian Ocean, smiling as she thought of Maya's joy when she discovered her gift the next day.

'All packed I see?' Agatha smiled, stepping from her place behind the bar to give Katie a farewell hug, her silver bangles jangling as she reached up to push her bushy salt-and-pepper curls from her eyes so she could peer more closely at her expression. 'Ready to go home?'

Katie nodded. 'Thanks, Aggie, for everything.'

'It's me who should be thanking you, darling. You've made a real impact in our cookery classes over the last few weeks. Your fabulous cake-decorating skills have definitely inspired a couple of our young students, particularly Maya, to take up sugar craft as a career, maybe in one of the big tourist hotels around the resort. That cake you created for Ed and Claire's engagement yesterday was an absolute masterpiece!'

'Oh, I loved making it just as much as your wonderful students did.'

Katie didn't add that her involvement in the project hadn't been purely altruistic; being busy had helped to keep her demons at bay. She wished she could stay longer, to continue to support Agatha's venture, but sadly her money had run out.

'Any news on the job applications?'

Katie grimaced, slumping down onto one of the tall bar stools with a view that would cause even a seasoned travel photographer to salivate – golden sandy beaches framed with whispering palm trees set against a backdrop of infinite azure skies. Add to that the bougainvillea and sweet jasmine twisted around the café's eaves, the brightly coloured surfboards ducking and diving on the waves, and the scattered offerings the locals left to appease the gods, and Katie completely understood why tourists thought the Balinese lived in paradise.

'Nothing yet,' she mumbled, tucking a stray tendril of her ruffled blonde bob behind her ear and taking a sip of the iced mint tea Agatha had set in front of her, relishing the tang of the fresh peppermint crashing over her taste buds.

Katie had shared her story with Agatha: every pain-filled detail of the wedding that had never happened, as well as the mortifying mistake she had made at work, which had culminated in her being fired from her dream job with François Dubois – supplier of bespoke celebration cakes to the rich and famous.

Even now, her cheeks flushed at the memory of the expression on the hot-tempered chef's face when he'd received a call from a TV soap actress to inform him of her disgust when, surrounded by family and friends, she had sliced into her birthday cake to find it was filled not with soft, lemony sponge, but soft, meaty dog food. It seemed that, in her trauma-filled state after Dominic's betrayal, Katie had inadvertently delivered a cake destined for a celebrity couple's beloved chihuahua's birthday instead. She had been fired on the spot and it was only now – four weeks later and thousands of miles away – that she was able to see the funny side of what had happened. However, gossip travelled like wildfire in the higher echelons of the cake-making business and the story was bouncing all over London. Perhaps she should be thinking of a change in career direction?

'Good.'

'Good? Why is it good?'

Jobless, skint and heartbroken was not the preferred state of affairs for a twenty-eight-year-old former wedding cake maker to the stars, despite the bombshell that had shattered her world.

'Because I have a proposition for you.'

'You do?'

Katie stared at Agatha, taking in the vibrant orange kaftan, the statement necklace made from wooden beads the size of golf balls, and the calm, worry-free expression on her kind face. Her friend's lithe frame and peaceful disposition were testament to her often-stated view that yoga was not just exercise, it was a way of life, but Katie hoped that Agatha wasn't going to suggest she join her for a session before she left for the airport. It would take more than a few hours of yogic harmony to change her internal dialogue of doubt from high-speed chuntering to calm, blissful acceptance, and if there was one thing she had avoided since arriving in Bali it was anything that would require her to confront her innermost emotions.

'Here.'

To Katie's surprise, Agatha reached into her handbag and,

with a theatrical flourish, produced a brown paper envelope, causing a waft of her signature jasmine perfume to invade the air between them.

'What's this?'

'Open it.'

Katie held Agatha's gaze for a moment, confusion and curiosity chasing each other's tails through the avenues of her brain. What was going on? She ran her finger under the flap and peered inside to see a large, old-fashioned iron key.

'It's a key?'

'It is.' Agatha smiled, clearly enjoying Katie's bafflement.

'What's … what's it for?'

'Something that's in my past but could be in your future.'

'My future? What do you mean?'

Katie met her friend's eyes and her heart softened. She had only known Agatha for a few weeks, but, as a fellow lover of all things culinary – particularly cake-related – they had formed an instant connection the moment she had sauntered into her Balinese café in search of a decent coffee. Their bond had deepened when they discovered they were both escapees from relationship trauma, and they were able to offer each other emotional support.

Katie had thought *her* story was painful until she heard what Agatha had been through. A former food tech teacher, her new friend had had the shock of her life when she had stumbled upon her Deputy Head husband in the broom cupboard with the gym mistress. So, after receiving the all-clear from her breast cancer diagnosis, she'd mothballed her café in a picturesque village in Cornwall to pursue her lifelong dream of attending a yoga retreat in the Balinese countryside. She'd loved the island so much she'd ended up staying, spending her divorce settlement on a dilapidated restaurant overlooking one of the most spectacular beaches in Bali. The thatched roof might let in rain and a myriad of exotic insects, but the place thrummed with positivity, cheerfulness and calm, just like its owner.

Never one to rest on her laurels, Agatha not only provided her customers with fresh, fragrant food, a listening ear and sage advice, but she also ran a cookery school in a small wooden annex at the back of the café. There she taught disadvantaged teenage girls to read, write and improve their spoken English – hence the Kindle Katie had slipped into Maya's bag – alongside the culinary skills needed to secure employment in the luxury hotels along Sanur Beach and Nusa Dua.

Agatha said she was creating good karma in the only way she knew how.

'This is the key to my café in Perrinby. I thought, as you don't have a job to go back to … well, I thought you were just the person to give it a new lease of life. What do you say?'

Katie opened her mouth but no words came out. All she could hear was the tooting horns of the ubiquitous scooters the local residents and tourists loved so much, mingled with the chirp of crickets and the soft melody of Gamelan music.

'I … you … you want me to run a café in Cornwall?'

'Yes, it might need a lick of paint, but all the bills are paid for the next three months – rates, utilities, insurances, that sort of thing – and you have all the right qualifications and skills to make a go of it.'

'Oh, Aggie, I … I'm sorry, no, I can't …'

'Of course you can, darling. I'm happy here; Bali is my home now, and I've no intention of returning to my old life in the UK. But it would be great not to have the place empty, especially as it used to be such a hub of the community with all the locals popping in. And I was thinking if you could breathe new life into the place, turn a bit of a profit, then perhaps some of those profits could be used to help with the cookery school. I'd love to take on more girls, vary the recipes we've been experimenting with so that the restaurant's customers don't get bored with the same old chocolate chip cookies after you've left. You know those banoffee cupcakes you made last week were the fastest selling dessert item in the history of Agatha's Beachside Café.'

'No, what I mean is …'

Agatha leaned forward, her eyes filled with sincerity and encouragement, but she had misinterpreted Katie's reluctance. Katie opened her mouth to explain, then closed it again. Agatha had thought she'd demurred because her offer was too much, too generous, and of course it was both of those things. But what she had really meant was that she *literally* couldn't do it. She couldn't do it because after what had happened with Dominic, she had no energy, no self-belief, no desire even, to spend the next twelve weeks of her life revitalising a run-down café in a part of the country she'd never been to and where she knew no one. She was bound to make a mess of it – just ask François about the doggie-cake debacle.

Agatha realised what was causing Katie's hesitation and she reached out to lace her fingers through hers, a gesture that caused tears to prickle at her eyes.

'Darling, you can do anything you put your mind to! Now is the perfect time to decide what exactly you want your future to look like. It's time to pursue your own dreams, just like Dominic is doing.'

A flash of pain scorched through Katie's veins as she thought of her ex-fiancé living the high life in the bars and nightclubs of Ibiza where he was trying to make it as a musician. The vibrant Mediterranean island was where Dominic, along with his best man Iain and six of his closest friends, had flown off to for his long-anticipated stag weekend, but what had totally floored her was that whilst his friends had returned home after their three-day sojourn of drink-fuelled revelry, Dominic had not. Instead of a text telling her he'd landed safely at Gatwick, she'd received one informing her that the wedding was off because he 'needed some time to think about whether marriage was the right way forward for him'.

Not only that – it had turned out that he had also emptied their wedding account of every last penny and then disappeared from her world, neatly avoiding all her efforts to contact him. If it hadn't been for her best friend, Cara, would-be chief bridesmaid, travel agent and eternal optimist, coming to her rescue with a suggestion that she transfer the already-paid-for honeymoon to something that had been on her bucket list for years, she would be looking at her sanity in the rear-view mirror.

'Katie, darling, I know what happened with Dominic was devastating, but you can't let what he did define you. Since you arrived here in Bali, I've seen lots of guys show an interest in you, but you've always turned them down. I know it's hard, but you have to learn to trust again – not everyone is like Dom.'

Katie smiled at Agatha who, by making such a generous offer, had just bestowed her with the first vote of confidence she'd had for years. However, whilst she had been open about her heartache over Dominic, she hadn't told her new friend that her issues ran far deeper than her ex-fiancé's rejection, and anyway, despite her gentle urging, she had no intention of letting anyone into her heart ever again.

'So, what do you say? Will you do this? It's the perfect solution, even if I do say so myself.'

'I don't know, Aggie ...'

Katie fiddled with the plaited leather friendship bracelets at her wrist, and when she raised her eyes and saw the hope shining in Agatha's kind, chestnut-coloured eyes, a new emotion joined the maelstrom of doubt in her chest.

Guilt.

Agatha had been through so much in the last year – her husband cheating on her, a difficult divorce, gruelling treatment for breast cancer – yet here she was chasing her dreams with vigour, with a smile on her face, a song in her heart and an eye on helping others to do the same. She loved what Agatha was doing in Bali. She loved the fact that everything her students created in her cookery school was sold in the café – nothing wasted, nothing without purpose. She wanted to help her, wanted to give something back, something more than just her Kindle. And if she did this, at least she would be busy and it would keep her abandonment demons bay.

So, trying her best to hide the reluctance in her voice, she met Agatha's gaze and nodded.

'Okay, I'll give it a go.'

'Oh, that's wonderful! I'm so pleased. I'll leave you to do your own thing, but what I'd really like you to do is to use some of that amazingly creative talent I've seen you display in the kitchen to come up with a new name for the café. Agatha's Beachside Café is a perfect name for a restaurant in sun-drenched Bali, but for the Cornish coast it just sounds so dull and boring, don't you think? Not to mention the fact that I'm over six thousand miles away and have most definitely served my last cream tea. I know you'll come up with something much more enticing to the discerning customers of Cornwall.'

'Are you … are you sure?' gasped Katie, her brain completely bamboozled by what was happening. Rename the café?

'Never more so, darling. I have complete faith in you.'

She was probably the only person on the planet who did, mused Katie as Agatha wrapped her in another jasmine-scented hug.

Over her friend's shoulder, Katie surveyed the Balinese restaurant, trying to ignore the tightening knot of anxiety in the pit of her stomach. Okay, so she might have graduated top of her class at catering college, and she *had* worked for one of the most celebrated confectionery chefs in the whole of London, but she knew nothing, nothing whatsoever, about what it took to run a village café other than what she had learned whilst helping Agatha in the cookery school and the beachside restaurant.

She decided that the least she could do was take a trip down to Cornwall to have a look at the café, give it a lick of paint and a couple of weeks, a month max, then she could admit defeat, scuttle back to London and return to her former life, minus the fiancé and the prestigious job. She only hoped that Cara's sofa was available because she couldn't afford to keep her flat on without Dominic's contribution towards the rent.

However, as Katie slid into the back seat of her airport taxi and joined the flow of bustling traffic, mingled in with the panic, the self-doubt and the fear of failure, was a tiny sparkle of excitement as ideas began to ricochet around her brain. By the time she was seated on the plane next to a woman who took bling to the next level, she was brainstorming menus – perhaps with a Balinese as well as a Cornish twist – and ideas for the perfect name for her new venture.

Chapter 2

Katie inhaled a deep breath, her heart hammering out a concerto of anguish as she realised that, at that precise moment, she should have been walking down the aisle to pledge her everlasting love to Dominic. Instead, she was standing on the doorstep of a quaint seaside café boasting a location that would have caused even the most jaded of estate agents to drool: to her left the pretty village green, complete with duck pond and whitewashed bandstand with a splash of late spring daffodils; a little further to her right a golden sandy beach, currently playing host to a handful of intrepid holidaymakers and a gaggle of bobbing sailboats.

One of the techniques Agatha had taught her when she'd arrived in Bali, battered and broken, and thinking she might keel over from the enormity of everything that had happened to her in such a short space of time, was to force herself to focus on the present. So, with difficulty, she erased the painful wedding day image that had popped into her head uninvited, slotted the heavy iron key into the lock, pushed open the door and took a few moments to survey her surroundings.

Even though the fabric of the building seemed structurally

fine, there was at least six months' worth of grime to tackle and a brigade of dust bunnies danced on every available surface, not to mention the faint aroma of disinfectant and neglect. It was a world away from the shiny, stainless steel kitchen she was used to in London where she had created her sugar-paste masterpieces under François' expert tutelage.

But that life was in the past, a place she knew she shouldn't linger for long, so she raised her chin, squared her shoulders and resolved to channel her inner Agatha as something else her friend was fond of quoting sprang to mind – every difficult journey started with a single stride. She closed her eyes and conjured up the vision that had morphed from blurry to crystal clear as ideas had bombarded her exhausted brain on the flight from Bali to Singapore, Singapore to Heathrow, and whilst she was handing over the keys to her sunny flat in Hammersmith to her po-faced landlord who couldn't wait to move the next tenant in.

Now that she could see the interior of the café, its dimensions were even better than she had dared hope. Golden shards of sunlight flooded through the magnificent bay window, which was encircled with an upholstered window seat that Katie could already see draped in the turquoise, lemon and white batik throws she'd brought back from Bali, then softened with a battalion of embroidered cushions.

She wanted to create a calm, welcoming ambience where her customers could relax and take a few precious moments away from the hustle and bustle of everyday life, so she would transform the clinical ice-blue walls with a fresh coat of ivory – or perhaps saffron? – paint and hang dreamcatchers and hand-painted papier-mâché mobiles from the ceiling. She thought of the set of carved Balinese masks she'd tucked into a corner of her suitcase, intended as a gift for Cara but which she now planned to repurpose as wall art. She knew Cara wouldn't mind; what she'd never had, she'd never mourn.

The thought of her best friend sent a warm feeling through

Katie's veins. Cara was the first person she'd called when she'd cleared customs, and her friend had been delighted to hear she was home, but less so that she was heading straight off to a tiny village in Cornwall to open up a mothballed café instead of partying hard in the wine bars and nightclubs of the West End – her personal prescription for the recovery from heartbreak. However, after listening to Cara rage for a couple of minutes about 'Dastardly Dominic, the Destroyer of Dreams', she had skilfully turned the conversation round to one of their favourite subjects – food.

'I want the café's menu to reflect not only the essence of Cornish cuisine, but also to include a few Balinese flavours too, as a nod to what Agatha's trying to do in Bali, Carr. I also want there to be as little waste as possible so I'm going for a pared-down choice of savoury dishes and cakes, and as far as possible, I want the ingredients to be fresh, locally sourced, and free from artificial additives. The coffee's going to be Fairtrade and there'll be a selection of herbal teas, and all the crockery and cutlery will be recyclable with zero use of plastics.'

'It's a fabulous mission statement, Katie. Agatha's Beachside Café sounds like the sort of place I'd love to spend a couple of hours aligning my chakras.'

Katie had wanted to keep their conversation upbeat and positive so she hadn't gone on to confide in Cara that she only had three months to make her venture work. Three months! It wasn't long to totally transform this careworn Cinderella into a sparkling princess *and* turn a profit so the business could not only pay its own running costs, but also make a contribution to Agatha's much-loved cookery school. Maybe if she was reopening the café in the summer months when the tourists descended on Cornwall in their droves, but it was the beginning of March.

Suddenly, the warm feeling in her chest was replaced by a ripple of panic as reality slapped her in the face like a wet fish. Doubts started to circle and the bubble of enthusiasm for her new adventure burst, sending her fragile confidence crashing down. There was no way she could do everything she had planned by herself, and have the café open before the Easter holidays in three weeks' time. Even if she threw herself on the mercy of the artist who owned the attractive gallery next door, offering to cook him or her an authentic Balinese meal in exchange for a few hours with a paintbrush (and sweeping brush), it was still a pointless exercise.

And yet, what else did she have to do?

She couldn't go back to London – she had nowhere to live. And she would go stir crazy moping about in the flat above the café unless she filled every minute of her day with physical activity so that the demons who pursued her every waking hour would not follow when her head hit the pillow. And last, and by no means least, she had to give it a shot for Agatha's sake, didn't she?

Katie gave herself a shake, stepped over the threshold, and turned a complete circle, taking a mental inventory of the eclectic mix of varnished pine tables and chairs crying out for a coat of pastel pink and sky blue, maybe peppermint green and soft ivory, until her gaze landed on the wide expanse of white marble countertop. A familiar tingle fizzed at her fingertips, and the urge to break out the bottle of antibacterial spray became too much to resist.

She kicked the door shut behind her, smiling at the jolly jingle of the brass bell, and went off in search of a pair of Marigolds so she could make a start on pacifying the insistent call of her hygiene monsters. The craving to scrub, to clean, to polish, was almost overwhelming – an itch that she was desperate to scratch. When she had started to work for François Dubois her colleagues had initially teased her about her preoccupation with cleanliness until they realised that it was a trait that only extended sessions with a trained therapist could cure – something she had refused to consider. She knew what the root cause of her issues was and she had no intention of going there.

Anyway, she had managed to banish her Queen of Clean tendencies when she'd met Dominic and had started to believe that, maybe, at last, there was someone in her life she could trust not to abandon her. Of course, things hadn't turned out that way and so her demons had poked their heads above the parapet once again. Her pragmatic side told her that she had to come to terms with the fact that the only person she could truly rely on was herself – but that thought terrified her so she had shoved it into the darker crevices of her mind to be unravelled at a later, much later, date.

Having gathered a selection of cleaning products from the cupboard under the sink, Katie dragged her suitcase up the flight of stairs at the back of the café and ditched it in the flower-bedecked bedroom overlooking the village green. She took a moment to appreciate the uninterrupted expanse of the deep blue ocean that could be seen from the elevated vantage point, then she skipped back down to the kitchen, filled a bowl with hot soapy water, grabbed a pair of ancient yellow Marigolds, and made a start on the bay window, the focal point of the whole café.

Before she knew it, she was in the zone, humming a Balinese tune whilst scrubbing away the tension of her long journey. She almost had a coronary when the front door burst open causing the brass bells to jangle with ferocious indignation.

'At last!'

Katie's heart crashed against her ribcage. She spun round so fast that instead of greeting the café's first visitor with grace and poise, her foot landed in the bowl of now-murky water sending a splash of heat to her cheeks.

'Ooops,' she muttered, trying to quash a nervous giggle whilst surreptitiously removing her soaking-wet Skecher and making a valiant attempt to compose herself in the face of the tall, dark, handsome stranger standing in front of her, eyeing her up and down as though she was the local comedy turn, before shooting out a smooth, well-manicured hand.

'Greg Forbes, Forbes & Mortimer,' he said, gifting her with a smile so white she almost reeled from the glare. His eyebrows rose high into his forehead as if expecting her to recognise him, and what? Swoon?

Katie accepted his outstretched palm, totally unprepared for the strength of his handshake, and couldn't prevent a small yelp from escaping her mouth, which she managed to disguise as a cough.

'Katie Campbell. Pleased to meet you, Greg.'

She took in his broad shoulders, clad in a beautifully cut designer jacket, with a starched white cotton shirt cracked open at the neck to reveal just a tantalising glimpse of mahogany chest hair. Their handshake had given him the opportunity to reveal a chunky gold Rolex, which he shook back into his cuff, his lips turning upwards slightly as he saw his mission had been accomplished.

Katie smirked. Whilst recent events had reminded her that she wasn't the *best* judge of character in the world, even the most unobservant of onlookers would have guessed which business Greg was in, if not from his sartorial choices, then certainly from the way his sharp eyes flicked around the room, sizing up its ample proportions, its southerly aspect and tantalising glimpse of the sea, whilst the words 'beachside' and 'bijou' were clearly zooming around his brain. She chanced a quick glance out of the window and when she saw the shiny BMW Z3 with alloy wheels and tinted windows lingering at the kerb like a sleek black panther ready to pounce on its unfortunate prey, her suspicions were confirmed.

'Good to meet you, too, Katie. You've no idea how happy I am to see you here.'

Greg stuffed his hands into the pockets of his suit trousers and settled his gym-toned buttocks against one of the tables as if he owned the place. A burst of heavy, spice-infused cologne mushroomed into the air between them like a nuclear fall-out cloud, causing Katie's nostrils to tickle and her lips to twitch. Greg met her eyes, bared his teeth again and, even though her heart was frozen in an impenetrable block of ice and she was completely immune to any kind of flirtation or flattery, Katie knew she was about to be treated to a high-octane charm offensive.

'I've been trying to locate the owner of this beleaguered little place for months. No one in the village seems to have the faintest idea where the elusive Agatha Carmichael might have disappeared to. Of course, it didn't take much digging to find out what happened, and I'm the last person to blame her for escaping to pastures new. Can I ask, are you a relative of hers?'

'No, I'm …'

'Good, good, well, Katie, I might just be about to make your friend Agatha a very happy woman.'

'You are?'

Greg vacated his perch on the rickety table and went to peer out of the newly sparkling front window that overlooked the row of shops on the other side of the village green – a hairdresser's, a smart bridal boutique, and a pretty florist's shop whose plate-glass window was filled with a cornucopia of colours – before twisting his head to survey the art gallery next door with the matching bay window. However, it was when his gaze settled on the sparkling sea to his right that she saw his lips twitch into a satisfied smile, and she could almost see the pound signs rolling through his eyes like a fruit machine.

'So, if you'd just give me Ms Carmichael's contact details, I'll be on my way and you can get back to your … your scrubbing?'

'Oh, yes, yes, of course, I'll just …'

'You know, instead of spending your holiday in Cornwall cleaning, you really should take in a few of the wonderful wine bars and seafood restaurants the area has to offer. If you need someone to show you around, I might be able to find a window in my diary next Tuesday?' offered Greg in the affected drawl that seemed to match his personality perfectly.

Katie found her handbag and began to riffle through the assorted paraphernalia until she located her mobile phone, praying that it still had a trickle of battery left. If she was even remotely thinking of re-joining the dating game, which she definitely was *not*, Greg Forbes would not be a swipe right!

'Actually, I'm not on holiday. I'm staying in Perrinby for a couple of months, but I don't think I'll have much time to do the tourist thing, I'm afraid.'

She turned round to find that Greg had followed her across the café to the marble counter and was standing peering over her shoulder; so close that when she saw the glint of expectation in his eye she was reminded of a pet ferret her ten-year-old neighbour had kept when she was growing up with her mother in Norfolk, which caused her to pause as she scrolled through her list of contacts.

'What do you want Agatha's number for exactly?'

'I'm going to make her an offer she can't refuse.' He smirked, raising his bushy eyebrows in a suggestive manner as he continued to loom over her, invading her personal space.

A niggle of anxiety began to worm its way through Katie's stomach, so she moved away from him towards the front door in case she needed to make a swift get-away. And yet, her curiosity was piqued.

'What kind of an offer?'

'Well, I would have thought that was obvious.'

Greg looked at her as though talking to a particularly dense toddler, his nose wrinkled with disdain as he reached into the inside pocket of his jacket, revealing an expanse of purple silk lining, and whipped out his business card with a proud flourish.

'Here!'

He handed Katie a rectangle of thick cream parchment embossed with gold lettering, which confirmed that Gregory A. Forbes was indeed the CEO of Forbes & Mortimer, high-end property developers.

'As I said, I've been trying to contact Ms Carmichael for some time, but she's proved as elusive as the Scarlet Pimpernel. Maybe she should consider taking up a position as an international spy!' Greg laughed at his own joke, a braying guffaw that reminded Katie of a strangulated donkey. 'Once she's heard what I'm prepared to shell out to add this scruffy, run-down shack to my portfolio, I'm sure she'll snap my hand off.'

The niggle of discomfort morphed into anxiety, but for a totally different reason.

'May I ask what you intend to do with the café?'

'And the flat upstairs – is it one bedroom or two, by the way?'

'It's two, but …'

'Even better!' Greg's eyes glinted like the diamond in his pinkie ring. 'It'll make a superb luxury apartment for some wealthy escapee from the London rat race to enjoy a taste of the real Cornwall, and, as an added bonus, once the renovations are complete it'll add a little bit of sophistication to this run-down seaside village. Any idea who owns the field at the back of here with those awful wooden hobbit houses on?'

Katie worked hard to conceal her reaction, to maintain her expression of polite interest in Greg's plans. Two things bounced around her brain as she slipped her phone into the back pocket of her jeans whilst Greg took the liberty of poking around in the kitchen – opening cupboard doors, switching on the lights, and generally impersonating the equivalent of a used car salesman kicking the tyres.

First of all, she knew there would be a reason why Agatha hadn't left a forwarding address with one of the other business owners in Perrinby, and she should check in with her friend before handing over her personal details. But secondly – and this was the overwhelming emotion swirling around her veins – what if she could do this? What if she could make Agatha's Beachside Café a success? And how would she know unless she tried?

She glanced out of the bay window at the spectacular view

of the beach beyond; the sand washed in a golden glow from the midday sun, a lone jet-ski rider skimming the surface of the waves like a pond-skater, a toddler collecting pebbles and shells in her castle-shaped bucket. Closer to home, she could see the ducks going about their daily business, and the owner of the bridal boutique in the process of waving goodbye to a beaming client and her chattering entourage. Ignoring the stab of pain that the unbridled joy on the bride-to-be's face caused her, Katie made her decision.

'I'm sorry, Greg, but I think I should check with Agatha before I hand over her phone number.'

She gave him her brightest smile, but to her utter astonishment Greg's face clouded, his jaw tightened and he whipped his fists from his pockets, slamming them down on the wooden table in front of her with such force that he sent a chair, and her heart, crashing onto the floor.

'God! Will you just hand it over? Anyone would have thought this Agatha woman's one of those privacy-obsessed celebrities instead of a common-or-garden domestic science teacher on the run from her failed marriage.'

Katie gaped at Greg in astonishment, but before she could say anything further the door of the café burst open to reveal a man with the most piercing blue eyes she had ever seen, his unruly blond curls sporting a natural just-tumbled-from-bed look, and his previously white T-shirt covered in splashes of paint and clay.

Despite the tenseness of the situation, her first thought was where had he left his surfboard?

Chapter 3

'I heard shouting. Is everything okay? Oh, it's *you.*'

The tone of her saviour's voice told Katie everything she needed to know – and that she had been right to withhold Agatha's details from the self-styled property tycoon. Obviously she wasn't the only one to have fallen foul of his demands.

'Don't worry, I'm leaving. I need to take a shower after spending time in this rat-infested place!' spat Greg, all previous charm evaporated as he turned to face Katie, his index finger raised. 'But make no mistake – I'll be back. And a word of advice from the wise: if you're thinking of trying to revitalise this "cute little Cornish café", then you're onto a loser. No one with an ounce of commercial acumen would even contemplate opening a new business in a village like this.'

Only when the roar of the BMW's powerful engine had melted into the distance did Katie allow herself to sink down onto one of the battered wooden chairs, her whole body besieged by a sudden bout of trembling, her heart beating hard against her ribcage after the unexpectedly upsetting encounter.

'Are you okay?'

'Yes,' she muttered. 'Thanks.'

But she wasn't. Her anxiety demons, so close to the surface

since Dominic had thrown a grenade into her carefully constructed world, had broken free of their shackles and were gleefully rampaging around her body, making it difficult for her to breathe. All she wanted to do was grab her antibacterial spray and launch into a marathon of frenzied cleaning until they retreated back into their dark and dingy cave, but she couldn't do that with an audience – that wasn't the relaxed, karma-infused first impression she had wanted to project to potential customers.

'I'm sorry to say it, but you don't look okay.' The beach-boy-lookalike smiled as he ran his fingers through his tousled curls. 'I'm Oscar, by the way, Oscar Spencer. I run the art gallery and ceramics studio next door.'

'Katie Campbell, deluded newbie café manager.'

Oscar laughed, his vivid blue eyes crinkling attractively at the corners. 'Look, why don't you come over and I'll make you a coffee?'

'Thanks, I'd love that.'

She gave Oscar a grateful smile and followed him to the adjacent building, a mirror image of the café, but that was where the similarities ended. In complete contrast to the dowdy duchess next door, the gallery was filled with warmth and light and the heady fragrance of freshly brewed coffee, buttery croissants and the wisp of citrusy cologne. The walls, ceiling and elaborate cornices were painted in gleaming white paint, and the wooden floorboards had been stripped back and whitewashed. It was fresh and clean and the perfect backdrop for the main attraction – the artwork, which adorned all available surfaces.

Everywhere she looked there were canvases of all different shapes and sizes; some mounted, some framed, some showcasing muted watercolours, others vibrant pastels, but all depicting local scenes of the Cornish countryside and, of course, the beach. Interspersed between the paintings and pencil drawings were hand-thrown ceramic pots, quirky sculptures made from drift-wood and sea glass, and on a paint-splattered easel in the far corner stood a huge canvas that Oscar had clearly been in the middle of working on when he'd heard Greg's outburst, depicting a family picnicking on a windswept beach, the parents relaxing on a red-checked blanket alongside a wicker basket, smiling indulgently at the two young boys scampering across the sand, their faces wreathed in joy as their blond hair burgeoned in the breeze. It was the best piece in the room and Katie couldn't take her eyes from it.

'Coffee. The answer to all life's traumas.'

Oscar handed Katie a mug that in a previous life had advertised a local newspaper but now sported splodges of clay and sunflower-yellow paint. She smiled her thanks and took a sip, inhaling the delicious, taste-bud-tingling aroma that she relied on to wake her up every morning.

'So, welcome to Perrinby. I'm sorry I didn't come round to introduce myself earlier but I had no idea that Agatha had decided to lease the café. I hope your encounter with our local property rottweiler hasn't put you off. I've only been here for six months, but I can assure you that everyone in the village is exceptionally friendly and welcoming. We all have as little to do with Greg Forbes as possible in case he swoops in and snatches our "prime seafront real estate" from under our noses.'

'Ah, so that's why no one would hand over Agatha's details?'

'Yes. Oh, no, you didn't …'

Katie laughed at the look of panic that spread across Oscar's handsome face.

'No, I didn't, but I nearly did.'

'Thank God for that.' Oscar swiped the back of his hand across his forehead in a theatrical gesture, his lips twisting into a cute smirk before becoming more serious. 'Forbes & Mortimer has already been instrumental in killing off one community over the border in Devon after the company bought up two vacant shops, eradicated every last smidgeon of character from the buildings, and then sold them on as second homes, despite the objections of the local residents who were desperate to maintain a viable business community. It wasn't long before the only remaining shop closed down and now the village has no amenities whatsoever, which is something the people of Perrinby are fighting to avoid.'

Oscar grabbed a white wooden chair and swung it round to sit astride, peering at Katie from over the rim of his coffee cup with interest.

'So, is running a café in Cornwall a long-held dream of yours?'

Oscar was regarding her with such obvious hope that she averted her gaze to concentrate on her own coffee. How could she confess that her plan was to give the café a quick lick of paint, toss a few colourful throws and woven mats about the place and then, when the whole enterprise failed on its feet, she would post the keys back to Agatha and admit that her friend's faith in her had been misplaced?

'I ...'

'*Salut!* Am I right in thinking you're our new arrival? *Cherie*, welcome.'

Before Katie knew what was happening, she found herself engulfed in a fragrant hug and in receipt of two exuberant air kisses. When she was eventually released, she saw a tall, slender guy, dressed head-to-toe in black – hand-stitched leather loafers, designer jeans and skin-tight T-shirt that accentuated his impressive physique – with a skin-care regime to rival the world's top models and a manicure that caused a spasm of jealousy. With his sexy French accent and neatly barbered mahogany quiff, he was the complete opposite to the surfer-dude look Oscar rocked.

'Katie, allow me to introduce you to Javier Bertrand ...'

'Oscar, darling, you know my friends call me Jay!'

Katie laughed. 'Hi, Jay, pleased to meet you.'

'Likewise, darling. If there's one thing this village desperately needs, it's fresh faces. Has Oscar told you that we threw a spectacular party when he arrived to take over this gorgeous little art gallery? Bunting, toffee apples, chocolate brownies, mulled wine, fireworks, the lot!'

'It was Hallowe'en, Jay!' Oscar smirked, rolling his eyes in Katie's direction. 'And if that party *was* for me it was more likely to send me running for the hills – some of those costumes were particularly gruesome, especially Ruby's. Coffee?'

'Oh, you're an absolute saviour! Not a drop has passed my lips since five o'clock this morning. I've had a particularly highly strung bride to talk down from a precipice of panic after her nan told her that according to some ancient folklore yellow roses are a no-no at a wedding. And then Talia messed up the Bradshaw order, sending Arthur Madeley's funeral wreath to Gertie Farrier's sixtieth birthday celebrations. You know, that girl is a complete liability – I have no idea how Agatha put up with her at the café.'

'Talia used to waitress for Agatha before she left for Bali,' explained Oscar as he handed a black coffee over to Jay. Katie couldn't prevent a splutter of amusement from escaping her lips when she saw Jay's upper lip curl at the sight of the misshaped earthenware mug covered in dribbles of bright orange oil paint. 'And in case you haven't guessed, Jay owns the florist's shop across the road – Bootylicious Bouquets – although he also doubles up as custodian of the village grapevine.'

'Is it wrong to take a healthy interest in other people's business?' And as if to prove himself worthy of his Badge of Honour, Jay removed his gold-rimmed John Lennon sunglasses and fixed Katie with his razor-sharp hazel eyes, making her feel as if he was scouring her soul for her innermost secrets. 'So, Katie, how do you know our wonderful Agatha?'

Katie had no intention of sharing her full history with Oscar and Jay. She knew the pain of her broken relationship reflected in her eyes; she was dealing with that, but it was still a work in progress. She didn't want them to feel sorry for her, to know that someone she had invested her trust in had gone on to abandon her without so much as a backward glance. Coming to Cornwall was an opportunity to start again, and that meant disguising her broken heart and shattered dreams.

'Oh, I met her when I was on an extended backpacking holiday in Bali and we clicked straight away. I loved what she was trying to do there, especially the cookery school she's set up to train disadvantaged teenagers in the skills needed to find work in the hotels, guesthouses and restaurants in Sanur. I helped her to run a couple of workshops on sugar craft – which is kind of my specialised subject.'

'So she's doing okay over there then, is she?' asked Jay, his features softening.

'More than okay.' Katie laughed, her thoughts scooting back to her new friend and the person she had to thank for setting her on the road towards a new future. 'She's really embraced the Balinese way of life; she practises yoga daily, wears a sarong, leaves regular offerings for the gods, and is giving lots back to the local community.'

'And she's managed to chase away the demons of her past?'

'Absolutely! I can honestly report that she's happier than she's ever been – her words, not mine. Whenever I was in her company, no matter how hot and sweaty the kitchen got, I felt calm, relaxed – as though the turmoil of the outside world was a million miles away. Actually, I'm thinking of adding a twist of Balinese serenity when I revamp the café – focusing on kindness and consideration for others – as well as trying out a few Indonesian cake recipes alongside the typically Cornish fayre.'

Katie could hear the note of pride in her voice and her cheeks coloured. She was surprised she felt so attached to her idea when it was currently only an image in her imagination, albeit a vibrant one.

'*Alors*, I love it!' declared Jay, his eyes sparkling with excitement. 'Great branding choice – I can totally picture the ambience of *le petit café* from just those three little words – kindness, community and cake. I see natural fabrics, carved wooden mobiles, maybe a wind chime or two, and I *might* be able to rustle up some gardenias and frangipani for a little floral authenticity. So, are you planning to completely redecorate?'

'I was, but to be honest, I'm not sure I'm up to the task …'

'Well.' Oscar laughed, running his paint-encrusted fingernails through his curls and making them stand to attention. 'If you need any help in that department, I'm a dab hand with a paintbrush, even if I do say so myself.'

Katie hesitated. Was it fair to drag Oscar into a doomed project? Surely he had better things to do with his time than decorating a shabby old café. However, she could see from the excitement on his face that his offer had been genuine, not to mention the fact that she could do with all the help she could get if she was to have any chance at all of throwing open the doors before Agatha's money ran out.

'Thanks, that would be great.'

'Good answer!' pronounced Oscar, jumping up from his chair. 'And when there's work to be done, there's no time like the present. In fact, I've got a couple of tins of white paint left over from when I did this place somewhere. Hang on, I'll go and fetch them and we can make a start this afternoon.'

Katie watched Oscar disappear through a door at the back of the gallery where she caught a tantalising glimpse of a potter's wheel and an industrial-sized kiln. She looked away when she saw him bend down to collect a packet of paintbrushes, his tattered jeans tightening to enhance the curve of his taut buttocks, the sleeves of his T-shirt straining against his muscular biceps.

'Gorgeous, isn't he?' Jay smiled, a teasing twinkle in his eyes. 'Erm … I …'

'If my heart hadn't already been snatched by a certain cordon bleu chef …' he mused wistfully.

Jay was right. In another world, in another life, she could see herself enjoying more than just Oscar's laid-back, friendly company. However, love, in all its guises, was a foreign country

26

for her – a place where she had no intention of straying. And yet, there was something about Oscar that drew her towards him, something vulnerable in his demeanour, something that he too was hiding from the world. She could see it in his eyes, in the fleeting shadow of sadness that was probably only apparent to someone who had suffered a similar trauma. But that was neither here nor there; relationships meant rejection and she had resolved to never trust anyone with her fragile heart again – even if he did look like a blond Aidan Turner.

Oscar reappeared, clutching two large tins of brilliant white emulsion in one hand, three smaller tins of paint in the other, and a battery of rollers, brushes and cloths poking out from a bright orange bucket that was hanging over his wrist.

'Okay, so I have pink sorbet, peppermint green and periwinkle blue. What do you think?'

'Absolutely perfect! Just what I was planning for the tables and chairs.'

'And, of course, it's a yes from me,' added Jay.

'Okay, let's go!'

Katie found she was grinning. A session of extreme painting was just like a session of extreme cleaning and she suddenly couldn't wait to get started. She said goodbye to Jay who had to dash back to his shop to make sure Talia hadn't killed off all his flowers, not to mention his business, and she and Oscar carried the decorating materials into the café. When the bell tinkled its welcome, an unexpected feeling of homecoming suffused her chest – which lasted all of five seconds until Oscar uttered his next sentence and sent her spirits crashing to the ground.

'You're going to love it here, Katie. I can't wait to tell everyone that our little village café will be open for business next week. It's exactly what we need to help revitalise our community, just like Agatha is doing in Bali. It's the perfect way to keep wolves like Greg from lingering around our doors.'

Oh, God, what had she done! If she couldn't make a success of the café in the next three months, not only would she be letting Agatha down, it looked like she'd be letting the whole community of Perrinby down too.

Chapter 4

'Oh my God, Cara, I've never been so exhausted in my entire life!'

Katie sat at the breakfast bar in the galley kitchen in the flat above the café, her chin in her hand as she filled her best friend in on the trials and tribulations of her first day in Perrinby. She had approached the afternoon's decorating challenge in the same way as she approached her need to scrub everything until it sparkled – with obsessive enthusiasm. She just wished she could spring-clean her life in the same way.

Every muscle in her body, including some she hadn't even known existed, screamed its objection to the unaccustomed exertion, but that was nothing compared to the emotional turmoil churning through her veins as she realised the extent of the task she had taken on.

'What? You mean you haven't spent the day sunbathing on those gorgeous Cornish beaches, treating yourself to a seafood lunch at a coastal shack hidden in the sand dunes or hooking up with a bunch of hunky windsurfers?'

'That's what I *should* have been doing. What's the point of spending the whole day and half the night painting the café and all its furniture when it's obvious that the practical solution would be to just sell the place to Greg, then Aggie can use the

29

proceeds to invest in her café in Bali and the cookery school and …'

'And you can run away and continue to lick your Dominic-shaped wounds?'

'No. It happens to be the sensible business option …'

'Why do you think Agatha hasn't done that already? The café's been empty for six months. If she wanted to sell it and use the proceeds to expand her business empire, then don't you think she would have put it up for sale when she decided to stay on in Bali?'

'I suppose …'

'When she gave you the key, she was clear what she wanted you to do. To give the café a new lease of life, hopefully generate enough income to keep it ticking over and, if possible, make a contribution to her pet project in Sanur.'

'But what's the point? The whole thing's doomed to fail, so why even try? The bills are only paid for the next three months so that gives me until the end of May. No one with an ounce of commercial acumen would even contemplate opening a new business at this time of the year in these economically uncertain times.'

Katie cringed when she realised that she had inadvertently strayed into Greg-Forbes-speak.

'But what do you have to lose? Agatha will still be in the same position whether the café's a success or not. I'm batting for the winning team – Team Katie. Look, darling, I know your self-confidence took a bit of a knock when Dom …'

'A bit of a knock? I sent my fiancé off on a stag weekend to Ibiza. And. He. Never. Came. Back! That's not just careless, it's tragic!'

'Katie …'

'*And* he stole every last penny we'd saved to pay for the weeding – ten thousand pounds! I don't have a bean to my name.'

'Okay, okay, so you've experienced a life-changing event. But another way of looking at it is that you've been given the opportunity to reassess your life goals and to pursue a new direction. Don't forget, I know you better than anyone. The only reason you weren't out there chasing your lifelong dream of owning your own cake-decorating business was because you were too busy helping Dastardly Dominic to chase his! I loathe what Dominic did to you, Katie, but you know what? A small part of me sort of respects ...'

'Respects?'

'Yes, I *respect* that he knows what he wants and he's single-mindedly going for it. It's time for you to accept what's happened, put it behind you and move on, too.'

'Oh God, oh God ...'

Katie dropped her head onto the countertop. Surely her best friend, her staunchest supporter when her world had imploded, wasn't defending what Dominic had done? She knew that the first stage in recovery from any trauma was acceptance – but how could she accept what she couldn't understand? Dominic still hadn't returned any of her calls, and apart from that solitary text he'd sent telling her the wedding was off and he was staying on in Ibiza, he'd not even had the decency to take the time out of his busy schedule to explain to her the reasons why he had left her in such a cruel and humiliating way.

What had she done wrong? If he wouldn't tell her, how could she get closure, like Cara was suggesting, or even start work on self-improvement?

But then Dominic wasn't the only one who had left her without a backward glance and she suspected that even if he *had* afforded her the respect of coming back from his stag weekend to tell her face to face why he was breaking off their engagement a mere four weeks before their wedding, she would still harbour these feelings of self-doubt. To recover, *properly* recover, from the agony that slumbered like a lead balloon in the pit of her stomach, there was someone else she needed to have that talk with and she had no intention of going there – it was too painful, as well as too late.

'I wasn't going to tell you, but I bumped into Iain last week,' continued Cara, her voice carefully level. 'Apparently, he still gets the odd email from Ibiza, and he told me that Dominic's just landed himself a residency at one of the big hotels in San Antonio. You know he's wanted to be in a band since he could hold a microphone and it looks like, at last, his ambitions have come to fruition.'

'Only because he could afford to live for free on our wedding fund.'

'I'm not condoning what he did, I'm simply saying that unless you chase your dreams, *single-mindedly* and without concern for anyone else, then no one is going to do it for you. This is your chance, Katie, now, down there in Cornwall, and you have to grasp it with both hands and hold on tight for the bumpy journey ahead, even if there's no safety net to catch you if you fall. So what if you fail? What's going to happen? Agatha's going to shrug her yoga-toned shoulders, meditate on it for a while at one of those spiritual retreats she loves so much, and then put it down to experience. She'll be no worse off than when she handed you the key.'

'Apart from the cash she's transferred into my bank account to buy ingredients for the menu.'

'Look, maybe you're right, maybe she will decide to sell and if she does, that's her prerogative, too, and if everything goes pear-shaped, as you seem to want to believe it will, then there'll always be a space on my sofa for you.'

'Thanks, Cara.'

'So, tell me what this Cornish property mogul is like? Is he tall, dark and broodingly handsome like Aidan Turner, all bare-chested, rippling biceps and wielding a scythe – just how I like my men?'

'No, Cara, he's not.'

'Are you sure?'

'Even if he *were* attractive – which he's not – he's the village's sworn enemy. If I even so much as shared a coffee with him, I think I would be lynched.'

'Mmm, you know me, always up for a challenge when it comes to love. Remember Luke?'

'He wasn't a challenge; he was a liability.'

Katie giggled as she remembered the hapless actor Cara had dated in the months leading up to Christmas the previous year, during which he spent most nights at the local theatre rehearsing for his role in the town's pantomime. They had nabbed front-row seats, arrived early with huge bags of popcorn and a sneaky bottle of Prosecco, only to reach the end of the production with no idea which part Luke had played ... until he emerged, grinning, from backstage with the pantomime horse's head under his arm.

'And what about the artist guy from next door? Oliver, did you say his name was?'

'Oscar.'

'Like the golden trophy? Is *he* a potential love interest?'

Oh no! Cara was from the same school of soul-scouring as Jay when it came to slicing through her carefully crafted defences, so she knew she needed to feign nonchalant disinterest and construct her reply with caution.

'I'm not going to fall into your trap, Carr. Oscar is simply a kind neighbour helping out a fellow business owner. After all, it's in his interest for there to be a thriving café next door to his art gallery. You never know, after indulging in a pot of Earl Grey tea – which, I'll have you know, is grown right here in Cornwall – and a slice of my deliciously fragrant carrot-and-walnut cake – which will be made with organic carrots – a customer might be more inclined to pop in and browse his hand-thrown mugs and matching cake stands. Anyway, he's probably got a girlfriend.'

'Ah, so you *have* thought about his relationship status.'

'No, I have not!'

Cara laughed and Katie joined in, enjoying the therapeutic effect laughter delivered, which went some way to ease the tension that had been steadily mounting as her few days in Perrinby wore on and she realised how much work she had to do before the café would be ready to serve its first infusion of peppermint, chamomile or lemon verbena tea. Suddenly, the task ahead didn't seem quite so insurmountable when she had Cara in her corner, shaking the cheerleading pompoms.

In fact, if she ignored the intimidating spectre of Greg Forbes lurking around on the periphery of her brain, the thought of being proactive in making a new future for herself as Cara had advocated, of reconfiguring her dreams without having to take account of anyone else's, ignited a tiny spark of optimism – something that had been in short supply since Dominic had left.

'So you'll give it a go?'

'Yes, I will.'

Her spirits edged up another notch at having made a final decision to commit to the project. Running away was the easy option, but she had done that and bought the tie-dye T-shirt in Bali. Now it was time to face her future head-on and follow the right path, not the one of least resistance.

Chapter 5

The next week was filled with a flurry of activity. Whilst she had a clear vision of how she wanted the café to look, she still had a great deal of work to do on preparing what was going to feature on the menu. It was important to her that the café offered fresh and above all delicious dishes, whilst keeping in mind her other requirements – locally sourced and with an aim to produce zero food waste, which she hoped to achieve by offering a pared-down list of items on the daily menu.

She also wanted to reduce her use of plastic and place recycling at the heart of everything she produced. However, her vision was about more than the setting and the food, it was about the ambience, the tranquil atmosphere, the experience of spending a few precious moments indulging in a short break from the constant hustle and bustle of daily life. She would take Jay up on his offer to supply her with fresh flowers and she intended to approach the local college to enquire if any of their music students would like their song list played at the café – she wanted to continue what Agatha had started in Bali and give something back to the community.

She had also decided to use the last of her savings – money she'd put by to surprise Dominic on their wedding day with a voucher for an all-day session in a recording studio so he could make a professional demo of his music, plus whatever was left of her security deposit after her landlord sent her the snagging list – to invest in new aprons, tea towels and table linen made from organic cotton and embroidered with a seaside-inspired design. Now that she had made a commitment to the café, she intended to give it everything she had. If nothing else, hard work had the benefit of keeping her demons at bay and she was pleased to see that she hadn't thought of her ex-fiancé living the high life on their hard-earned wedding fund for over thirty minutes – that was progress, wasn't it?

However, as the week sped by and opening day loomed, it became increasingly apparent that she couldn't run the café by herself – she needed help. She needed an experienced waitress, someone who could slide straight in and hit the ground running, and before she had thought it through properly, she had shared her dilemma with Jay who had nipped over for a cup of his ubiquitous black coffee and a slice of the caramelised apple cake topped with cider buttercream and hazelnut brittle that she had been trialling that afternoon.

'Oh my God, darling, I have the perfect solution!'

'You do?'

'Yes! Hang on.'

And to her surprise, he popped the last of his cake into his mouth and shot out of the café leaving an industrial-strength cloud of oriental aftershave in his wake. Every day that week Jay had made it his mission to call on her, to ask how she was getting on, never deviating from his favourite outfit of black dress pants and an open-necked black shirt with sleeves rolled up his forearms to reveal a tantalising ripple of espresso-coloured hairs. She wondered if he'd been a model on the Parisian catwalks before coming to run a florist's shop in deepest darkest Cornwall and if so, why he had given it up. There was a story there and she intended to find it. Jay wasn't the only purveyor of grapevine gossip.

Within minutes, Jay reappeared holding a huge bouquet of pale-pink roses aloft, which should have been her first clue.

'Ta-dah! These are for you, darling.'

'Thanks, Jay, I—'

'And allow me to introduce you to the wonderful Talia. Talia, this is Katie Campbell – she's the brave soul who's taken over this abandoned old café from Agatha and is intent on turning it into a sparkling princess fit to greet her very own Prince Charming. And guess what? She's looking for a someone to provide all her waitressing needs!'

Jay looked so pleased with himself that Katie relegated his previous comments about Talia's floral ineptitude to the back of her mind – maybe she was better at serving salmon sandwiches than twisting twine around tulips. Anyway, desperate times called for desperate measures if she was going to be ready to open the café on time tomorrow night.

'Hi Katie, I've heard all about you from Oscar.'

Katie took one look at the erstwhile trainee florist and liked her immediately. With a sleek sheet of toffee-coloured hair poking from under a clashing moss green hat that looked like it had been hand-woven from floristry tape, she looked more sixties flower-power girl than twenty-first-century teenager. Instead of the standard outfit of knee-less washed-out jeans and T-shirt, she sported a geometric-patterned jumpsuit and a pair of raffia wedges.

'Hi, Talia, it's great to meet you.'

'Oh, I knew I was going to meet you today, *and* that you would be offering me my old job back.'

'You did?' Katie smiled, wondering how she could possibly have known that when she hadn't known herself.

'Yes, it was written in the stars – well, my horoscope to be precise. I'm a Libra, you see, and today is the day when I'm going to be offered something that's going to change my life for ever.'

Katie's heart sank. Not another resident of Perrinby whose

future she held in the palm of her hand! She didn't think she could cope with the pressure. Maybe it would be better all-round if she found someone else to help her in the café – on a temporary basis, on the understanding that it would be a strict three-month contract only – instead of being the person responsible for Talia's destiny. She could feel a headache coming on just thinking about it.

'Oh my God. These are just amazing! Did you make them, Katie? They're like something out of a French patisserie shop window!'

Talia reached for one of the clotted cream cupcakes decorated with swirls of home-made strawberry jam buttercream and topped with sugar-paste butterflies that Katie had made the previous night when the sleep fairies had eluded her. It had been a while since she had really indulged in a session of extreme cake baking and sugar crafting, and she had pulled out all the stops just so she could convince herself that she could still produce a cake worthy of tempting the paying public to part with their cash.

She had also whipped up a huge chocolate sponge, covered it with ganache and decorated the top with the immortal words: Agatha's Beachside Café. The result, at two o'clock in the morning, had added another golden coin of contentment to her depleted coffers, knowing that in culinary terms at least, she could still hack it – there was not a splodge of dog food in sight!

'I'm glad you like them – they're for the launch party tonight, and I've just got to put the finishing touches to two vats of home-made soup.'

'Which, might I add, smells absolutely divine,' said Jay, laying his palm on his chest as he inhaled the fragrance of lemon grass and coconut milk. 'I'll be waiting in line on your doorstep at six o'clock sharp.'

'Count me in, too,' announced Oscar, appearing on the threshold, snatching up one of the cupcakes and devouring it in one mouthful as though not a crumb of sustenance had passed his lips all day. He then rolled his eyes in theatrical ecstasy when the flavours hit his taste buds. '*Am … az … ing*! You should do this for a living.'

'Funny.'

Katie paused to take in everything she had achieved in the space of just over a week. The window seat was now upholstered in a vibrant multi-striped fabric – with a couple of cream lamb's wool rugs she'd found in Agatha's old bedroom to add some texture – upon which she had arranged a cornucopia of cushions, from fuchsia to orange, turquoise to saffron, embroidered, sequinned, and tie-dyed. There were dreamcatchers and wind chimes and fairy lights framing the window and several exotic flower arrangements that showcased Jay's indubitable talents to perfection.

To break up the clinical starkness of the white walls, Oscar had donated several of his more exuberant paintings, and along with the pastel-painted furniture, the eclectic vibe was complete. Bright spring sunlight sliced through the wide bay window and a CD player pumped out a mix of soft jazz tunes. Even without the benefit of customers, the whole café exuded a laid-back, positive, relaxing feel that she hoped reflected what she was trying to achieve: a place to escape and enjoy a treat that wouldn't cost the earth – in both senses of the word.

She loved it all, but she knew the reason everything was on track for that evening's launch – to which she had invited all the local business owners and their families – was down to the energetic enthusiasm and hard work of Oscar and Jay. It was truly community spirit in action from the outset and she vowed to offer them her own support in return.

'What's this?' asked Talia, peering into a huge glass jar that Katie had given pride of place on the marble counter.

'That's just an idea I had …'

Katie paused, unsure whether her new friends would laugh at what she had done.

'Are these Post-it stickers?' asked Oscar, sticking his hand into the container and choosing a luminous yellow one. *A compliment costs nothing.*

'It's my good karma jar. It's filled with inspirational quotes and ideas on how to add just a tiny bit of kindness to everyone's day.'

'Wow, that's a fantastic idea! My turn, my turn,' declared Talia, pushing a bemused Oscar out of the way and dipping in, pulling out a Kermit-coloured piece of paper. '*Follow your Dreams.* Oh, oh, I've got an idea for one. Can I add it to the jar?'

'Of course, that's exactly what I was intending.' Katie smiled, pointing to a selection of Post-it pads and a handle-less mug crammed with different coloured pens.

'Mine's *Dance Naked in the Rain!*'

'I'm adding *Take a Moment to Smell the Roses,*' said Jay, reaching for a pen.

'What about *Don't Sweat the Small Stuff?*'

'What about *Treat Yourself to one of Ruby's Marvellous Manicures?*' suggested a voice with a singsong Caribbean accent from the café's front door.

'Katie, this is Ruby who owns the village's fantastically fabulous hair salon and beauty parlour,' announced Jay as though introducing Katie to the patron at the Royal Spring Ball. 'What this lady can't do with a comb and a can of extra-strength hairspray isn't worth knowing about.'

'Hello, Katie, welcome to Perrinby.'

'Thanks, Ruby.'

'Well?'

Ruby turned to face Jay with her hands on her ample hips, a look of impatience on her attractive face. Katie immediately understood how Jay maintained such an impressive beauty regime – it was obviously courtesy of Ruby.

'Oh, my God, darling, I'm *sooo* sorry! I'm late for my waxing, aren't I?'

'By fifteen minutes!'

'Come on, Talia, Oscar, let's leave Katie to don her glad rags and do something with that wild hair of hers for Perrinby's party of the decade.'

Katie watched everyone follow Ruby across the village green before returning to the kitchen, a place she was much more comfortable in.

Chapter 6

Anxiety gnawed in the pit of Katie's stomach as she stirred in the last of the ingredients to the two huge pans of soup she had prepared using the vegetables she'd bought from the organic farm in the next village, giving one an Indonesian twist and the other a Cornish flavour with a generous dollop of cream from a local dairy. She had arranged the cakes, all seventy-two of them, on the pretty vintage cake stands loaned to her by Talia's mum, Zoe, who ran the bridal boutique, and there were matching teacups and saucers that Agatha had used in the café.

Finally, she managed to carve out ten minutes to hop into the shower and rinse off the day's grit and grime before pulling on a short tangerine-coloured shift dress she'd bought for the equivalent of few pounds at a Balinese night market. A surge of contentment washed away her earlier bout of apprehension as she added the necklace-and-bracelet-combo her mum had sent over from Greece to wish her luck for the grand opening the following day, along with a letter insisting that Katie posted lots of photographs of the event on her social media accounts so she could show off her wonderful daughter's achievements to all her fellow horse-obsessed friends at the riding retreat she helped to run in the Cretan countryside.

A smile tugged at Katie's lips when she thought of all the support and encouragement she had received from her mum in the weeks following the implosion of her carefully planned wedding arrangements, particularly the threat she had issued to fly over to Ibiza and scour every bar and nightclub in San Antonio until she found Dominic so she could punch him in the nose and give him a piece of her mind. A rush of much-needed confidence spread through her veins. If her mum could embark on a brand-new life among strangers – *and* in a completely different country – after everything she had been through, then she could too.

'Hi, need any help with anything?'

'Oh, hi, Oscar. No, I think everything's sorted, thanks.'

Katie was delighted to see that Oscar had dressed for the occasion, sporting a pair of splatter-free dark-blue jeans and a freshly laundered pale-pink shirt with the cuffs turned back to show off his tanned forearms, with his halo of golden curls as wild as ever. Despite being sworn off romance for life, she could still appreciate an attractive guy when she saw one. She felt a frisson of electricity shoot through her body when their fingers touched as he handed her a bundle of cards, sending a whoosh of delicious lemony cologne into the air between them.

'What's this?'

'It's a café-warming gift.'

Oscar reached out to select the first of the cards and took a step to the left, unravelling the banner as he went until the garland of letters, painted in the same pastel shades as the café's furniture, spelled out the words 'Welcome to Agatha's Beachside Café'.

'Oh, my goodness, thank you, Oscar. I love it!'

Before she'd connected her brain to its modem she had flung her arms around him and given him a hug, then shot backwards to smooth down the creases in her dress when she realised what she'd done – it was the closest physical contact she'd had with a man since Dominic and it felt weird. However, there was no awkwardness; Oscar simply beamed with delight at her reaction and set about draping the hand-made sign across the entrance to the café.

Next to arrive was Jay, carrying the biggest bouquet of frilly pink peonies Katie had ever seen, and accompanied by the most adorable labradoodle puppy sporting a gem-encrusted collar. Jay reached down to scoop up the little dog waiting patiently next to her master's hand-crafted leather loafers for an introduction. Katie wished someone would look at her with the same adoration she saw in the dog's chocolate-brown eyes.

'This little bundle of joy is Dotty. Say hello to our new friend, Dotty.'

'Woof!'

'Hello, Dotty,' said Katie, giving the dog a scratch between her ears and receiving a friendly lick for her trouble.

'Hey, everyone, it's me!' cried Talia, bursting through the door and sending the bell into a fierce frenzy of clanging.

It took Katie every ounce of her willpower not to gasp when she saw what her new waitress was wearing on her head that night. Without wanting to seem overcurious, she assumed that it couldn't possibly be what it looked like. Fortunately, Jay wasn't quite as circumspect after he'd popped his eyes back into their sockets.

'Loving the new hat, Talia!'

'Thanks, Jay. My horoscope said that if I wanted to make an impression tonight, I had to dress to impress so I thought I'd channel my inner unicorn. So ...'

'Ah, so that's a unicorn horn, then?' Oscar smirked, his lips twisting as he too tried to conceal his amusement. 'Any reason you chose to make it out of luminous pink satin?'

'Mum had a couple of metres left over from a bridesmaid's dress she made for Becca and Freddie's wedding next month, so I pinched it to make this. What do you think? Honestly?'

'It's ... well ... it's very ... *pointy*? But you know what? I'm not sure Perrinby is ready for such an exhibition of innovative creativity. Why don't you leave it in the kitchen until the party's over? I take it, then, that you're hoping that the object of your affections is intending to grace us with his presence this evening?'

Talia's whole face lit up. 'I hope so. And good karma dictates that as I helped him to blow up the Valentine's night balloons for the pub's Romance & Risotto night last month, then tonight could just be the night when he asks me out on a date. Things have a way of turning out right in the end.'

And Talia trotted off to the kitchen where, to Katie's relief, she removed her phallic-shaped hat and tied on her brand-new apron, an item of supreme good taste in rich cream linen with the words Agatha's Beachside Café embroidered on the front with peppermint-coloured thread. Katie didn't have the heart to tell Talia that, actually, sometimes things *didn't* work out in the end, so she crossed her fingers and sent up a missive to whoever was in charge of Talia's astrological chart that day to ask if they could weave a little magic in the romance department.

'Who's the object of her affections?' Katie asked Oscar, aware she sounded like a fully paid-up member of Jay's village gossip network.

'Ryan Murray – his parents own the Hope & Anchor. Talia's had her eye on him for the last few months ever since her horoscope told that her that one true love could be found among the hops and barley of ancient times, or something like that.'

'Well, if you want my opinion, he's crazy if he doesn't ask her out.'

'Oh, but the poor boy's terrified,' interjected Jay, a smirk on his face as he fed a morsel of apple cake to an appreciative Dotty.

'Terrified? Why?'

'Doh! Her mother runs the bridal boutique.'

'So?'

Oscar and Jay stood watching Katie, identical expressions on their faces as they waited for the penny to drop.

'Oh, so he thinks that if he asks her out for a coffee, he'll

45

end up kidnapped, dressed up in a morning suit and cravat, and frogmarched down the aisle before he has the chance to say, "hold your horses"? That's crazy!'

'Wait until I tell you about Talia's sister, darling. The very first guy Melanie took home to meet Zoe, our very own intrepid wedding dress designer and all-round bride whisperer, is living proof that Ryan's fear is no flight of fancy, but founded on fact. The poor man didn't stand a chance – the couple were married three months later and he's now the proud father of twin boys, a particularly energetic Jack Russell, and a bright-orange campervan. *Now* do you understand why Ryan's more of a let's-just-be-friends kind of a person? Anyone who so much as sets foot in Confetti Carousel is doomed! There's some kind of weird aura about the place. Maybe it's all the astrology stuff Talia's got going on, or it could be the crazy hat collection, I don't know, but you can't blame Ryan for giving it a wide berth. So, Katie, you are hereby warned … unless of course you're *looking* to get hitched in the next couple of months?'

Jay had meant it as a joke, but the mention of weddings caused a spasm of pain to slice right through her chest and drill deep into her heart and she knew her reaction showed on her face.

'Ooops sorry,' said Jay, his hand flying to his mouth in horror, yet his eyes sparkled with interest. 'Have I hit a bit of a nerve, perchance?'

'No, not at all. Now, let's crack open the fizz, shall we?' she said, turning her back on Jay and reaching for a bottle of sparkling wine she had sourced directly from the Cornish vineyard that grew the grapes.

Oscar had remained silent during Jay's monologue against matrimony, but he'd been watching Katie closely and decided to come to her rescue before his friend engaged his razor-sharp interrogation techniques any further.

'Okay, troops, it's exactly six o'clock. Positions please – let's make this launch party the best bash Perrinby has ever seen!'

46

Chapter 7

Famous last words.

It was as far from the *best party Perrinby had ever seen* as you could get. A total of seven people turned up and that included Oscar, Jay and Talia. After an awkward hour of forced jollity during which Katie's desire to grab the antibacterial spray became almost overwhelming, they admitted defeat and Jay took Dotty home, ostensibly for her late-night walk around the village green, but Katie knew he was going to knock on a few doors to find out why no one had turned up — she could almost hear the village grapevine humming.

'I'm so sorry, Katie, I don't know what to say,' murmured Oscar as he closed the door behind Jay.

'I'm going to kill Ryan when I see him,' declared Talia, removing her apron and hanging it on the back of the kitchen door. 'He promised faithfully that he'd come across with a few of his mates after the match finished.'

'It's okay, guys, it's not your fault,' said Katie, her light tone fooling no one. 'I'm not sure what I'm going to do with these two huge pans of soup, though, not to mention a mountain of cupcakes as tall as Everest.'

Silence reverberated around the little café that seemed to have lost all its earlier positivity and taken on the forlorn air of a wallflower left on the sidelines at a high school dance. The anxiety demons began to tighten their strings around Katie's throat, but she fought valiantly not to give in to their lure, determined to maintain a cheerful façade after everything Oscar, Jay and Talia had done to help make the café's launch a success. It wasn't their fault it hadn't worked out.

But what if it was a taste of things to come? What if, when the café opened to the public the next day, she had no customers? At this rate, she wouldn't need three months to convince herself that coming to Cornwall was a fool's errand. Perhaps she shouldn't even bother opening? Quit whilst she was ahead?

'You know, I read your horoscope this morning, too, Katie,' mused Talia, jumping up to sit on the marble counter, swinging her legs as she flicked her long butterscotch-coloured hair behind her ears and looking a lot younger than her eighteen years.

Oh no, thought Katie, *here we go*.

'You're a Leo, right?'

'I am, although I'm not sure I actually believe in—'

'So, your horoscope said, "Out of adversity springs good fortune" and you know what?'

'What?'

'That's exactly what's going to happen!'

Katie stared at Talia who was beaming at her and Oscar as though she'd just stumbled across the pot of gold at the end of the rainbow. It seemed that nothing could shake her belief in the ability of the stars to predict the day's destiny. Katie wondered if there was anything that would disturb her sunny demeanour – and she was reminded of a phrase Agatha used whenever she saw the hordes of backpackers begin their trek up Adeng Mountain – hope springs eternal in the young.

Ryan might have rained on Talia's parade that night, but she hadn't sunk into a maelstrom of self-pity like Katie had when Dominic had done the same thing. She had simply got on with her life with a smile on her face and a song in her heart, certain of the fact that when Venus was in the seventh house Ryan would come running. If anyone believed in the power of positivity it was Talia, and Katie realised she had the perfect employee for her café.

'Well, the *adversity* bit has happened, that's for sure,' Katie said, trying to make a joke of it. 'When exactly is the good fortune bit due?'

'Maybe it's not for you, but for someone else.' Oscar grinned, flashing Talia a meaningful look.

'What do you mean?' asked Katie, making a start on returning the cake stands to the kitchen and wondering how soon Talia and Oscar would leave so she could don her Marigolds and launch into a therapeutic marathon of scrubbing until every ounce of humiliation that was currently churning through her veins had been eradicated.

Why had she listened to Cara? Why had she deluded herself into believing that all she had to do was bake a few cakes and the customers would come running? She would be eating soup for her breakfast, lunch and dinner for the next month!

'Oh my God. Yes! Oscar, you are a genius. Why didn't I realise that's what the stars had in store?'

'Maybe they just needed a bit of a nudge?'

Katie paused in the doorway to the kitchen, bewildered at their jubilation.

'My sister Mel volunteers one day a week at the local soup kitchen over in St Agnes. Why don't we drive over there and donate the soup and cakes to a good cause? Isn't that the very definition of goodwill, thoughtfulness and community?'

Katie stared at Talia, the dreamy, quirky young girl who sent funeral flowers to birthday bashes, who left her fate to the whims of astrological forces, but who, in the face of disaster, could come up with something so perfect, so in tune with not only the café's aims, but which would surely meet with Agatha's approval as well.

'That's … that's a fabulous idea!'

To her surprise, tears smarted at the corners of her eyes as her respect for Talia ballooned.

'It's more than fabulous, it's inspired,' declared Oscar, slinging his arm around Talia's shoulders and planting a kiss on her cheek. 'Come on, let's get going – if we're quick we'll get there for supper time.'

Working in tandem, they loaded up Katie's hire car with everything they could fit in and then sang ABBA songs at the tops of their voices all the way to St Agnes. When they arrived, Katie's spirits soared with gratitude for the unquestioning support of good friends and good ideas, and she made a decision that surprised her.

'You know, I have a proposition. Why don't we make this a monthly thing? Soup & Song nights at Agatha's Beachside Café? It has a great ring to it, hasn't it? We could charge a small entrance fee and the proceeds and any leftover goodies can be donated to the soup kitchen? What do you think?'

Oscar met her gaze, his vivid blue eyes filled with an emotion she couldn't fathom. Fortunately, Talia broke the connection by pogoing up and down on the spot, clapping her hands and squealing her approval.

'It's a fabulous idea! Mel's going to be totally stoked. And I've had an idea, too.'

Oscar smirked at Katie as they carried the catering boxes inside the rather austere-looking red-brick church that housed the charity's venture.

'I've got lots of friends who are going to uni in September who don't know the first thing about cooking if it doesn't involve a microwave or a Pot Noodle. Why don't we organise a pizza and pasta-making night at the café, then all sit down to eat together, like they do in Italy? There's nowhere to go in Perrinby on a night-time apart from the pub, so I think it'll be really popular.'

'That's a date!' Katie smiled, knowing it was the least she could do.

'Yay! Awesome.'

Talia beamed as she skipped off to find her sister to tell her why they were there and to regale her with their future plans for the café inspired by her, which left Katie alone with Oscar.

'Thanks for helping out, Oscar. Who would have thought we'd end the night supporting the homeless?'

'Not a problem. Sometimes life doesn't turn out how we expect it to. The trick is to make the most of every opportunity that wanders across our path – good or bad.'

Again, Katie caught the shadow of sadness stalk across Oscar's eyes and she wondered if it was the right time to ask him what had caused it. She opened her mouth to reach out and offer a listening ear as so many people had done for her when Dominic had vanished from her life, but she stopped when Talia reappeared, accompanied by a tall, slender woman who could only have been Talia's older sister; not because they both sported a sheet of long, straight caramel hair but because Mel was wearing a hand-knitted waistcoat depicting what Katie had initially thought were daggers dripping in blood but which thankfully, on closer inspection, turned out to be exploding poppies. She imagined the two sisters growing up in the bridal boutique, experimenting with their own individual styles of attire from the off-cuts of bridal fabric whilst their mother created fairy-tale wedding gowns.

'Mel, this is Katie who's running Agatha's café now. You just have to come over with the other volunteers and sample her toffee-apple cupcakes with confetti sprinkles, which are to die for! Oh, and you met Oscar at the village Christmas party.'

'Hi, Katie, I don't know how to thank you for your kind donation. I have to admit the soup smells absolutely delicious – it'll be a real treat, but those cupcakes – I mean, wow! Were you planning a royal garden party? They're like, well, like miniature works of art. I think we've got a rival artist in Perrinby, Oscar.'

Mel's dark eyes reflected the sincerity and innate kindness that was clearly engraved in her heart as she chatted to Katie and Oscar, filling them in on the charity's aims and their lack of funds whilst leading them into the vast, careworn kitchen to unpack their cakes onto plates ready for the nine p.m. rush when the doors opened.

'Are you able to stay and help? Many hands and all that?'

'Of course,' chorused Katie and Oscar in unison, laughing at their respective enthusiasm.

For the next two hours, Katie worked alongside Oscar in choreographed harmony; Oscar sliced the bread that had been donated by a local bakery when their doors closed to their paying customers, and she spread the butter, all the while listening to Mel eulogising about the apricot-and-pistachio cupcakes decorated with lemon frosting. Other members of the volunteer team came over one by one to introduce themselves and to thank her for her generosity, and with every person who spoke to her, from teenagers like Talia to elderly pensioners, Katie grew more humbled by their effusive thanks.

Why hadn't she thought of doing this before? When she'd worked for François? There had been several instances when their experiments with the more exotic celebration cakes simply hadn't met the superior standards that François demanded, or that time when her colleague Sophie had spelled the customer's name wrong on a *Game of Thrones* birthday cake that had taken two weeks to create. François, in a fit of hot-tempered pique, had tossed the offending article into the bin. How many hungry people could that have fed? Heat flashed across her cheeks at the thought and she resolved there and then that her promise to make this a regular date in her diary would not fall onto the pile labelled 'good intentions' but would be a genuine commitment to contribute to those who found themselves in difficult circumstances.

A splash of shame joined all the other swirling emotions that evening had engendered as the patrons began to trickle in, each as diverse as the volunteers themselves, and she began to wonder about their histories. Everyone had a story to tell, and not every one had a happy ending. Why was she still lounging in a mire of misery over her cancelled wedding plans when her life could be so much worse?

Katie swallowed down a surge of remorse that threatened to send with it a smattering of tears as she ladled her home-made soup into a bowl and handed it to a woman who couldn't have been much older than herself. Two hours ago, she had felt like a complete failure just because no one had turned up to her launch party, but clearly fate had had something else up her sleeve for that night and she had been taught a very valuable life lesson.

A crystal-clear image of Agatha, dressed in her favourite turquoise kaftan, her eyes filled with approval and pride, floated across her mind's eyes and she understood completely what her friend was trying to do in Bali despite her own dance with the heartbreak harlots.

No matter what happened – with the café, with Dominic, with her parents – she should pin a smile on her face and count her blessings every single day because there was *always* someone, somewhere in the world worse off than she was.

Chapter 8

The day of the Grand Reopening of Agatha's Beachside Café dawned with a clear blue sky, and a scant breeze tickling through the daffodils on the village green where the ducks went about their daily business without a care in the world. Katie woke to a symphony of early morning birdsong and the rhythmic crashing of the waves on the nearby beach, something she hadn't experienced since moving from Norfolk to London six years ago where her wake-up call was more usually the cacophonous roar of commuter traffic, intermittent car horns and screeching brakes.

She jumped out of bed and straight into the shower, spending an extra few minutes on her hair so as not to frighten the customers into thinking she was auditioning for a role as Worzel Gummidge's younger sister. Then, she skipped down the stairs to make a start on preparing the food for the day ahead and to give the café a last wipe down before she flung open the doors to the hungry hordes of Cornwall.

Apprehension swirled through her chest, but it was mingled with a healthy dollop of excitement and anticipation. The café reflected the setting she had hoped to achieve, the menu showcased a variety of delicious dishes made from as many locally sourced ingredients as possible, and she had an amazing waitress who, although on the dreamy and forgetful side, had a heart of pure kindness, which meant more to her than the ability to get an order right.

But more important than all of those things, Katie hoped that the café would be a happy place filled with chatter, laughter, music and the fragrance of freshly ground coffee, buttery pastry, and exotic spices.

'Hey, Katie, do I have time to grab a coffee?' Talia beamed as she breezed in through the back door clutching a home-sewn tapestry bag out of which poked a bunch of glossy magazines, which she whipped out and handed to Katie.

'What're these for?'

'I only had enough money to buy five, but I've texted Mum and she's promised to go over to the newsagent's in St Ives to get the rest after she's done Grace's final dress fitting for her wedding next Saturday. Did I tell you how Grace met her fiancé Daniel?'

A sudden whoosh of sadness invaded Katie's heart, so she quickly changed the subject, keen to avoid a wedding-related story, even if she wasn't sure what she was letting herself in for instead.

'Why do you want more than five magazines?' she asked, hoping that Talia wasn't going to spend the whole of their first day flicking through the pages of *Vogue* and *OK!* and *Hello!*

'Why do you think? To read our horoscopes!'

'Ah, yes, of course. Silly me.'

'I've already read mine, and I think today is going to be an amazing success, but you need to read yours. And just in case we need an extra bit of luck, I've brought a green malachite stone to put in the kitchen, which will bring good fortune for the café.'

Talia wriggled out of her bright-orange padded jacket that made her look like an over-ripe satsuma and reached for her apron. When she turned around, Katie couldn't stop herself from doing a double take when she saw what Talia had chosen to wear for their first day.

'That's a ... rather striking T-shirt, Talia.'

'I knew you'd like it! I designed it myself, you know.'

'Yes, I thought you might have done.'

Katie found it difficult to avert her eyes from the medley of assorted pastries printed onto the front of Talia's T-shirt, unsure whether the young woman was aware of the rather inappropriate positioning of the Chelsea buns or whether she had actually designed it that way. She had never been more relieved at her foresight in ordering their personalised aprons, which would cover the offending article of clothing.

'Why don't you pop your apron on while I sort out the coffee?'

'I adore these aprons, Katie – especially how we've got our names embroidered on the front, too, so the customers can call us by our names. It's just so much more friendly.'

At nine o'clock on the dot, Katie asked Talia to accompany her to the front door and together they performed a mini-opening ceremony by turning the sign from Closed to Welcome! Their first customer, a harassed-looking mum with a toddler asleep in her pushchair, gave them a grateful smile and ordered an almond milk latte, a piece of home-made caramelised apple shortcake, and helped herself to one of Talia's magazines.

After that there was a steady stream of people, mostly tourists on their way to seaside villages further down the coast or visiting the Eden Project, but a few curious locals also stopped by and lingered long enough to exclaim their delight at the quirky, colourful décor and to assure Katie that after they had devoured a slice of her banana and honey flapjack topped with pearls of rich dark chocolate, they definitely felt the effects of the relaxing, calming ambience she was aiming to achieve.

At lunchtime, Talia's mum and sister arrived to swell the numbers, along with several of Talia's college friends, and Katie suddenly realised that the young waitress had cajoled, bribed and threatened them into coming, just in case there was a repeat of the previous evening's dearth of patrons when the café had resembled the dining room of the *Marie Celeste*.

'I love what you've done with the place, Katie, and in such a short space of time.' Zoe smiled, digging into a slice of Bakewell tart made with apricot jam and topped with rose-infused icing whilst Mel devoured a huge helping of black cherry and sprout cake with gusto before learning what gave the cake its unique green colour and staring at Katie in horror.

'Thanks, I did have a lot of help, though. And Talia has been amazing.'

'Yes, Talia told me about last night – I'm sorry that happened, Katie. But I hear it hasn't put you off and that you've got another soup night organised for next month? I think it's a great way to diversify and to showcase the businesses in Perrinby as well as do your bit for charity. Are you planning any more events to build up the business?'

'I am, actually. Oscar's offered to put on a drawing class, Jay has promised to do a flower-arranging demonstration ...'

'Oh, I'm definitely up for that one,' said Mel, beaming, totally unaware that she had a dusting of icing sugar across her cheek as her mother leaned forward to remove it with an indulgent smile.

'I'd love to lead a session, too,' said Zoe, tucking the edges of her short bob behind her ears in an identical gesture to Mel and Talia. 'Although I'm not sure how many people would want to come and learn how to make a wedding dress. What if I joined forces with the ladies from my WI and we held one of our Knit & Natter get-togethers here? We've been meeting in members' homes since the library closed down.'

'That would be ...'

The door sprang opened and Katie beamed when she saw who her visitor was.

'Ruby, over here!' called Mel, waving at the village beautician and hairdresser. 'We were just talking about holding a few themed nights here at the café to drum up business. How are you fixed to do a beauty night? Nails, make-up, aromatherapy, that sort of thing?'

'Count me in.' Ruby grinned, her singsong accent conjuring up images of warm, sun-drenched beaches and swaying palm trees on a distant Caribbean island.

'Well, you'll all have to wait your turn,' declared Talia, setting a cappuccino and a slice of rocky road down on the table in front of Ruby. 'Because the first event on our list is a pizza-making night. I've already invited all my friends and if *anyone* fails to turn up, like last night, then they'll have me to answer to!'

'Does that include a certain young man who lives at the Hope & Anchor?'

'It might,' said Talia, her eyes sparkling in anticipation, completely unfazed by his previous reticence to have so much as a coffee with her. 'Remind me to research what pizza toppings encourage feelings of romance in the consumer.'

'Well, I think oysters are supposed to be an aphrodisiac?'

'Ergh, gross! I'm not serving Ryan those.'

By the time five o'clock came around, Katie's shoulders ached and her feet felt like they were encased in blocks of concrete, but she had made a bunch of new friends – Ruby and Zoe amongst them – and, even better, she hadn't had time to allow her thoughts to linger on what Dominic was getting up to in San Antonio; a feat she would have thought impossible yesterday.

'Thanks for all your help today, Talia. I couldn't have done any of it without you.'

'No probs – see you tomorrow.'

No sooner had she waved goodbye to Talia and pulled down the blind on the café's front door, than there was a knock on the back door. She was surprised at the nip of pleasure she experienced when she saw Oscar's face peering through the window.

'Hey, how did it go?'

'Really well, I think. It's early days, but I don't think we've poisoned anyone, and our tip jar is full. Want a coffee?' She smiled as she indicated for him to grab a seat in the window.

'No, actually, I'm here to issue my own invitation.'

'Oh ...'

'I thought, well, after your first full day, that you must be exhausted and the last thing you'd want to do was cook dinner so ... why don't you come over to the flat and I'll cook *you* dinner? Nothing fancy, spaghetti is the extent of my culinary expertise, I'm afraid, but I've got a decent bottle of Chianti? What do you say?'

Katie knew he was just being neighbourly, but her whole body froze as she struggled to formulate a reply. Have dinner with him? Just the two of them? Alone in his flat above the art gallery? A swathe of panic prevented cogent thought for a few long seconds.

'It's okay if you've got something else planned.'

'No, no, it's very kind of you, but I ...'

Katie watched the hope in Oscar's eyes seep away and she felt awful. What was the matter with her? Why couldn't she enjoy a meal with a friend who had done so much to contribute towards that day's success? If nothing else, it would give her the opportunity to weave into the conversation the fact that she wasn't interested in joining the dating scene, just so that there were no misunderstandings from the outset – not that he'd given her any indication that he was interested in her that way.

'Actually, thanks, Oscar, I'd love that.'

'Great. See you at seven.'

Katie watched him walk back to his gallery with a spring in his step and wondered why he didn't have anything else better to do than take pity on the exhausted café manager from next door. Perhaps he made it a point of principle to cook dinner for every new village arrival, but she discarded that thought immediately.

Again, she wondered what Oscar's story was – if he'd only been in Perrinby for six months, where had he been before, and what had caused that wisp of sadness that his cheerful demeanour couldn't mask?

Maybe she would find out that night.

Chapter 9

Katie stood on the doorstep of the Perrinby art gallery and studio clutching a bottle of wine, regret zooming through her chest. Whilst she owed Oscar a great deal of gratitude for all he had done to help her to get the café ready on time, and for rescuing her launch night from the ashes of complete disaster, she felt awkward and it was taking all her willpower not to spin around on her sparkly sandals and run away.

Yet, when she saw Oscar's smiling face appear at the glass door, her doubts melted away. This wasn't a date, she chastised herself, it was a relaxed supper between two friends, and when he led her upstairs to a light and airy apartment that was surprisingly homely – in complete contrast to the stark white walls and bleached floorboards of the gallery and studio – the delicious aroma of roast garlic floated through the air and her stomach growled, and after her first few sips of the promised rich, ruby-red Chianti, she began to relax.

'I learned how to make spag bol at university and now it's a weekly staple,' Oscar explained as he divided the steaming pasta into two bowls and added a dollop of tomato sauce to each of them. He indicated the coffee table where two large saffron-coloured cushions awaited – the perfect setting for an impromptu supper between friends. 'What do you think?'

'It's delicious, even better because someone else has made it for me,' she said, twirling her fork and taking care not to splatter the sauce on the T-shirt she'd bought from the Pasar Sindu night market in Sanur – fathoming out how to work Agatha's ancient washing machine was next on her list of tasks to master.

'Does a love of baking run in your family?'

Katie couldn't help but laugh. 'No way! My mum struggles to boil an egg.'

'Does that mean your father does all the cooking?'

Katie ignored the familiar sinking feeling in her stomach; she was used to fielding this question and had an answer ready.

'My parents divorced when I was twelve. When I left home to work in London, Mum moved to Crete, to a small village outside Chania, where she runs a horse-riding retreat for exhausted professionals – but she employs someone to do the catering.'

'Is that where you learned to create those amazing cakes? London?'

'Yes, I used to work for François Dubois – he's famous in the celebration cake business.'

'God! I've heard of him. My mum ordered one of his five-tier masterpieces for my dad's sixtieth a couple of years ago.'

'Yes, he's like the Michelangelo of the sugar-paste world.' Katie laughed, taking another sip of her wine, relishing the taste of rich red berries, mingled with a hint of dried oregano, balsamic vinegar and espresso coffee. Every mouthful conjured up an image of the rolling hills of a sun-filled Tuscan hillside, complete with terracotta-roofed villages, arrow-straight cypress trees, and swathes of smiling sunflowers dancing in the fields. 'So, I assume you studied art at university?'

'Actually, I studied architecture, would you believe? But my passion always lay in the field of painting, right from the moment my aunt bought me an easel and a box of watercolours when I was ten years old. My parents have never forgiven her.'

Oscar laughed, but he avoided meeting her eyes and she suspected that here lay the origin of the almost intangible melancholy that lurked just beneath the surface, only detectable by those who had experienced a similar trauma.

'So what did you do after you graduated from university?'

'Joined the family's architecture firm in Pimlico.'

'That must have been exciting. What made you give it up and come down to Cornwall?'

'Sometimes something happens and you realise that life is short and unless you chase your dreams with determination and passion, time will run out.'

His use of those words caused a switch to trip inside Katie. What was it with people who insisted you should follow your dreams without any consideration for the ripple effect on those around you? She had seen that particular trait in action and it wasn't pleasant. She wondered whose heart Oscar had broken to follow *his* dreams and resolved to ensure their relationship remained at the friendship end of the spectrum despite the tickle of interest that had been burgeoning as the night progressed and she got to know Oscar better and liked what she saw.

Whilst hope might have broken through the steel-encased box she had consigned it to, she hadn't discarded all her common sense!

'Thanks for the pasta, Oscar,' she began, suddenly keen to reacquaint herself with her pillow.

'You're welcome, but before you go, I want to show you something.'

Oscar unfurled his long legs and held out his hand to help Katie up to her feet. To her surprise, when his palm slid into hers it felt like the most natural thing in the world. She allowed herself to be guided to the top of the stairs that led back down to the studio where she paused at the window overlooking the field at the back of their building.

'I love those wooden pods. They look so magical, as though a platoon of hobbits is about to scuttle out and hold a party when no one is looking. Why are they empty? I'd have thought with the Easter holidays in full swing, they'd be booked out by the glamping brigade?'

'Didn't Agatha tell you?'

'Tell me what?'

'She owns them, too.'

'Really? No, she didn't mention that.'

'Just a word of caution. Don't mention it to Greg if he comes knocking again.'

'Actually, he's already asked me if I know who owns the site.'

'I'm not sure what Agatha's got planned for it, but she'll make her own decision in her own time. I think Jay mentioned a couple of months ago that she may be thinking of asking someone to get the site ready in time for the summer holiday season, but that's a couple of months away.'

They had reached the foot of the stairs. Oscar paused at the door that led to the room at the back of the gallery and when he pushed open the door, Katie gasped.

'Wow!'

She couldn't think of another word to describe the place that contained everything an avid pottery enthusiast could possibly need. The longest wall housed a battalion of wooden shelves groaning with equipment, tools, ceramic pots filled with implements, and plastic bags containing large slabs of brown clay awaiting the caress of its owner's hands. On the opposite wall, the shelves showcased the finished products; some destined for the kiln, some awaiting the paintbrush: jugs, vases, bowls, mugs in various shapes and sizes and in various stages of production. In an alcove off to the side stood the industrial kiln she had seen on her first visit to the gallery, and at the back of the room were two potter's wheels, still, silent, waiting patiently to be pressed into service.

'Have you ever thrown a pot?'

'Not unless you count the time François told me he hated my depiction of a bichon frise on the top of one of our doggie celebration cakes and expressed his displeasure by hurling a plate at me.'

Oscar laughed, his eyes crinkling attractively at the corners and Katie's longing for her bed vanished.

'Want to have a go?'

'What, now?'

She laughed at the incongruous suggestion, then she realised he was serious.

'No, no, I'd be useless.'

'I don't think so. I've seen your cake sculptures, and sugar paste is just edible modelling clay – *and* we bake it in the oven afterwards – what's the difference?'

Oscar had already sliced off a chunk of clay and slammed it down onto the turntable, cocking his leg to sit astride the wooden seat and setting the wheel in motion. As Katie watched on in fascination, he began to coax the unremarkable lump into a perfect sphere before he jumped up and held out his hand.

'Your turn.'

'Oh, no, I really …'

But Oscar wouldn't take no for an answer and Katie ended up sitting on the narrow wooden plank that masqueraded as a seat, its pitted surface still warm from his buttocks. She placed her palm tentatively on the slippery wet clay, enjoying the feel of the smooth material as it rotated slowly through her fingers.

'Now push your thumbs down into the middle.'

'Like this?'

The ball of clay started to wobble and shift on the turntable.

'Hang on.'

Before she could say anything, Oscar had scooted into the seat behind her, reached his arms around her waist and taken hold of her hands to guide her thumbs into the clay and then ease them slowly, gently upwards, teasing the sides of what would be her very first ceramic dish into shape.

'Keep your hands firm and steady,' urged Oscar, softly.

But Katie couldn't concentrate. All she could think about was the way the taut muscles of his abdomen pressed against her spine, and the whisper of his breath on her earlobe sent spasms of long-forgotten desire through her frozen veins. Goose bumps rippled across her naked forearms as she grappled with every ounce of her willpower to ignore her body's treacherous reaction and forced her brain to take over control.

How could she be having this reaction when her heart was still smarting from Dominic's rejection? It didn't make sense.

Confusion swirled and when Oscar leaned even further forward, his chin over her shoulder, she stiffened and suddenly all she wanted to do was escape from the intimacy of the moment, her emotions flowing like wildfire through a cornfield. She jumped from the seat so quickly she stumbled and as she reached out to steady herself, she knocked a pale-blue ceramic vase from the shelf onto the floor.

'Oh, I'm so sorry! So sorry!'

She knelt down to collect the shattered pieces, her cheeks burning, but Oscar got there before her, and simply scooped up the bits and tossed them into the bin.

'Are you okay?'

'Fine, fine. Yes, I'm fine. I just, well, I should go. Thanks for dinner, it was delicious.'

And before Oscar could ask her why she was acting so crazily, she dashed from the studio and out of the gallery, and she didn't look back until she was safely locked in Agatha's bedroom, her breath coming in spurts as she looked out of the window at the rippling expanse of the sea over the dunes, and then down onto the village green below where she spotted Jay taking Dotty for her last walk of the day.

Katie groaned, knowing immediately that he had witnessed her flight from the gallery, her suspicions placed beyond doubt when he glanced up at the window, his lips stretched into a broad grin as he gave her a little finger wave.

She didn't have to be Einstein's younger sister to know what would be the main topic of the next morning's gossip schedule.

Chapter 10

The weeks following the grand reopening rushed by in a frenzy of activity and at the end of each day Katie was too exhausted to even contemplate anything beyond taking a shower and falling into bed.

Their hard work was paying off, though, and every day more and more customers crossed the threshold; some expressing their delight at the exotic décor while others commented on how much they enjoyed the music – a mix of soothing Indonesian Gamelan interspersed with the more cutting-edge tunes composed and performed by Talia's friends and fellow students from the local college who were studying music. Her 'pay it forward campaign' was proving popular, too, and on several occasions, customers had agreed to round up their bill, or had returned the next day with a donation for the local food bank – something Zoe and her friends at the WI were heavily involved in.

However, the icing on Katie's self-confidence cupcake had been the day when a well-known celebrity chef who lived in a small village further along the coast had graced them with her presence, exclaiming with delight at the slice of beetroot and fresh fig loaf she had ordered to accompany her skinny latte and asked for the recipe. When she left, she promised to let Katie know if she decided to use it in her upcoming *Cornish Cornucopia* cookbook.

Talia had proved to be a godsend. Unsurprisingly, she knew the routine backwards, as well as most of their more local customers, chatting cheerfully about a myriad of subjects and urging them to sample that day's specials as well as encouraging them to take advantage of, or contribute to, their Kindness Jar. Every morning she arrived clutching their horoscopes – which she had printed off from one of her favourite astrology websites – then spent the rest of the day pointing out to Katie how accurate they were in the most highfalutin way.

Perrinby's answer to Mystic Meg also continued to turn up for work in increasingly bizarre outfits: a denim jacket decorated with paperclips, a waistcoat made from what looked like woven straw, and a wide variety of knitted bobble hats sporting fruit and vegetables made from felt instead of the usual pompoms. Katie couldn't prevent a smile from tugging at her lips when she thought of the conversation she'd had with Talia just that morning when she'd arrived at the café wearing a luminous pink fez topped with a pair of curtain tie-backs.

'I love your hat, Talia. Very unusual. Have you ever thought of a career in millinery?'

'In the military? No way! I'd be useless – and I hate khaki. It doesn't suit my colouring.'

She'd giggled. 'Not the military, millinery – making hats.'

'Oh, right, no, not really. I want to go travelling first. I'm saving hard and I'm researching an itinerary. Just think, this time next year I could be waitressing at the Balinese branch of Agatha's Beachside Café. That would be a dream come true!'

Katie finished wiping down the last of the tables, then glanced at her watch, aware she only had a couple of hours before she had to switch the Closed sign back to Welcome! and launch the first of the café's activity evenings – Talia's pizza-making night. However, she desperately needed to replenish her energy levels, so she set the kettle to boil, made a mug of Earl Grey tea, and allowed herself a few quiet moments to ponder how far she'd come in such a short space of time in her favourite spot in the café.

From her vantage point on the window seat, she sipped her tea, smiling when she saw the lights flick on in the gallery next door as twilight began to tickle at the rooftops. The first time she had bumped into Oscar after their supper *à deux* had been a little awkward, but his unrelenting cheerfulness had ensured the feeling was fleeting. She resolved to return the gesture – but maybe with a trip to one of Cornwall's wide sandy beaches or sheltered coves further down the coast instead of a cosy meal in her flat because she was determined to ignore the mischievous elves of attraction who seemed bent on pushing her in his direction.

However, she didn't want to lose him as a friend. Not only did she enjoy his easy company, she also felt a certain affinity with him, as though they inhabited the same wavelength, and her curiosity mounted every time she tried to figure out what was eating at his heart. It occurred to her that if she shared a little of her own personal background, he might be willing to open up to her.

But was she ready to do that?

She had successfully sidestepped his question about her father when it had come up in conversation over their bowls of spaghetti bolognese, but maybe she should have grabbed her courage by the scruff of its neck and spilled out the whole sorry saga that had plagued her life for far too long. Maybe confiding in someone who knew nothing about what had happened would prove easier than raking things over with a close friend, like Cara, who was aware that despite banishing her anguish to the deepest crevices of her heart, the embers of hurt still smouldered, always there, biding their time, waiting to pounce when she was at her most vulnerable to deliver a fresh wave of pain.

Thankfully, her internal monologue of self-examination was

brought to an abrupt halt by a knock on the door, and she experienced a sharp jolt to her heart when she saw a face peering through the window at her until she realised who it was and leapt from her seat to let him in.

'Need an apprentice sous chef?'

'I'd love one.'

'Great!' Oscar beamed, his piercing blue eyes filled with the same excitement she'd seen on Cara's nephew's face whenever she suggested they rustled up a few home-made gingerbread men to decorate with multi-coloured icing and Smarties.

Working in synchronised harmony, they spent the next hour in the kitchen experimenting with a number of pizza dough recipes. When Katie had settled on the perfect consistency, she made a huge batch, separated it into twelve individual portions, and they began the task of stretching and kneading the dough, which, she had to accept, Oscar proved to be extremely proficient at.

'Looks like you've done this before?'

'I haven't, but it's just like kneading clay.'

'No, it's not!' She laughed. 'You can't do this with clay.'

Katie had intended to stretch out her ball of dough as far as she could to demonstrate its excellent elasticity, but the dough snapped and a dollop of the mixture ended up on the front of Oscar's navy-blue T-shirt. He held her gaze for a long second, then glanced down at the splodge of pizza dough on his top, his eyebrows twitching with mischief, and before Katie knew what was happening, she had received a dousing of flour as payback.

'Hey!'

Not to be outdone, she picked up a wooden spoon, dipped it into the bowl of home-made passata she had spent the afternoon preparing, and tapped Oscar's nose with it, giggling with delight at the shock on his face as he reached up and removed the tomato sauce with the tip of his finger then tasted it.

'Mmm, delicious, but I think I prefer it on a sizzling hot pizza.'

'Me too.'

Katie leaned forward to deposit her kneaded ball of pizza dough into one of twelve lightly oiled glass bowls for proving before the students arrived at seven o'clock, but Oscar misread her intentions. As quick as a flash, he grabbed hold of her hands and wrapped his arms around her waist to stop her from depositing another splash of tomato sauce on his face. She spun round, her chest pressed against his, their lips inches apart, his breath causing tingles of attraction to sweep through her veins.

She smiled, surprised to find she was enjoying their brief sojourn of closeness so much, before she gently pulled away, heat flooding her cheeks, to finish covering the bowls with the red-and-white gingham tea towels she had bought especially for the event.

'Thanks, Oscar, I don't think I would have got everything finished without your help.'

'No problem, I've had fun. You know where to find me if there's any pizza left.'

'Somehow I don't think there will be.' She laughed as she untied her apron and hung it on the back of the kitchen door. 'Twelve ravenous teens? I think you should make alternative arrangements for your dinner this evening.'

'Good call.'

Oscar ran his fingers through his messy curls, depositing a sprinkle of flour onto the bench top like falling snowflakes, causing Katie to reach for a cloth and the antibacterial spray. She had the distinct impression that he was about to comment on her obsession with hygiene but he thought better of it, and instead made his way towards the door.

'Okay, see you later. Good luck. I hope the night's a runaway success.'

'So do I. The café can't afford another disaster.'

Even before the brass bell on the back of the door had stopped tinkling, Katie was rushing up the stairs to shower and change and make herself presentable for her debut role as an evening class presenter. As she ran a comb through her unruly locks and added a slick of mascara and lip gloss, she sent up a quick prayer to the director of her fate that at least eight pizza lovers turned up because that was her break-even figure and she couldn't bear to contemplate making another loss.

But she needn't have worried because at seven o'clock on the dot, twelve of Talia's closest friends, including Ryan, bowled into the café filled with chatter and enthusiasm, ready to be guided through every stage of preparing a pizza from scratch.

'Hi everyone, and welcome to Agatha's Beachside Café's very first pizza-making night. I hope you'll all have lots of fun, but I'm sure you'll agree that the best bit will be the taste-testing part at the end. Now, as you can see, I've set out twelve separate sets of ingredients around the table, so if you'd all like to take a place, we'll get started.'

'Oh, wow, I adore these cute little aprons,' cried Sara, Talia's best friend, striking a pose in her embroidered apron as if she were about to launch herself down a culinary catwalk – with her six-foot frame and long glossy mahogany hair, she could easily have given an Italian fashion house model a run for her money.

'Me too,' agreed Talia, wriggling out of a neon-green jacket bedecked with what looked at first glance like cotton wool balls but on closer inspection turned out to be a flock of sheep and newborn lambs as a nod to the season. 'And I absolutely *lerrrve* these paper chef's hats, Katie. Can we write our names on them?'

'That's exactly what I want you to do.'

A cacophony of excitement followed as the gang of friends spent the next few minutes personalising their hats, offering suggestions, adding cartoons and doodles as well as their names, until Katie eventually managed to call the proceedings back to order.

'Okay, shall we make our pizzas?'

'Yay!' came the rousing response.

For the next ten minutes the group studiously followed Katie's step-by-step instructions on how to make a basic pizza dough with flour, water, sea salt and dried yeast, giggling as they got their hands covered in the gooey, sticky mess.

'Now comes the fun bit. Sprinkle a little flour onto the table, turn out the dough and gather all the bits together. Then, holding one side with your fingers and using the heel of your other hand, you pull it, like this, then you fold it, like this, you pull it, you fold it, you pull it, then fold it, then you turn it round, grab the end and start all over again, pull it, fold it, pull it, fold it.'

'How long do we have to do this for?' asked Talia, brushing back an escaped tendril of hair with her forearm and dousing her forehead with a smudge of flour, causing her friends Marcia and Callie to giggle.

'Ten minutes or so until the gluten in the dough develops and we get a stretchy, pliable consistency. Then we shape the dough into a ball, like this, and place it into a lightly oiled bowl, cover it with clingfilm or a tea towel and leave it to rest for two hours.'

'Two hours! But I'm starving,' declared Ryan, eliciting a chorus of agreement from the other males in the group, all of whom had worked hard on their kneading technique, producing perfect balls of pizza dough, unlike several of Talia's girlfriends who were struggling to get the rhythm right.

Katie laughed. 'Don't worry, Ryan, in true *Blue Peter* style, here's some balls of pizza dough I made earlier, with a little help from Oscar, which are proved and ready to go. You can take the dough you've just made home with you for another time.'

'Phew!' said Ryan, his green eyes filled with relief as he theatrically ran the back of his hand across his forehead, before casting a surreptitious glance in Talia's direction from beneath his lashes that only Katie saw.

'Okay, so as you can see, this dough that was made earlier has doubled in size. Now, turn it out onto your floured pizza bases, press the middle with your fist, like this, turn it and repeat, turn it and repeat, until you have a pizza shape. See how soft and pliable the dough is?'

'Yay! Watch this.'

And to Katie's amazement the class was treated to an impromptu display of pizza twirling by Ryan's friend Marc, the one who had supplied their music for the evening via his iPhone, but whose talents clearly extended to culinary exploits as well. With a practised flourish, he tossed his circular dough into the air, spinning it on the tip of his finger before pirouetting on his toes and catching the Frisbee-like base on his way back round, for which he received an exuberant round of applause and high-pitched whistling.

'Wow, that's amazing,' gasped Katie, joining in with the clapping.

'My uncle owns a pizzeria in Naples. We visit him every summer and he taught me how to twirl pizzas almost as soon as I could walk. It's actually an important part of our cultural heritage, but all I'm interested in is eating them.' Marc laughed, his cheeks glowing with a mixture of pride and embarrassment at having such an avid audience.

'Let's all give it a go,' declared Ryan, throwing his dough into the air like a miniature pancake, except his manual dexterity was nowhere near as graceful as Marc's.

'Argh! Ryan, cut it out!' squealed Talia, cowering with her hands over her head as the spinning pizza came in to land on the top of her head, knocking her chef's hat to the ground.

'Ooops, sorry, Talia.'

Ryan rushed to Talia's aid, removing his pizza base and then gently tucking stray strands of hair around her ears in a gesture that caused Katie's heart to melt. She saw his freckled face colour as he scooted back to his place at the table and there was no doubt whatsoever in her mind that the feelings between the pair were mutual.

'Okay, let's move on to the pizza toppings, shall we?'

'Yay! The best bit!' cried Marc and Ryan in unison.

Katie and Talia retreated to the kitchen to collect the pre-prepared dishes of ingredients with which to decorate their pizzas; from the classic passata, mozzarella and fresh basil leaves, to favourites like pepperoni, mushrooms, grilled peppers, black olives, and the less conventional but no less tasty chopped red cherries, goat's cheese and rocket or strawberries, crumbled feta and balsamic glaze. Katie had even sourced a tub of Italian ricotta – which she had sweetened with icing sugar – bowls of sliced peaches, apricots and kiwi and a bottle of runny honey for those participants who had a sweet tooth and wanted to experiment.

'Oh my God, Ryan, can you get any more pepperoni on there?' Talia giggled, standing next to him as he covered every square inch of his pizza with the sliced meat before finishing it off with a drizzle of olive oil.

'I like pepperoni. Anyway, what's that on yours?'

'Strawberries.'

'You don't put strawberries on a pizza – it's sacrilege,' announced Marc with conviction. 'My Uncle Gino would have a coronary.'

'Well don't tell him.' Talia laughed, adding a handful of crumbly goat's cheese and finishing the whole thing off with a sprinkle of rocket leaves. 'Mmm, delicious!'

'Okay, if everyone's happy with their creations, Talia and I will bake them in the oven. While you wait for them to cook, there's a selection of drinks and antipasti over there, so please just help yourselves.'

When everyone eventually sat down together to munch on their pizzas, Katie took a moment to count her blessings. She knew her face was glowing like an over-ripe tomato, and her hair had ballooned into a halo of curls, but she didn't care because the laughter and animated conversation that buzzed through the café was enough to bring tears to her eyes. Teenagers often got bad press, and there was very little to keep them occupied in

Perrinby, but here they were bonding over something as simple as iced lemonade – made from real lemons – and pizza.

She hoped that in some small way she had taught them a skill they could take with them when they moved on to the next stage of their lives whether that be university or college or the world of work, as well as showing them how enjoyable preparing their own meals from scratch could be, especially if they then went on to share the product of their labours with a group of friends. And at the end of the session, when Ryan stood up to deliver a vote of thanks, she was delighted to hear the barrage of requests for the pizza-making night to be repeated the following month.

'Thanks, everyone. I've had lots of fun, too.'

After refusing all offers to help with the tidying up, Katie accepted a dozen fist-bumps and several hugs, then locked the café's door, pulled on her Marigolds and filled a bucket with warm, soapy water, relishing the task of scrubbing away every last speck of flour and splatter of tomato sauce from the wooden tables. When she finished, a warm glow of contentment washed through her whole body, which increased further as she totted up her takings for the night. Even though she had supplied the drinks – all of them non-alcoholic – free of charge, the café had still made a small profit.

Maybe she could have a future at Agatha's Beachside Café after all.

Chapter 11

Katie was about to climb the stairs to fix herself a cup of chamomile tea before answering the siren call of her pillow when she heard a knock on the front door. Her heart performed a swift somersault of alarm and her first thought was whether she could get away with ignoring it. After all, the café was clearly closed and even the most avid addict of chocolate chip cookies couldn't possibility expect to feed their craving at ten thirty at night.

Then another more worrying thought skipped into her exhausted brain. Surely it couldn't be Greg paying her a night-time call? She would take the chocolate chip cookie enthusiast over the property tycoon anytime. Her quandary was ended by a buzz from her phone telling her that Oscar was on the doorstep, his mouth watering at the possibility of leftover pizza.

With a grin stretching her lips, she skipped back down the stairs and wrenched open the door, surprisingly thrilled to see his smiling face and the way his eyes lit up when he saw her – or that could have also been her confirmation that there were indeed a few slices of pizza left.

'Although I'm not sure the toppings will be your first choice.'

'What do you mean?'

'Well, Talia in particular went a little off-piste with her

selection. Apparently, the stars told her that she would have a fruitful evening and she chose to interpret that vague promise with the creation of a "fruit-laden" pizza, so there's either a slice of what she called her banoffee pizza …'

'What on earth is banoffee pizza?'

'Pizza with chocolate spread, sliced bananas, and toffee sauce drizzled on the top, or you can have a slice of Margarita.'

'Margarita, please.'

'Thought you might say that.' Katie giggled, leading Oscar into the kitchen where she set the kettle to boil and handed him a slice of cold pizza, which he devoured as though he hadn't eaten for days. 'Want another slice?'

'Sorry, I've spent the whole evening painting and time seems to have run away with me. I forgot to eat and I'm suddenly ravenous. I hope you don't mind me throwing myself on your mercy?'

'Not at all. In fact, you're doing me a huge favour by helping me to cut down on waste. I hate throwing good food in the bin, and I couldn't sell this pizza in the café.'

Katie set down all the leftover pizza, including the banoffee version, on the table in front of Oscar and watched in awe as he finished every last morsel, washed down with two mugs of black coffee.

'Delicious! Remind me to tell Talia that she might be on to something with that pizza – it was surprisingly good.'

'I'm sure she'll be delighted.'

'I suspect you're exhausted after the day you've had?'

'I am, but that's okay, I've enjoyed every minute, *and* I've made a small profit tonight.'

'That's great news.' Oscar smiled, suddenly leaping up from his chair. 'Come on. All work and no play and all that – you need a breath of fresh Cornish air!'

'Oh, actually I was just …'

Katie thought of her warm cosy bed waiting for her to snuggle into, then looked at the boyish exuberance on Oscar's face as he held out his hand to guide her out of the café and she could think of nothing she would like more than to take a stroll around the village green before she indulged her aching bones in the regulatory eight hours of sleep.

'Hang on while I grab my coat.'

She skipped to the cupboard under the stairs, grabbed her denim jacket and linked her arm through Oscar's as they made their way towards the duck pond where its residents had turned in for the night just like the rest of the inhabitants of the village. The Hope & Anchor was also in darkness and when she glanced at her watch, she was shocked to see it was almost midnight and her alarm clock would be waking her up in less than six hours. Yet, her earlier tiredness had lifted and all she could think about was enjoying the company of this kind, thoughtful man who was leading her towards a scarred wooden bench inside the bandstand where they sat for a while in contemplative silence.

'You know, Talia might have a point.'

'What do you mean?' asked Katie.

'The stars *are* beautiful, and maybe they *do* have a role to play in our destiny.'

Katie gazed at the speckles of infinite light overhead and a blanket of calm descended over her whole body. The last few months of her life had been filled with turmoil and trauma and she had cried more tears in that short period of time than she had since, well, since she was twelve years old. But sitting there, staring up at the inky black sky, she realised that every cloud did have a silver lining, even if it took time to find it among all the pain and the angst and the swirling distress. Her heart had cracked in two when Dominic had abandoned her, but she now knew that given time it would mend and she would be a stronger, if different person, for it.

She turned towards Oscar, to thank him for his support that day, not just in the café's kitchen, but for his thoughtful suggestion to get away from the chores for a few moments of peace and reflection. However, when she saw his expression, she paused. She knew when she thought or spoke of Dominic, her emotions were always written clearly on her face for all to see, but the look in Oscar's eyes was something much deeper, much more painful, and her heart gave a nip of anxiety.

'Oscar, are you okay?'

'Sure,' he said, automatically, as though he had been asked that question many times before and given the same practised, non-committal answer, just as she had when he had asked about her father.

Katie was about to take the hint, but changed her mind. While she didn't want to meander into territory that was none of her business, she was equally keen to offer him the same support he had given her.

'You don't look okay.'

'Sorry, I guess I'm just tired from spending too much time submerged in my painting. As soon as I pick up a paintbrush, the whole of the outside world and all its tasks and challenges just seem to slide away and the only things spinning through my mind are colour, and mood, and perspective, and creating the best picture I'm capable of.'

'So you don't regret switching from architecture?'

'Not at all.'

'And what do your parents think about your career change?'

'When I first left university, they were adamant that the best thing to do was to join their thriving practice, get some experience under my belt and relegate my passion for painting and ceramics to a spare hour here and there that I could carve out of my day. Of course, I never managed to find even a few minutes, and as time went on the craving to create didn't diminish, it grew. I didn't want to let them down, but I also didn't see myself like them in ten or fifteen years' time, running the practice alongside them.'

'So you decided to move on?'

'Something like that.'

There, she saw it again, that tightening around his jawline as he held back on his emotions, that flicker of sadness scooting across his eyes, that pulling away from her, physically as well as emotionally. And then she understood – Oscar's parents were disappointed about his decision, and maybe more than that; maybe they were angry at his decision to reject everything they had offered him to go off chasing his own dreams many miles away in Cornwall. Despite the situation being the complete opposite to her own, with her parents living their own best lives – one in Edinburgh, one in Greece – she understood how he must be feeling.

'I'm sure your parents will come round, Oscar. You've only been here for six months. Just give them time.'

Oscar stared at her, his forehead creased, his eyes filled with bafflement.

'I don't ... never mind.'

Katie had been so engrossed in their conversation that she had failed to notice that a bank of dark, bulbous clouds had scudded across the sky, playing a hasty game of hide-and-seek with the moon, and now preparing to deposit their contents on the unsuspecting onlooker.

'I think it's ...'

But it was too late; the heavens opened and sent down a barrage of rain with alacrity.

'Oh my God!'

'Come on!'

Oscar laced his fingers through Katie's, yanked her up from the bench and, with his arm hooked around her shoulders, sprinted from the bandstand, past the pond where the ducks had sensibly taken shelter beneath a clump of reeds, and headed for the café's front doorstep. Within seconds, she was soaked to the skin, her hair glued to her cheeks, her teeth chattering with cold. She struggled to find the key and when she eventually inserted it into the lock and tumbled into the café, she had never been so grateful for its warm embrace.

'Hey, you're shivering.'

Before she knew what was happening, Oscar had slid his arm around her waist and pulled her towards him, his soft breath warming her cheeks, his deep blue eyes for once devoid of their habitual mischievous glint. When he reached up to brush a damp tendril of hair from her forehead and gently tuck it behind her ear, Katie couldn't prevent a gasp from escaping her mouth as fizzles of desire shot the full length of her body. She felt as though she was teetering on the edge of a precipice, trying to make a decision whether to take a step back or jump into the unknown.

She met Oscar's gaze and suddenly they were kissing and the real world receded into the inconsequential; she was no longer shivering from the cold, but from the way Oscar's lips seemed to fit hers to perfection, from the way she felt both safe and so vibrantly alive in his arms, from the delicious sharpness of the sensations that swirled through every part of her being. She loved the way he laced his fingers, those strong, firm fingers that moulded clay into works of art by day, through her thick curls and caressed the nape of her neck with his thumb, exploring every single vertebra with a silky touch before peppering her collarbone with scrumptious kisses.

Wow, wow, wow, wow, wow, were the only words Katie was capable of thinking. There might be a storm raging outside on the village green, but a veritable bolt of lightning had just crashed through the café's windows straight into her chest. Was this what Cara was talking about when she spoke of waiting for a 'sign' when she kissed the various men she dated? She wasn't sure, but what she was feeling at that very moment was so radically different from anything she had experienced before and that shocked her to the core.

The realisation that Dominic had never made her feel like this brought her rushing back to reality, and she saw that Oscar's eyes had widened in surprise, too, mingled with something else she couldn't fathom. She took a step back, confusion flooding her brain, words failing her for a few seconds as her body swirled with a maelstrom of emotions. With supreme effort she managed to arrange her facial expression into something approaching normal and said the first thing that came into her head.

'Okay, better get to bed.'

She cringed at how that sounded spoken out loud, but fortunately Oscar came to her rescue.

'Yes, it's late. Thanks for the pizza. I'll catch you later.'

And he was gone, leaving her to stare after him through the bay window, his hands thrust into the pockets of his jeans, his shoulders hunched against the worsening rain and the weight of the world, and, leaving aside her own rampaging thoughts, Katie knew for sure that Oscar's issues ran far deeper than what his family thought of his change of career direction. There was something gnawing away at Oscar Spencer, and she wondered whether he'd had his heart broken too.

Chapter 12

Katie climbed the stairs to her bedroom, her brain working overtime as she attempted to work through what had just happened. Why had she decided to take the leap from friendship to something more complicated when she was still hurt over the way Dominic had treated her? And, more worryingly, why had she experienced such an intense reaction to Oscar's kiss? What did it mean?

She stripped off her rain-splattered jeans and hoodie and replaced them with a pair of pyjamas Cara had bought her for Christmas. As she slid between the sheets, her mind wandered to the precise moment she had unwrapped the carefully selected gift – fashioned from fluffy fabric bedecked with cupcakes and donuts – and Dominic's scathing comments that even his seven-year-old niece wouldn't be seen dead in such tasteless attire. She had wanted to retaliate with a vociferous objection, to tell him she adored them and that Cara had hit the nail on the head with her present – more so than Dominic had with the shiny Gaggia coffee machine that had been on his own shopping list for months – but she hadn't wanted to spoil the day by starting it with a row.

She hadn't admitted it out loud, but she was aware that Cara and Dominic had always had a lukewarm relationship, with Cara making a point of calling Dominic out every time he made a flippant comment about baking cakes not being a real job, or when he 'forgot' to attend François' fiftieth birthday party because Spurs were playing in the FA cup that night, or refused to organise a celebration when Katie won a prestigious competition for the best depiction in sugar paste of a London landmark. The latter occasion had been the only time Cara had taken Katie to one side, her hazel eyes filled with genuine concern, and asked gently whether Dominic was truly 'the one', or whether she just craved the security of being in a steady relationship after what had happened between her parents.

She accepted now, with the benefit of hindsight, that Cara had seen what she'd been unable to; that she deserved someone who rejoiced in all her achievements, large and small, someone who sang about them from the rooftops, not brushed them under the carpet as insignificant and unworthy of recognition. Had she really allowed her unresolved issues over her parents' divorce to colour her choice of partner? She had loved Dominic, and so had been quick to overlook his indifference towards her ambitions, to excuse his lack of interest in her dream to rival even François as a cake maker while he focused exclusively on his own goal to become a successful musician.

As she lay in Agatha's narrow guest bed, staring at the shadows dancing across the ceiling, she wondered how she would she react when – and she knew that eventually there had to be a *when* – Dominic finally called her to wax lyrical about how his decision to stay on in Ibiza had paid off? Despite his lack of contact over the last eight weeks, she knew he wouldn't be able to resist having an 'I told you so' conversation, and whilst she was still a mixture of bewildered and angry at the way they'd broken up, she was aware, deep inside, that there was still unfinished business between them.

The smiling face of her mother flashed across her mind. Katie had always admired the way she had handled the devastating blow that, after fifteen years of marriage, her father was leaving them to pursue a new life in Edinburgh with his dental hygienist. Oh, there had been tears, but with the help of her wide circle of friends and fellow equine enthusiasts, there had been acceptance along with frequent week-long trips to Spain, to Greece, to France, to volunteer at a variety of equine sanctuaries – her personal remedy for healing the cracks in her heart.

Then, as soon as Katie had left home to pursue her catering career in London, her mum had announced that she intended to fulfil a long-held dream of setting up a horse-riding retreat in the scenic hills and valleys of western Crete. Within a matter of weeks their house in Norfolk was on the market and she had made an offer on an in-need-of-a-little-love farmhouse in one of the whitewashed villages just outside Chania.

Katie smiled, the sleep fairies keeping their distance as she meandered along the road of reminiscence, when she remembered how wonderful her mum had looked when she'd met her for the first time at Chania airport after her relocation; tanned, lithe and filled with inner peace. Later, when they were sitting on the terracotta-tiled patio overlooking the Mediterranean Sea and sipping on a glass of the local ouzo, she had plucked up the courage to ask her how she felt about her father's infidelity. Her mum had placed her hand gently on Katie's arm and told her that she had forgiven him, that she had moved on, and that that was what Katie had to do, too.

She had ended her sun-drenched holiday filled with purpose, but as soon as she'd landed back in drizzly London, her demons had scoffed at her good intentions and once again it was easier to avoid reaching out to build bridges. Then she had met Dominic, and she was over the moon to have found someone who told her that he would love her for ever, someone who would never abandon her for a colleague and hot-foot it to Scotland at the first opportunity.

The sensible side of her brain had told her that it was the perfect time to begin dealing with the issues of insecurity and abandonment that had haunted her since she was a teenager. She had been terrified of raking up the past, but when Dominic slotted a pretty diamond solitaire onto the third finger of her left hand, she experienced a burst of self-worth, of certainty that she could conquer anything she put her mind to. Even her previously constant urge to grab her Marigolds and scrub away her feelings of rejection diminished to merely intermittent, and she no longer had to hide behind the fact that a keen interest in extreme hygiene was a necessity in her line of work.

So with Dominic and Cara's positive assurances ringing in her ears, she had agreed to call her father to tell him she was getting married and ask him if he would walk her down the aisle.

It was time to be brave.

That was over twelve months ago, but she could still remember with absolute clarity the emotions that had spun through her body as she'd cradled her phone in the palm of her hand for what felt like an eternity, her stomach churning, her knees a little weak and wobbly at the thought of what lay ahead, but she knew she had to do what her mother and Cara had been urging her to do for years.

After inhaling a few steadying breaths, she'd scrolled through the numbers in her contacts and stopped at the one she had stared at so many times but never had the courage to dial, until then.

'Hello?'

Even now, lying in a tiny bedroom above a café in Cornwall, and after everything she had been through since, she could still hear the irritation in the voice that had retained its Norfolk accent and sent her memories scooting back to her childhood.

'Hi, Dad, it's Katie.'

'Oh, Katie. Gosh, what a surprise!'

She had no idea what caused it, but she had suddenly decided this was the sort of conversation she wanted to have face to face.

She would take a trip up to Edinburgh, with Dominic at her side for moral support, and meet her father for a coffee; maybe they could stay over, explore some of the capital.

'Dad, I'd really like to talk to you.'

'Okay, right, I ...'

The complete lack of enthusiasm in his tone didn't deter her. She had known her call was a surprise for him.

'So, I thought I'd take the train up to Scotland at the weekend and we could ...'

'Oh, Katie, no, no, don't do that. I can't ... I have something else planned this weekend. It's Joanne's Sweet Sixteen party and we've organised a big do at The Balmoral. Maybe we could meet up in a couple of weeks? I'll give you a call, shall I, after I've discussed it with Sue? I have your number now.'

'Dad, I really want to ...'

'Sorry, Katie, I really have to dash. I'm actually in the process of collecting Joanne's birthday cake – sugar-free, of course.' Her father had laughed and Katie had almost lost control of her emotions as she recalled the constant battle cry of her dentist father about the evils of sugar. 'I'll call you.'

And the line had gone dead and she was left sitting there, the phone still pressed against her ear, struggling to corral the maelstrom of confusion swirling through her veins, trying to understand what had just happened.

Katie remembered every word, every inflection, every hurtful nuance as though it were yesterday. She had felt shock, sorrow, but also anger and indignation that her father could be so excited about his stepdaughter's birthday party when he had never even attended hers – sixteenth, eighteenth or twenty-first – despite having been invited. Nor had he showed up at her engagement party, although he and Sue had sent a gift – a couples' dental plan for the next two years, which Dominic had thought was hilarious.

When her anger had subsided, the pain had set in, the raw, energy-sapping hurt at what had been yet another rejection.

She had been stunned, dumbfounded even, at the brusque way someone who was supposed to love her unconditionally had spoken to her, and her hygiene monsters, so recently banished into the cleanliness wilderness, had threatened to once again rear their ugly heads.

However, with her wedding to organise, and François giving her more responsibility at work, she had managed to put the disappointment of her father's rejection into a sealed box and store it there for later dissection. She never had returned to that unenviable task, which had been made even harder after Dominic had called off the wedding, but after the last few weeks in Cornwall and the events of that night, she knew with more certainty than ever that until she dealt with her ever-present fear of abandonment, her demons would continue their persistent pursuit.

Now that the café looked as though it *could* be a viable business, and she *could* be sticking around for the foreseeable future, she resolved to take a break from the hustle and bustle of life as a busy café manager and carve out some 'me time', something she had resolutely avoided for as long as she could remember.

And no matter how attracted she was to Oscar with his cheerful, laid-back approach to life and just-tumbled-out-of-bed hair, the last thing she needed was further complications.

Chapter 13

The next event to be held at the café was one Katie had been looking forward to, mainly because it didn't involve her as the presenter. Jay had been planning his flower-arranging tutorial for the last two weeks and the highly anticipated event was due to take place at seven o'clock that evening. She had prepared several pitchers of home-made lemonade, made three huge chocolate, orange and frangipane tarts, a batch of buttery Cornish fairings, as well as a classic Victoria sponge cake which she had decorated using that evening's theme as inspiration – a sugar-paste depiction of a pretty wildflower garden complete with bumble bees and butterflies frolicking among the leaves and the grasses.

Despite the success of Talia's pizza-making night, and the steady increase in the café's footfall, Katie still couldn't quash the niggle of anxiety that agitated at her chest at the thought of a potential repeat of the dire launch-night attendance figures and what she was going to do with all the cake and the armfuls of flowers Jay had delivered that afternoon and then spent an hour organising into individual bundles, if no one turned up.

She checked her watch – six thirty, only half an hour to go, time to have a quick shower and wash her hair so she didn't scare the natives. She tossed her antibacterial spray into the cupboard under the sink – which now resembled a miniature Aladdin's cave jam-packed with every eco-friendly cleaning product available on the British high street – and she was halfway up the stairs when there was a knock on the door.

Surely no one would turn up so early?

She trailed back down to the café and wrenched open the door, the cheerful smile of welcome slipping from her lips when she saw who her visitor was.

'Oh ...'

Without waiting to be invited in, Greg pushed past her, his eyes flitting around the room, his lips twisting in derision at the colourful décor.

'Oh my God, where've you hidden the Dalai Lama?'

Greg snorted at his own joke, a sound that grated on Katie's rattled nerves.

'I wouldn't mind a slice of that cake, though? Where did you get it? It's amazing!'

Katie bristled, fighting an internal battle between remaining polite and professional or demanding that he leave the premises. Clad in another well-cut designer suit with lavender silk lining and a tie to match, the cloud of cologne was even more powerful than the last time he visited. However, his demeanour was exactly the same: arrogant with just a snippet of malice, and whilst good manners always pipped rudeness in Katie's book, she was determined to keep their second meeting as short as possible.

'What do you want? I'm expecting guests.'

'I heard through the grapevine that your launch party was a wash-out and you had to offload the mountain of food you had left over. No business can sustain that sort of loss, so I'm here to offer you a little of my hard-won expertise and to tell you that there's no shame in admitting defeat and pushing on to the next project.'

'Greg, I appreciate ...'

'Not everyone is cut out to run a small business,' he continued as though he were a keynote speaker at a conference for entrepreneurs. He squinted at one of Oscar's more gregarious paintings. When he turned back round to meet her gaze, she was surprised to see genuine concern in his eyes. 'Why are you doing this to yourself, Katie? What are you trying to prove, or perhaps I should be asking, who are you trying to impress?'

'I'm not …'

'Anyway, I won't keep you. I just wanted to give you this.'

Greg reached into the inside pocket of his jacket and whipped out a large white envelope, brandishing it in front of her face.

'What is it?'

'A letter I'd like you to deliver to your friend Agatha Carmichael. If you persist in refusing to hand over her telephone number or her email address, then I want you to give her this. It's a formal offer for the building – the café and the flat upstairs.'

When Katie didn't take the envelope, he left it on the table and strode towards the door.

'Holiday homes are not the bête noire people think they are. They can be good for the local economy, bring in a whole host of visitors who spend their money in the shops and businesses. It's a win-win. I'll leave you to your event. Ciao!'

Katie closed, and locked, the door behind him, her emotions churning as she watched his BMW roar away. She picked up the envelope as though it were a grenade about to explode, and a nugget of dread imbedded itself into her chest as she realised that she no longer had an excuse not to contact Agatha and tell her about Greg's interest.

Now he had made his offer in writing, it was serious.

However, her telephone call to sunny Bali would have to wait until the following morning because she could see Jay making his way across the village green looking like a film star attending his first première, and ten minutes later he was launching into his very first flower-arranging class.

'Okay, everyone, brace yourselves for a night of floral

fabulousness! I've brought roses, tulips and carnations as well as sunflowers and delphiniums and gypsophila, and by the end of the evening I promise that everyone will be going home with a bouquet of bootyliciousness.'

Jay beamed at his gathered audience, a selection of mainly women with a few token athletic-looking men with great tans from the local tennis club where Jay was a member of the Sunday morning league. Everyone watched spellbound as he selected several random stems and twisted them together to create a posy worthy of a celebrity bride, before finishing it off with a candy-striped ribbon, curling the ends with scissors. It was like watching a magician at work as he switched to showcase a different trick, this time producing an arrangement of huge smiling sunflowers and pale blue delphiniums, blushing with delight when he received a flutter of applause.

'Okay, so now it's over to you.'

An explosion of high-pitched chatter filled the café as the group rushed for the tables where the various stems had been set out alongside a mound of glossy foliage and a selection of ribbons and bows, whilst Katie, Talia and Zoe adjourned to the kitchen to make a start on the refreshments.

Katie had decided it was the perfect event to introduce the herbal teas she had sourced from an estate in Cornwall where they actually grew tea as well as offering locally produced cordials – elderflower, apple, even rhubarb and chilli, but of course, in pride of place was the wildflower cake, which was receiving compliments abound.

'What do you think?' asked Ruby, holding up a bunch of roses the same colour as her nails that day.

With her ample curves encased in a figure-hugging jumpsuit and her profusion of corkscrew curls held back in a matching bandana to highlight her fabulous cheekbones, the village beautician and hairdresser could give Jay a run for his money when it came to attire fit for treading the red carpet – although Jay definitely had the edge in the perfume stakes. In honour of his presenting debut, he smelled like he'd spent the night in a Parisian lady's boudoir. In fact, the whole café was awash with a potpourri of competing fragrances; from Jay's oriental spice-infused aftershave, the myriad of aromas from the fresh flowers, and the perfumed tea lights scattered around the café, not to mention the sugary desserts and the herbal teas.

'It's fabulous, Ruby!'

When it was time to cut the cake, Jay was handed the knife and a wide smile stretched his cheeks as if all his birthdays had come at once. He was clearly having the time of his life, flitting backwards and forwards between the various groups, tweaking the arrangements, twisting the wire, adding alternative colours to enhance the mix that turned a mediocre bunch of random flowers into a splash of vibrant artistry, or advocating the less-is-more approach by sticking to a simple colour scheme and adding lots of foliage.

'Have you got any tips on how to keep cut flowers fresh for longer, Jay?' asked a buxom woman with a short ebony bob and a fringe skimming her eyelashes, sitting with the yummy mummies group.

'Yes, I do. My first tip is to trim the stems daily, using a sharp knife or a pair of scissors, making sure you cut on the diagonal, and to change the water frequently, too.'

'I love these sunflowers, Jay. Just seeing them makes me smile.'

'They're also said to bring good luck, and that their presence fills your home with safety and protection.'

'That's great! I can do with all the luck I can get,' announced Ruby's friend Willow who was clearly competing for the top slot in the extreme-clothing competition with a pair of neon-green hot-pants worn with paisley-patterned tights. 'I've got my mother-in-law coming tomorrow for a week and she just loves to criticise the way I do things in the house.'

'Why don't you make a posy especially for her, tell her you

chose the flowers because they represent her personality. If that doesn't soften her hard edges, I recommend an infusion of chamomile, fennel and lavender tea.' Jay smiled, his eyes glinting.

'Great idea!'

When it was time to leave, everyone sang Jay's praises at the tops of their voices, and as the door closed for the last time, Katie dropped down onto a chair and heaved a long sigh of relief.

'Thanks, Jay, that was a huge success.'

'Of course it was, *cherie*. With my talent for floral artistry and yours for sugary magnificence, how could the evening be anything other than a terrific triumph?'

'True, true.' Katie giggled. 'I'll give you a hand to pack up the leftover flowers, shall I?'

'Oh, just leave them – they're bruised, I can't sell them in the shop. Look, why don't I make a couple of arrangements for the café?'

'Thanks, Jay, but I think the place already looks like an extension of the Eden Project.' She pointed to three huge displays of peach gladioli, pale yellow carnations and ivory tulips.

'Can I make a suggestion, then?'

'Sure.'

'Why don't you take them over to the care home in Bradbury? I go down there once a month to do a demonstration for the ladies there, and they adore the flowers.'

'What a wonderful idea! I'm sure Talia will hold the fort in the morning.'

'Great, here's the address. Ask for Hector. He's a friend of mine from the gym; tell him I sent you. Be careful though, he's bound to rope you in for something or other. Those OAPs have the best social life this side of the West End of London! Last weekend he booked a juggler to come in and show them circus skills – hilarious!'

'I don't mind doing a cake-decorating demonstration one day,' said Katie, her brain already scooting towards possible themes.

'Thanks, Katie, you're a sweetheart!'

'I am?' She laughed.

'Yes, you've only been in Perrinby for a few weeks and already you've made a huge impact. The whole village is much more vibrant; these themed nights are inspirational and I love how you've included the whole community, and don't think I haven't noticed that you've put a smile on the face of our resident artist.'

Heat rushed to Katie's cheeks. She had bumped into Oscar a couple of times since the night of the storm, but each time she had been with either Talia or Zoe or Jay. However, as she had expected, there had been no awkwardness between them, just the same good-humoured, friendly banter that she'd come to expect from Oscar – although that obviously hadn't fooled Jay. There had been no mention of their brief embrace, of the shock its intensity had instilled in both of them, and she had to admit to being relieved because she was still working on what it meant.

Jay had been watching her expression as though able to see exactly what was swirling through her mind, and, satisfied at what he'd seen, he leaned forward to deposit *les bises* on her cheeks before collecting the huge white cardboard box the flowers had been delivered in.

'Later, darling! Say hi to Hunky Hector from me!'

As Katie filled a bucket with hot soapy water and set about returning the café to its pristine glory, her spirits edged up a notch. So far there had been the failure of the launch party but two successes with her themed evenings – she hoped that her fortunes were beginning to turn and the gods were at last smiling on her and Agatha's café.

It was early days, but could Perrinby become her new home?

Then her eyes snagged on the envelope Greg had left earlier and her heart bounced down to her toes. Okay, so people might have turned up to the pizza-making night and the flower-arranging demonstration – and to her delight they had both made a small profit – but a modest return on the evening's investment wasn't enough to grow a successful business, despite having produce left to contribute to good causes.

However, it was only the beginning of April; she still had a couple of months left to build on what she had achieved so far and the summer tourist season was fast approaching, which could only be a good thing for a pretty Cornish café overlooking a typically English village green and a mere stone's throw from a gorgeous sandy beach.

Thinking of gorgeous sandy beaches, another beach six thousand miles away flashed into her mind, this one fringed with swaying palm trees and drenched in golden sunshine, the fragrance of red hibiscus and pink bougainvillea wafting through the warm air and the sound of gentle music lingering on the breeze.

She missed Agatha and their easy friendship and she knew she couldn't put it off any longer – she had to call her and tell her about Greg's offer.

Chapter 14

Katie shouldn't have felt relieved, but when she phoned Agatha the next morning, the call went straight to voicemail. When she checked her watch and saw it was two o'clock in the afternoon in Bali, she realised that her friend would be in the throes of one of her cookery school tutorials. She left a message asking her to call her back, then sent Talia a text to ask if she would mind opening up because she was taking a trip over to Edgemont Manor.

It was the first break from the café she'd had since she'd arrived in Cornwall, and, in honour of the auspicious occasion, she pulled on a pair of floral cropped trousers and a vibrant yellow T-shirt, then fixed her hair into a short ponytail with one of the unicorn bobbles Talia had gifted her.

She skipped down the stairs, a dash of contentment flooding through her veins at the sight of the early morning sunshine slicing through the bay window giving the café the air of a magical exotic paradise. The faint sound of birdsong sent her spirits up another notch, as did the lingering aroma of jasmine and gardenia from the flower arrangements that had spent the night in a sink full of water. She wrapped the bouquets in a damp tea towel and carried them like precious artefacts to her hire car for the short drive over to the care home.

Katie took her time navigating the serpentine roads. Hedgerows, resplendent with late spring blossom, provided the perfect backdrop for the daffodils dancing their final jig as they said goodbye to April and ushered in May. It was a world away from her former work commute in the capital, pushing through a brigade of office workers in their identikit suits, their eyes on the bottom line instead of the horizon. The toxic stench of traffic fumes had made her eyes water, but here in the most southerly county of England a crystal-clear breeze wafted through the car window, bringing with it the scent of hawthorn and sea salt as she headed further down the Cornish coast.

A smile twisted her lips when she thought of the jolly phone call she had made to Jay's friend Hector, especially when he'd said he would have a pot of Tregothnan tea and a round of warm, buttered crumpets ready for her arrival. She switched on the car radio, turning the dial until she found a soft classical melody, and it wasn't long before a pair of impressive pillars, topped with miniature stone lions, hove into view and she crunched down the gravelled driveway, the old-fashioned black lampposts and rhododendron bushes providing a welcoming guard of honour.

The property itself was like something from a TV period drama, with mullioned windows flanking both sides of a huge oak front door and a shiny brass plaque confirming that she had arrived at Edgemont Manor. She parked her car in the visitors' car park and took a moment to appreciate the extensive, wraparound gardens – this was definitely the sort of place she would like to spend her later years, especially when she saw the croquet lawn. She checked her watch again and realised her journey hadn't taken her as long as she had expected and that she was forty minutes early for her appointment with Hector.

Surely he wouldn't mind if she took a stroll around the gardens?

She made her way across the paved terrace on the south side of the manor house, down a flight of steps and through a small formal garden complete with neatly clipped box hedges and a goldfish pond watched over by a pair of wooden benches for the residents to rest awhile and drink in the spectacular Turneresque view. She continued walking, past an avenue of laburnum trees, and on towards a large Victorian greenhouse, its door ajar in a gesture of invitation – a temptation she couldn't refuse.

She pushed the door open and stepped inside, closing her eyes briefly to inhale the smell of fresh green leaves and potting soil. Then she came to an abrupt halt, her heart crashing with unexpected ferocity against her ribcage and sending painful sparkles of electricity radiating out to her fingertips.

'Oh my God!'

She rushed forward and crouched down next to an elderly lady, crumpled in a heap on the mosaic brick floor, her lined face pale, her silver hair dishevelled, but her pale-blue eyes still held a defiant sparkle despite her discomfort.

'What happened? Are you okay?'

'I am now you're here, dear. I think I may have twisted my ankle.'

The woman looked decidedly peaky and for a split second Katie's mind went blank with panic, then she switched to autopilot, spotted an ancient rattan chair at the far end of the greenhouse and rushed off to collect it.

'Here, let me help you.'

With supreme gentleness, Katie manoeuvred the elderly woman into the seat, rolling her eyes when she spotted the surprisingly trendy leopard-print shoes with a kitten heel, which almost certainly had contributed to her fall. The footwear made her think of Cara, another confirmed shoe connoisseur – as far as her budget would allow. She took hold of the woman's age-speckled hand, the skin papery thin, and gently rubbed warmth back into her fingers, relief flooding her veins when she saw the colour return to her face.

'Thank you, that's much better.'

'How long have you been lying there?'

'About an hour, I think. I take a stroll over here every morning – to commune with nature, talk to the plants, hug a few trees. Maisie says I'm going doolally but I just tell her that if it's good enough for royalty then it's good enough for me. I'm Dorothy, by the way.'

'I'm Katie, Katie Campbell. Now, if you think you'll be okay for a few minutes, I'll go and fetch some help.'

'Oh, I'm fine now, dear. Just a sprain, nothing a cold press won't cure. But I do think that if you hadn't been passing, then it could have been curtains for me. Jim, that's the manor's head gardener, doesn't start his shift until one.'

The thought caused a sharp spasm of shock to nip at Katie's heart and she gave Dorothy a smile.

'I'm still going to get help.'

She patted her hand, then sprinted across the lawn to the conservatory that ran the full length of the back of the manor and housed the breakfast room where there was a gasp of surprise when she burst through the French doors and grabbed the first uniformed person she encountered to explain, breathless, what had happened.

Within minutes, a well-oiled rescue mission had been mounted and Dorothy was wheeled like the Queen of Sheba, her foot elevated, back to the house and treated by the designated first aider who gently chastised her for leaving the house without telling anyone. She was then stationed in a sunny corner of the conservatory to receive a steady flow of well-wishers.

'I don't know what to say,' said Hector, a chubby thirty-something with a friendly face and a penchant for the excessive use of hair gel – even a force-ten gale would have struggled to dislodge his sculptured quiff, the colour of a fox's tail. 'First you bring us several stunning bouquets to brighten up our darkest corners, then you save the life of one of our most loved residents.'

'Oh, I don't think I …' began Katie, warmth scooting into her cheeks.

'Old ladies don't last long on cold, hard floors, my dear.' Hector smiled, his kind eyes wrinkling at the corners as he brushed away her protests. 'And you're not leaving until you've had a hot cup of tea and one of Cook's famous cherry and almond scones. Off you go. I think Dorothy has finished regaling her audience with the finer details of her morning's adventure. She's ninety-two next birthday, you know. Doesn't look a day over seventy, if you ask me. Hope I have such good skin when I'm her age – doubt it though – I love a bit of Santorini sunbathing. Go on shoo!'

Katie smiled as the care home's manager trotted off towards the kitchen. She made her way over to the large, light-filled conservatory, complete with chequerboard floor, the chairs and occasional tables the pawns and the knights on horses. The room was decorated with an array of old-fashioned houseplants, and if she stood on her tiptoes and looked out of the window, she could see the merest glimmer of the Atlantic Ocean shimmering in the distance.

'How are you feeling?'

'Oh, right as rain, dear, right as rain. Come, sit.'

Dorothy indicated a peacock-blue wing-backed chair, which looked stiff and unwieldy but was in fact very comfortable. Katie turned to smile at her new friend, but before she could say anything, Dorothy had launched into her cross-examination.

'Hector tells me you own the café in Perrinby?'

'Oh, no, I don't own it, I'm just … well, I'm just managing it for a few months until …'

'You know, it was always a dream of mine to own a little village café,' mused Dorothy, her pale blue eyes lingering on a random point on the distant horizon. 'I used to be a Nippy at the Lyons tea rooms in Piccadilly just after the war, you know. We didn't have much in those days, but us girls made our own entertainment – it was the most exciting time of my life.'

'Oh, that must have been …'

'Met my Arthur there – he'd pop in on his way home from work, always sit at the same table, always order the same thing. The other girls used to tease me rotten! By the time he'd eventually plucked up the courage to ask me for a date, I'd already planned our wedding. Things moved much faster in those days. Oh, he looked so handsome on our wedding day.'

Hector arrived to break the flow of reminiscences, holding a wooden tray laden with a silver teapot, milk jug and china cups and saucers, as well as a cake stand sporting fresh-from-the-oven scones, strawberry jam and a pot of the famous clotted cream. He performed his tea-pouring duties like a seasoned professional and then retreated to complete his morning's chores after telling Katie to stay as long as she liked.

'Do you have children, dear?'

'No, no, I don't.'

'Me neither. It was the only hiccup in what's been a very happy life. When Arthur and I married I left the tea rooms and went to work as his secretary in his accountancy practice and we were very comfortable. I've been all over the world, you know, but there's nowhere quite as lovely as the Cornish coast. Just look at that view!'

'It *is* beautiful here.' Katie smiled, taking a sip of her tea and feasting her eyes on the expanse of deep blue sea, its surface glistening beneath the strengthening sunshine as colourful tourist boats made their way to secret coves.

'Are you married?'

The question took Katie by surprise and she knew her reaction showed in her face.

'Oh, I'm sorry, dear.' This time it was Dorothy's turn to reach out for Katie's hand and give it a warm squeeze, wincing a little as she leaned forward in her chair. 'Have I stumbled on a sore subject?'

'No, not at all …'

'Want to tell an old lady what happened to cause that grimace? If there's one thing I've learned in this long life, it's that it's good to talk – to empty out all that useless clutter we carry around with us, get rid of all the mess and tangle of thoughts before we start to fill our mind up again with more inconsequential stuff that we let upset us and stand in the way of making us happy.'

Dorothy held Katie's gaze and simply waited, her eyebrows raised in expectation, knowing full well that she had cut through Katie's shaky defences and seen the raw, gaping wound within – *she really did have to work on her acting skills!*

Still, Katie hesitated. Agatha was the only person outside her immediate circle of friends she had confided in about Dominic, but for some reason she couldn't quite put her finger on, Dorothy reminded her of Agatha – maybe it was the west country accent.

'My fiancé broke off our engagement a month before the wedding. We were supposed to have been married six weeks ago, but when he went off for his stag weekend in Ibiza, he … well, he never came back.'

'And what did he say when you asked him why he did that?'

'No, that's the thing. After his text to tell me the wedding was off, Dominic refused to answer any of my calls. In the first couple of weeks I rang him almost every hour, begging him to explain what had gone wrong, but all my pleas went to voice-mail. I called every one of the friends who went with him, but of course, they didn't want to get involved. I've even been to see his parents, Bill and Jackie, whom I have to tell you are mortified about what happened.'

Katie decided to leave out the bit about Dominic emptying their wedding coffers – it was just too embarrassing to admit that she had intended to marry someone who would do such a horrible thing.

'In fact, they ring me every fortnight, just to make sure I'm okay. I don't think Dominic has spoken to them either, or maybe they're just telling me that, I don't know.'

'That must be hard. Not knowing the reason why he jilted you like that.'

'It's the hardest thing. This might sound stupid, but I had no idea there was anything wrong. Okay, I admit there were a few arguments, but who isn't stressed when they're planning a wedding – there's just so much to do. But to ditch your fiancée without saying anything and expecting your best man to field all the increasingly hysterical questions? Poor Iain, I don't think he's recovered from the trauma.'

Katie gave a joyless laugh as she recalled the excruciating conversation she'd had with Iain when she'd called him – before Dominic's text had arrived in her inbox – in a complete panic thinking Dominic had been in an accident on the way home from the airport, *not* that he hadn't even been on the plane!

'Are you angry with him?'

'I was. Who wouldn't be? He didn't just let me down; he caused a lot of hurt and inconvenience to a lot of people.'

Katie paused as she thought of her mother's threat to catch the next flight to Ibiza, and Cara who had stormed over to Iain's house and refused to leave until he'd told her where Dominic was staying, which he had done – Cara could be fierce when she needed to be – but when Katie had called the B&B, Dominic had, probably sensibly, moved on.

'And that's why you're down here in Cornwall, is it? To make a fresh start?'

'Something like that.'

'So, tell me about your little café.'

Feeling on safer ground, Katie filled Dorothy in on her vision for Agatha's café: the locally sourced ingredients, zero food waste wherever possible, and with community at the heart of it all. Dorothy clapped her hands with delight, declaring herself exceedingly jealous and promising that when her ankle was better she would pay Katie's new venture a visit.

The old adage was true, time did fly when you were having

fun, and when Katie looked at her watch, she was shocked to find it was after eleven o'clock. Spending the morning with Dorothy had chased away her anxieties over the future of the café as they gossiped about fancy cakes, herbal teas and whether you put the cream or the jam on a scone first.

'You have to move on, my dear. You know that, don't you? There's nothing to be gained from wallowing in "what might-have-beens". You have to put what your fiancé did down to one of life's many learning experiences – there'll be a few more of those along the road, I can assure you of that. It's how we deal with disappointment that dictates whether we have a happy and fulfilling life.'

'But how can I …'

'Look how far you've come in just a couple of months. A trip halfway around the world, starting your own business, making new friends, saving old ladies' lives!'

'Dorothy …'

'Will you do something for me, Katie?'

'Of course.'

'Will you promise me that you won't hold what Dominic did against every other young man within a twenty-mile radius? You have to find a way to take a leap of faith again, to give your heart to someone new and to trust them to love you back, even if it didn't work out the first time. If you don't, then you risk leading a very lonely life. I've seen it in the residents who live here – heard their sad stories of regrets. Please, Katie, don't find yourself in a place like this, looking back and saying those dreadful words none of us should ever say – "if only I'd …" My mother, bless her heart, always used to say that it's better to have loved and lost than never to have loved at all. And that's where you'll always hold the winning hand over Dominic – you loved. You experienced that wonderful emotion that some people wait a lifetime for and still never experience. Losing it is painful, but it's better than the bleak loneliness of the alternative.'

Katie stared at Dorothy, temporarily lost for words.

'Thanks,' was all she could manage to say.

Clearly, long days in the care home had given Dorothy time to reflect on life in all its myriad guises and, whether knowingly or not, she had cut straight to Katie's emotional core. Katie reached out to give her new friend's hand a squeeze and made to get out of her chair, but Dorothy hadn't finished delivering her pearls of wisdom.

'However, I think, my dear Katie, that your difficulties go far deeper than what your fiancé did to you. Am I right?'

Katie contemplated asking Dorothy to explain what she meant, but of course she didn't need to. Her issues with abandonment *did* go beyond her broken engagement. Her relationship with Dominic, even in the good times, had merely papered over a gaping wound she had carried around with her for years. His leaving had ripped off the temporary sticking plaster and delivered a fresh burst of pain because she hadn't faced the root cause and allowed it to heal. She knew what she had to do, but she simply couldn't face it. She didn't have the emotional strength, not now.

But if she didn't, would she be sitting in a chair similar to Dorothy's, filled with regrets that she hadn't found the courage to face her demons head-on before it was too late?

Chapter 15

'What do you think of my new dress?' asked Talia a few weeks later as she removed her coat and proceeded to perform a catwalkesque strut through the forest of tables in the café, her skirt swishing around her knees as she paused to flick back her hair and pout to an invisible camera.

'It's …'

Katie's jaw dropped, at a complete loss for words until she realised that the fabric was printed with cucumbers and green tomatoes and not the more risqué image she had initially suspected.

'Yes, it's lovely. Cucumbers … it's an unusual print for a dress material, don't you think?'

'Well, this is a café. And we do use lots of cucumbers. I've been experimenting with my Skechers too. Do you like them?'

Katie had been too preoccupied with Talia's dress to notice her shoes, and when she looked down she couldn't stop the guffaw from erupting from her throat.

'Oh, I'm sorry, Talia. I … well, it's a bold choice of accessory, that's all.'

'I think they look amazing!'

Katie wasn't sure she agreed with her. Talia was probably the only person in the whole of Cornwall, or the UK for that matter, who thought that accessorising her shoes with Lego bricks was an avant-garde approach to spring footwear.

'They're certainly original. So, are you ready for tonight's event?'

'Absolutely!'

It was the first time they had organised an event on a Saturday night, but Katie thought it might appeal to a different kind of customer, someone who perhaps had child-care responsibilities or work commitments during the week, which could potentially widen the café's reach. The pizza night had introduced her to Talia's tribe who continued to pop into the café for a latte or a hot chocolate, and people still stopped her in the street to ask when Jay was planning to hold another of his floral fantasia shows.

There had been so much going on, so much to do in the café to make sure she added a little extra sparkle to her customers' morning coffees or afternoon teas instead of pandering to the whims of rich celebrities who ordered cakes for their pets, that she realised she hadn't been thinking of Dominic at all during the day, only in those quiet moments before sleep swept her down Morpheus's dark highway.

Progress indeed!

And despite the uncomfortable tickle of guilt for not trying to ring Agatha again, she was starting to think she could actually make a go of not only running a successful café, but also of her new life in a Cornish village where everyone had made her feel like she was an important, and valuable, part of the community. She hoped the Books & Bakes event that night would make a profit, like the previous two events, so she could report to Agatha how well things were going before she went on to inform her about Greg's letter that was currently on the coffee table in her flat, growing horns.

'So, what book have you brought tonight, Talia?'

'Oh, actually I couldn't decide so I brought two.'

Katie surreptitiously crossed her fingers behind her back that Talia's choice of reading material was more conservative than her choice of attire.

'One is a Harry Potter – which I love! And the other is a non-fiction book called *The Secrets of the Stars* about how we are all guided by the position of the stars at the time of our birth. What have you chosen, Katie?'

'I've chosen *Eat, Pray, Love* by Elizabeth Gilbert.'

'Sounds like the sort of mantra I could get into.' Talia grinned. 'It's perfect for our friendly little café's first book club.'

Katie didn't add that its relevance was purely coincidental and the only reason she had brought that book with her was because, embarrassingly, it was the only book she had with her; most of her possessions were still in storage until she decided where her future lay. She had bought it at the airport on her way out to Bali and the story had given her hope that maybe one day she too would be able to move on from the Dominic Debacle and find love.

She couldn't wait to meet the village's bookworms, and, as it was the inaugural meeting, the rules of the evening were going to be a little different. Everyone who had put their name on the sign-up sheet was asked to simply bring along a copy of their favourite book. As they indulged in tea and cappuccinos, each avid reader would be given five minutes to explain to the gathering why they had loved it, hopefully inspiring another reader to swap it with theirs and try out a book they might not have otherwise picked up.

'Wow, these courgette and walnut cupcakes are yummy!' swooned Talia, rolling her eyes in comic ecstasy as she licked the saffron buttercream from the ends of her fingers. 'And what are those?'

'Beetroot and fudge. I thought I'd let everyone have as many tea and coffee refills as they want, but make a charge for the cakes, the clotted cream scones and the cookies. Maybe if the book club idea takes off, we can rustle up a few Balinese-inspired desserts, such as laklak cakes – which are also gluten-free – with the money going to Agatha's cookery school project. What do you think?'

'I think it's a great idea! In fact, I think I'll whip up a quick poster to let everyone know about it so they won't be able to resist signing up for next month.'

'Oh, I … well, yes, okay.'

Katie watched Talia disappear into the kitchen and fire up her ancient laptop, then spent a few minutes making sure everything was perfect, wiping away an escaped crumb, and straightening the cushions on the window seat when she had an idea.

'I saw you and Ryan were getting on well at the pizza-making night.'

'We were, but he still hasn't asked me out,' grumbled Talia as her fingers flew over the keyboard.

'Then why don't you ask *him*? Nothing too intimate, just a coffee, or what about a trip to the cinema or a picnic on the beach?'

'Do you really think so?'

'Absolutely – it *is* the twenty-first century, you know.'

'True. Okay, I'll do that! What's the worst that can happen?'

Suddenly Katie regretted her decision to get involved in Talia's love life. What did she know about dating? She had just made a whole mess of her own attempt at a long-lasting relationship and she didn't want Talia to suffer the same consequences of picking the wrong person. Maybe Ryan's reluctance to ask her out on a date was down to more than the fact that her mum owned the local wedding boutique?

'Actually, Talia, I …'

'Here, what do you think?'

Talia dashed over to the printer and held up a poster sporting a riot of exotic colours, complete with emojis of flying parrots, swaying palm trees and smiling suns, interspersed with books and cupcakes.

'I love it. Thank you.'

'I'd love to visit Bali one day, you know. I've been saving up to go travelling for ages, but I don't think I'll ever have enough in the kitty to travel that far.'

'Well, when you're ready, let me know. My best friend Cara is a travel agent in London and she knows how to get the best deals out there on flights and accommodation. She'll fix you up and make a few suggestions on how to save money.'

'Wow, that's amazing. I'll definitely …'

'*Salut, mes cheries*! I'm here to bestow your evening with a sprinkle of glamour and literary fabulousness. I couldn't decide whether to go for *The Perks of Being a Wallflower* or *The Best Exotic Marigold Hotel*, so I plumped for one of my absolute favourites – *Hollywood Wives* by Jackie Collins! Now, Katie, where shall I park these gorgeous yellow roses that I spent ages arranging into the shape of a book? I thought you could raffle it off at the end of the night with the proceeds going to Agatha's cookery school project?'

'Oh, Jay, that is so kind of you.'

Katie beamed at Jay, and, as words temporarily failed her, she reached out to give him a quick appreciative hug instead, turning swiftly back to the kitchen so he didn't notice the tears gathering along her lashes.

'So, how many are we expecting at the Books & Bakes night? Did we get a last-minute surge of avid book lovers with insatiable appetites for sweet treats? The place looks like the set of *The Great British Bake Off* – not that I'm complaining of course, those cupcakes look am … maz … zing!'

'Actually, we had a lot more people sign up than I expected. If everyone turns up, including you, me and Talia, there'll be around twenty-five of us, and if everyone buys a cupcake or a slice of cake, then I think the night will be a financial success, too!'

'Which is what we're all aiming for. I know how difficult it is to make a profit during the off-season, but the summer months are nearly here, and I can assure you that trade will definitely pick up and you and Talia will be run off your feet.'

'Thanks, Jay. I'm really grateful for all your support – everyone in Perrinby has been so kind. You know, people are still talking about your fabulous flower-arranging night.'

'Of course they are, darling, of course they are!'

'Oh, Katie, I've just had a text from Marcia and Danielle. They went over to St Ives this afternoon to see a film and they thought they wouldn't be able to make it tonight, but they're on their way back. Can we squeeze them in, do you think?' asked Talia, peering at the screen on her mobile phone in delight.

'Absolutely! The more the merrier!'

Contentment swirled through Katie's chest as she busied herself with hanging up Talia's poster and adding extra chairs for any more last-minute arrivals. Ruby, and her best friend Willow – who swapped her weekday job in doggie day-care for the new title of 'nail technician' at the weekend – had said they were a 'definite maybe' if they could get out of the salon on time, and even the couple who supplied the café with locally grown organic fruit and vegetables had promised to come along if she didn't mind them talking about gardening books. Maybe Saturday nights were a good idea!

When seven o'clock rolled around, Zoe was the first to arrive with Mel and a gaggle of the mums from school in tow, all of whom kept up a constant stream of chatter that filled the café with a warm, welcoming and friendly vibe from the off. The burble of conversation, fed by plenty of tea, coffee and sugary treats, was taken to a new level when Ruby burst through the door, sporting the most striking of jumpsuits that would challenge even Talia for sartorial exuberance, followed by Willow who presented Katie with an envelope.

'What's this?'

'A voucher.'

'A voucher? What for?'

Willow glanced down at Katie's nails, her eyes filled with compassion, her perfectly shaped eyebrows raised and Cupid's-bow lips twisted into a sympathetic smile, sending a message that required no vocalising.

'Oh, it's a manicure! Thank you so much, Willow. I can't wait! I was actually planning on taking a little "me time" and this is the perfect gift.'

'Self-care is so important, especially for people who run their own businesses,' said Ruby, reaching out to squeeze Katie's hand meaningfully before weaving her way through the coterie of WI women who had commandeered the cake table, to greet Jay and Talia with enthusiastic hugs.

'Okay, everyone, if you could take a seat, we'll get started.'

It took another ten minutes to get everyone settled, then another five to find seats for three more late arrivals, Jay's tennis club friends who had travelled all the way from Redruth bringing an armful of books each, their faces filled with excitement when they saw the numerous tiers of goodies waiting to be sampled. The café had never been so full of people, with every chair taken and Marcia and Danielle relegated to the beanbags Katie had dragged down from the flat upstairs. She wished Agatha could have been part of the evening, to see how vibrant and alive the space was, to hear the animated chatter reverberating around the freshly painted walls, to inhale the intoxicating fragrance of freshly baked cakes mingled with spicy cologne (Jay's friends) and the hint of new books.

Heavenly!

'Right, I'll go first,' announced Ruby, her rich, melodious voice slicing through the cacophony and delivering a silence that Katie had been afraid she'd not be able to achieve. 'My choice for Agatha's Beachside Café's inaugural Books & Bakes night is a murder mystery set in St Lucia, which some of you might not know is the island of my birth …'

And from that moment on the evening flowed effortlessly

with each book lover extolling the virtues of their chosen read, followed by lively discussion and very little literary criticism from anyone who was familiar the books presented. Katie realised that might come at later meetings but that night it was clear the confirmed bibliophiles were keen to avoid any potential for disagreement until they got to know each other better, or maybe it was the soporific effect of hot chocolates with lashings of Cornish cream, copious cupcakes and lots and lots of laughter. When nine thirty arrived, everyone expressed their surprise at the swift passage of time when fun was being had by all, and every single bookworm asked to sign up for the Books & Bakes meeting the following month, promising to report on the books they'd chosen as well as bringing new books to swap.

By the time Katie closed the door behind Jay and his gang of tennis friends, she was buzzing with elation that the café had well and truly morphed from dowdy dowager aunt to delightful dazzling debutante. She couldn't wait to check the till, and the jar that had collected the money for the raffle tickets for Jay's flower sculpture and any other donations to Agatha's cookery school project.

'Why don't you come over to us for dinner, Katie,' suggested Zoe, her arms crammed with books. 'We're having a family curry night, with plenty of lager and red wine to wash it down with. We can take some of the leftover cakes over for dessert so they don't go to waste.'

'Yes, please come!' added Talia, bouncing up and down on the spot like Tigger on speed.

An unexpected whoosh of exhaustion washed over Katie and she suddenly just wanted to be alone to relish the success of the evening, to take her time tidying up and returning the café to its pristine glory so she could have the following day off to indulge in something that didn't involve baking, and cleaning, and shopping for supplies.

'Oh, thanks, Zoe, that's really kind of you, but you know

what? I think I'll clean up here and have an early night, maybe make a start on this book I got from Willow about the joys of meditation. It's been a really long week and I'm really looking forward to a lie-in tomorrow to recharge my batteries.'

'What do you have planned for your day off?'

'I haven't decided yet, but it won't be anything too strenuous. I'd like to explore a bit of the area, though.'

'Okay, well, if you're sure?'

'Absolutely. It's really kind of you to think of me, though, and I'd love to come over for dinner with you all another time?'

'We'd love to have you, Katie.'

Katie locked the door for the last time, turned the sign to Closed, and drew down the blind. She leaned on the glass panel for a few seconds inhaling a long, calming breath before setting the chairs onto the tables and attacking the floor with a mop, then moving on to fill up the dishwasher and wiping down the units in the kitchen. When her shoulders and neck started screaming in objection to the late-night exertion and her wrinkled red hands would have Willow exclaiming in horror, she checked her watch and decided to call it a day. She switched off the lights, carried the till drawer and the raffle money they'd raised for Jay's floral book arrangement upstairs and dropped down on the floor of the living room to count up the notes and coins.

'Fabulous!' She grinned, her heart ballooning at everyone's generosity.

She placed thirty-five pounds into an envelope to deposit in her bank account on Monday morning, and then transfer over to Agatha's in Bali. It wasn't a huge amount but it would go a long way in helping out the cookery school continue its objectives. However, when she moved on to tot up the café's takings from the Books & Bakes night, she had to repeat the task in case she had made a mistake in her arithmetic. Maths had never been her strong point at school – that was Cara's forte – but she was more than capable of adding up the pennies.

After the third time of counting with the same figure arrived at each time, Katie's earlier high spirits sunk to rock bottom; once again, despite the overwhelming success of the book club in social terms, the evening had been only a lukewarm *financial* success with merely a modest profit being made. She was grateful it wasn't a loss, but if the bills hadn't already been paid by Agatha, she wouldn't be able to meet them herself, let alone invest in a new dishwasher.

She got up from the floor and slid into one of Agatha's overstuffed armchairs, hugging a bright orange silk-and-sequin cushion to her chest for comfort. Just when she thought she had taken a step closer to her goal – that she could report to Agatha that her café was thriving again and when her three months were up there would be enough money to pay the bills – something popped up to take a swipe at her misplaced optimism. Tears prickled at her eyes and she had trouble swallowing because her throat was blocked by what felt like a mini pineapple.

Why had she allowed a glimmer of hope into her heart?

Why had she dared to think that she could make a new life in Perrinby when she should have known that it would take more than a couple of months to build a strong enough foundation for a business to thrive. How naïve she was to think that simply because she had given the café a lick of paint, a new menu and an environmentally friendly mission statement, then all she had to do was organise a few evening get-togethers and all in the field would be rosy?

And why hadn't Oscar come to the Books & Bakes night?

But then, why should he?

Maybe he had better things to do – a thought that caused a spasm of distress to shoot through her veins but she shoved it aside. Looking at the event dispassionately, perhaps spending a Saturday night talking about books did *sound* a little dry, even if it had turned out to be a riot and there had been oodles of cake and coffee and cheerful conversation.

Oscar was completely within his rights to spend his time doing whatever he wanted. Yet, being honest with herself, she had thought she'd forged a connection with him. Perhaps she had misjudged the situation – it wouldn't be the first time – and, like before, she was guilty of relying too heavily on others. They owed her nothing and were completely within their rights to decide to spend their Saturday nights elsewhere and quite frankly if something better had come up, then maybe she would have done the same.

She had made a mistake, but there was nothing to be gained from crying about it.

And hadn't she heard those very words of wisdom before? Spoken in a voice that was almost as familiar to her as her own? Suddenly she craved hearing it for real and she reached for her phone to dial the number, certain in the knowledge there would be a sympathetic ear on the other end of the line.

'Hi, Cara, how's London?'

'It's wonderful if you think staying in watching reruns of *Britain's Got Talent* on a Saturday night is the height of entertainment. Anyway, why are you ringing me? I thought you had that book club thingy tonight?'

'I did, I did, but ...'

'So what happened?'

To her embarrassment, Katie was suddenly ambushed by a wave of emotion and she had to battle to keep her voice even so as not to alert Cara to her regret that Oscar had preferred to spend his time elsewhere.

'Oh, don't get me wrong, it was a roaring success; plenty of bookish banter, a genuine interest in the breadth of people's reading choices, lots of compliments about the transformation of the café and the deliciousness and creativity of the vegan cupcakes, the cherry and almond scones, the rosemary and cheese shortbread biscuits, not to mention the oohs and ahhs over the spectacular floral arrangement Jay created in honour of the evening in the shape of a book.'

'But?'

'But despite the café being jam-packed with people – seriously we ran out of chairs! – I only made a small profit again. If I can't make money when the café is teeming with contented customers who love the place, love the food, and promise to bring their friends, then what's the point?'

'I'm so sorry, darling.'

'What am I doing here, Carr? It's all just too overwhelming. I'm worn out, I'm stressed and I've spent every last penny in my savings account. I think it's about time I accepted this whole café-managing thing is not going to work out.'

'So you didn't make a huge profit, but you also didn't make a loss! What did you think was going to happen, Katie? That you'd sail through every day on a waft of exotic incense and warm buttery pastry watching the cash flood in? You've only been there for six weeks and you've had three really successful events *and* you've made a whole host of people happy, as well as contributing to a charity for the homeless and putting smiles on the faces of the people over at the care home. Those are amazing things in anyone's book!'

'I know, but …'

'Look, just keep doing what you're doing until the three months are up and then take stock? If it doesn't work out, then you've given it your best shot. Agatha will understand, and the café will be in the same position as it was when you arrived, except with a new coat of paint, which can only increase its value if it's going to be put on the market. And I promise to have your sofa bed made up and ready for you, as well as a big welcome-home party.'

'Thanks, Cara, I needed to hear that.'

'And can I make a suggestion?'

'Of course.'

'Why don't you take Agatha's advice?'

'What advice?'

'To use some of your creative talent to come up with a new name for the café? As she rightly said when she handed you the key, she's six thousand miles away in gorgeous Bali and unlikely to be coming back to Cornwall anytime soon. Anyway, all your newer customers must wonder who the eponymous Agatha is because it's *you*, Katie, who's at the heart of the café now, not Agatha. You just need to have a bit more confidence and belief in yourself, and actually *own* this wonderful little Cornish café you've created.'

'I'm not sure, Carr, changing the name seems so … so disrespectful.'

'No it doesn't, it's exactly what Agatha wants you to do. In fact, *not* changing the name to herald new beginnings and attract more custom is flying in the face of the hopes and dreams she no doubt has for the café she loved for more than a decade.'

'Well …'

'Great, so what are you going to call it? Perrinby's Parlour?'

'Ergh, no!'

'The Karma Café?'

'Erm …'

'What about Katie's Kitchen?'

'Oh, no, I couldn't call it that.'

'Okay, okay, so what about The Cornish Kitchen?'

'Actually, I love that.'

'So, it's agreed?'

'Yes.' Katie grinned, her spirits soaring. 'Provided it's okay with Agatha.'

'And you'll email her as soon as we get off the phone?'

'Yes.'

'Promise?'

'Promise.'

'Yay! I foresee a bright future for Katie's Cornish Kitchen.'

'Thanks, Cara,' she muttered, suddenly overcome by a wave of emotion and keen to change the subject. 'So, enough about me, how did your date go last night?'

'No detonation of desire, I'm afraid, so another dud to add to the expanding list. I'm thinking of joining an evening class to meet some normal people for a change. I thought perhaps Italian conversation – I could really fancy a date with a tall, dark and handsome Italian guy.'

Katie laughed. 'Why would an Italian guy be attending a language class in Italian?'

'I'm talking about the tutor! I'm going to scour the Internet for a class led by a native-speaker – even if I have to travel over to Richmond or out to Hampstead. That's how far I'm prepared to go for the sake of my love life. Talking of love life, what's happening between you and the gorgeous painter guy from the gallery next door?'

'Oscar and I are just friends, Cara!'

Yet her stomach performed an uncomfortable somersault when her thoughts scooted back to the night they had sat in the bandstand staring up at the stars before dashing through the downpour to take refuge in the café and the kiss that followed. She thanked her lucky stars that Cara wasn't standing in front of her because she knew her friend would make it her mission to extract every last detail of their brief encounter before she could stop her.

'Best way to start a romantic relationship: friends to lovers. Heard of that?'

'Cara, you know I'm not ready to embark on anything new right now.'

'If you ask me, it's the perfect solution to putting the whole Dominic disaster behind you and moving on. Any chance you could send me a photo of him? I've been stalking your social media accounts for weeks and all I can see are photographs of a windswept beach, the inside of the café and all the delicious food – which is amazing and gorgeous and mouth-watering – but give a single girl a break here!'

'Cara …'

'Look, why don't you just spend your day off tomorrow doing all the things you love, like walking through a cornfield, or treating yourself to a fresh seafood lunch, or swimming in the sea. Have you forgotten that you were the county breaststroke champion for two years running when you lived in Norfolk? Even if you just go for a paddle – I hear the beaches are amazing in Cornwall, as is the seafood! You need to take a break from the constant slog at the kitchen sink and just breathe. Why don't you go and knock on your gorgeous neighbour's door and invite him to go with you? I recommend St Ives – I went there with Fraser when I was going through my phase of dating guys in kilts. Never did get to find out what he wore underneath, sadly.'

'Thanks, Cara. Did I ever tell you that you're the best friend a girl could ask for? You always know how to talk me down from the ledge. Ever thought of going into psychiatry?'

'Ditto! So you'll do it?'

'Yes, definitely. In fact, a day out in the fresh air sounds like the perfect therapy – even if it rains.'

'And what about asking Oscar?'

'Maybe. I'll sleep on it.'

'You do that. Oh, and one last thing before you go.'

'Yes?'

'Ask Oscar if he has a brother, or a cousin, or even a guy who does his accounts who might be interested in meeting a cute, twenty-nine-year-old travel agent who would rather be having adventures than selling them.'

Katie laughed. 'Will do.'

By the time she had finished bleaching the benches in the tiny attic kitchen, and sent a quick email to Agatha about the café's possible new name, her emotions had returned to an even keel. In fact, she was positively looking forward to her day out at the Cornish seaside, and she wondered whether she might persuade Oscar to join her.

Chapter 16

The meteorological gods were smiling that morning because when Katie drew back her curtains, sunshine poured in through the bedroom window. If she pushed her nose right up against the glass, she could see the sea, its smooth surface reflecting the battalion of fluffy white clouds scudding through the cerulean sky on their continuous journey towards the Scilly Isles and the Atlantic Ocean beyond. Seagulls ducked and dived between the waves in search of a tasty morsel for breakfast, their cries of delight upon making a successful catch causing a smile to tug at her lips.

While she waited for the kettle to boil, she cast her eyes over the picturesque view from the kitchen window at the back of her new home. It was such a shame the wooden glamping pods were empty because they were now surrounded by a resplendent tapestry of wildflowers, from bluebells to violets, from evening primrose to sea holly and pink campion. She wouldn't have been surprised to see a coterie of fairies prancing through the knee-high grasses on their way to enjoy a Sunday morning picnic.

Humming a random tune, she gulped down a quick coffee, hopped in the shower, pulled on a pair of skinny jeans, and stuffed her feet into her favourite Converse trainers. Then, before her courage failed her, she skipped over to the gallery and knocked on the front door, her heart hammering a concerto of anticipation.

'Oh, hi there, Katie.'

Katie couldn't help grinning at the sight of Oscar, lounging against the doorframe, his sleep-filled eyes peering at her though his ruffled curls, his frayed-at-the-knee jeans and crumpled T-shirt clearly grabbed in a hurry for the early morning call. If she were in the market for a Sunday morning date – which she was not – then she couldn't think of anyone better to spend that time with.

'Hi, Oscar. Fancy a trip to St Ives to check out the new seafood restaurant Jay's always going on about?'

'I'd love that – nothing better than good old Cornish fish and chips.'

'Great, I'll drive – see you in ten minutes.'

She spun on her heels and made her way back to the café to collect her coat and the keys to her super-shiny hire car that had so far only experienced a few short journeys, such as to the organic farm in the next village, to the soup kitchen, and to Edgemont Manor, none of which fell under the heading of leisurely. She gathered the straw beach bag she had brought back from Bali, tossed in a pair of flip-flops and on the spur of the moment added a swimming costume and beach towel – just in case. She thought of the joy that swimming had brought her over the years, of the medals and trophies she'd brought home from county championships and how her chosen sport had actually provided her with a focus when life as she knew it had imploded when she was twelve years old. Spending an hour in the pool didn't take away the issues she had to deal with, but the rhythmic movement of powering through the water calmed the turmoil for a while.

She had shelved her sport when she'd moved from Norfolk to London. Dominic had laughed at her when she'd suggested a trip to the local health club to work off some of the wedding stress with a few lengths and a lounge in the Jacuzzi. Then, when she had arrived in Bali questioning her sanity of travelling there alone, as soon as she slipped into the warm Indonesian Ocean, she could feel the anxiety slipping away from her body as she floated on her back, her legs and arms outstretched like a sun-worshipping starfish, the gently rippling water massaging her aching muscles. An early morning swim had once again been her daily therapy, which, along with Agatha's kindness and regular baking marathons, had helped her to come to terms with what had happened.

'I brought my camera,' said Oscar, climbing into the passenger seat with a professional-looking photography case. 'I hope you don't mind?'

'Not at all.'

She turned the key in the ignition but all that followed was a splutter followed by silence. She tried again and the same thing happened. Her heart sank.

'Oh no!'

She was grateful Oscar didn't make the usual patronising quip about having checked the petrol gauge – something Dominic did regularly – but it did look like the day off she had *so* been looking forward to was over before they had even left the village.

'I'm sorry, Oscar. Just when I thought my luck was changing.'

Katie saw a flash of indecision zoom across Oscar's face, but within seconds the smile was back on his lips and he offered a solution.

'I might have an idea.'

Oscar led her round to the lane at the back of the gallery where a low-slung vehicle slumbered beneath a scruffy green tarpaulin. Katie watched him reach out, grab the corner of the canvas and then hesitate, as though battling with a brigade of invisible tormentors, until in one swift action he whipped the cover away to reveal a Triumph Stag Cabriolet that matched his personality to perfection.

'Wow, great car!'

'It belonged to my brother, Harry,' he murmured as he ran his fingers along the roof, his eyes on some faraway adventure, until, with some difficulty, he returned to the present, inhaled a strengthening breath, then wrenched open the driver's door. 'Come on.'

Katie didn't have to be asked twice. She jumped into the passenger seat, relishing the faint smell of tannin from the black leather seats and the feeling of nostalgia the Seventies icon evoked. She wished she'd brought her oversized sunglasses and a headscarf so she could channel her inner Audrey Hepburn as they skirted the village green and headed out of Perrinby into the Cornish countryside on their way to lunch in St Ives.

Oscar flicked on the radio and, with the breeze casting her hair into the slipstream, she grinned when one of her favourite Beach Boys tracks blared out, and they spent the whole of the thirty minutes it took to drive to the coast singing sunshine-filled songs at the top of their voices.

When they reached the town, Oscar scooted into the tiniest of parking spaces and led her down a narrow, pink-hydrangea-framed pathway towards a whitewashed building with an outside decking area overlooked by a cluster of palm trees.

'Wow! What an amazing view. It's like something out of a holiday brochure.'

'Wonderful, isn't it?'

Katie took a moment to focus on the horizon where the deep turquoise of the sea met the aquamarine of a cloudless sky. As she watched the ebb and flow of the waves, all the stresses and strains of the last few weeks began to fall away, replaced by a feeling of complete and utter calm. Tiny yachts bobbed about on the water, their sails flapping like miniature handkerchiefs. Children ran around on the gloriously sandy beach whilst their parents relaxed on striped deckchairs or read their books under the shade of brightly coloured umbrellas. She closed her eyes and inhaled a deep breath, tasting the salty air, listening to the seagulls' piercing cry and the faint tinkle of music emanating from one of the sunbather's radios. It was a truly idyllic scene and her spirits soared as her stomach rumbled.

'Come on, let's grab a table before they all go.'

She followed Oscar into the restaurant overlooking the beach, taking in the fresh white walls showcasing a selection of watercolours from local artists, the vases filled with driftwood, pebbles and blue glass flowers, and the hand-painted wooden birds used as table numbers. They were shown to a table on the veranda, bedecked in a blue gingham tablecloth, which made the most of the spectacular view. A waiter handed them menus.

'There's only one thing to eat here and that's the grilled lobster,' said Oscar, pushing his curls away from his eyes only to have them fall back into place.

'Sounds fabulous.'

Oscar ordered for both of them, along with a jug of iced water for him and a glass of white wine for Katie, and when the waiter brought a basket of freshly baked bread and locally produced butter, they dug in as though they hadn't eaten for days.

'I could stare at that view all day,' sighed Katie, watching a jet ski bounce across the waves in the distance.

'Did you grow up by the sea?'

'Yes, in a tiny village on the Norfolk coast. I spent every spare minute of the school holidays at the beach, crabbing, building sandcastles, and later on swimming in the sea and messing around with boats.'

'Sounds idyllic to a boy who grew up in London – Pimlico to be precise. I'm a City boy through and through, I'm afraid.'

'That must have been exciting, too, with all the amazing galleries and museums and theatres on your doorstep.'

'It was okay, I guess. So what made you move to London?'

Their food arrived and the fragrance of warm seafood and

melted butter caused Katie's mouth to water and her taste buds to tingle in anticipation. She managed to control herself, though, and after a few mouthfuls of the most delicious lobster she had ever tasted, she answered Oscar's question.

'Well, after I graduated from catering college and Mum decided to relocate to Greece, my best friend Cara suggested we head to the bright lights of the capital to make our fortune.' She laughed at the memory of them setting out on their adventure into the big unknown. 'We both got jobs in the kitchen of a luxury boutique hotel in Mayfair, then a couple of years later, I landed my dream job with François Dubois, cake maker to the stars. François taught me so much and I loved every single minute I spent in his amazing kitchen.'

A sharp pang of loss hit her in the solar plexus and she gulped in a mouthful of the delicious Camel Valley wine to stop herself from succumbing to her swirling emotions.

'So why did you leave?'

She groaned inwardly. She had started this conversation to find out more about Oscar, not to open her old wounds. The rickety wooden table they were sitting at was small and she could feel his eyes resting on her, scrutinising her expression as he waited for her answer. Maybe this was her chance to expel the constant thrum of heartache by getting her story into the open, lance the boil so to speak, so she could move on. An image of Agatha floated across her vision, reminding her that it was good to talk about what had happened in the past. But could she do that with Oscar?

'I was fired.'

'Fired? What for?'

Oscar's eyes widened in surprise; that was clearly not what he was expecting her to say. A whoosh of relief flowed through her, thankful that she didn't look like the sort of person who made a habit of getting sacked on a regular basis. Then she laughed.

'Why are you laughing?'

'Oh, it's not funny. I was devastated and the timing couldn't have been much worse.'

'So what happened?'

Oscar covered her hand with his in a gesture of support, the intimate act sending sparks of electricity through her veins, as he waited for her explanation of the most bizarre reason to be sacked ever to be told.

'Okay, so in my defence I was under a *lot* of pressure. I wasn't thinking straight and I ...'

'What happened, Katie?'

'Well, François was flying out to his family's villa in Cannes the following week so he asked me to handle the delivery of a couple of celebration cakes he'd been working on for the previous two weeks. One was this amazing all-white confection with delicate filigree decorations and the other a three-tier cake iced in ivory and gold. You have to understand – they were both masterpieces of sugary confectionery, more edible sculptures than ...'

'Katie ...'

'So, I put the cakes in the van and drove, very carefully, first to a mews house in Kensington where I left the first cake with a neighbour as per the client's instructions, then delivered the second cake to a house in Knightsbridge.'

She didn't go on to say that she then drove to Cara's and spent the rest of the weekend alternating between sobbing her heart out and raging against the fiends of fate for throwing her life into such maelstrom of misery, as well as her bank balance.

'On Monday morning, when I got into work, all hell had broken loose. I've never seen François so angry, and that's saying something: he's a typical Frenchman full of fire and passion. I thought he was going to have a fit right there in front of my eyes. You know those cartoon characters who are drawn with steam coming out of their ears? Well, he managed a very good impression of one of those.'

'But why? What had you done?'

'Apparently I'd mixed up the deliveries.'

'Okay, I can see how mistakes like that can happen, and I understand how he would be upset, but to fire you on the spot? That's a bit harsh.'

'Oh, I don't blame him, to be honest. I'd have fired me!'

'You don't? You would?'

'Yes.'

'Why?'

Katie glanced out to sea, memories of the mortifyingly embarrassing incident swirling around her mind; another sip of the delicious dry white wine made right there in Cornwall should do it.

'You see, one of the cakes wasn't your typical fruit cake, or Victoria sponge, or even lemon drizzle, it was one of François' other specialities – a cake made from dog food and then carved into shape and decorated with fondant icing just like a real cake.'

'Oh. My. God. No way! Are you telling me that people order birthday cakes for their *pets*? That's well … that's totally crazy.'

'It's cute! The problem was, the one I dropped off at the mews house was the one destined for a celebrity couple's precious chihuahua's birthday bash, and not the birthday cake a TV soap actress was expecting for her birthday celebrations. Well, you can imagine her shock when the time came for the cake-cutting ceremony!'

Oscar's lips twitched as he tried to contain his amusement at the scenario Katie had painted, which caused her to giggle, then laugh at the incongruity of the story. Of course, at the time she had been mortified, had apologised profusely to an apoplectic François. Unfortunately, her contrition had been to no avail, even after she had sent the most expensive bouquet she could afford to the actress's house.

'Anyone can make a mistake, Katie.'

'Yes, but unfortunately it wasn't the first mistake I'd made that week. My mind just wasn't on my work because … because …'

She stopped. Now was the perfect time to spill the whole

sorry saga about Dominic. To just tag it onto the end of a conversation as the explanation for her actions that had led to her losing her job, but a tidal wave of dread rolled through her stomach at the thought of disclosing the details of her broken engagement and the words simply wouldn't come. Fortunately, Oscar came to her rescue.

'Well, maybe you should look upon the doggy debacle as a fortuitous accident.' Oscar grinned.

'Why?'

'If you hadn't been fired, then you would never have flown off to Bali, would never have met Agatha and never have come down to Cornwall to relaunch her Beachside Café.'

'True, but maybe that was a mistake, too.'

'What do you mean?'

'There's something I haven't told you about the café.'

'Really? What?'

She swallowed, determined that this time she would not baulk at confiding in Oscar. He was a fellow business owner, after all. He would understand the difficulties, her anxieties, her need to make the café a success, her desire to prove to herself and Agatha that the café could be profitable, as well as her guilt at not telling her about Greg's interest and the letter that was sitting on her hall table like a smouldering firework.

'Greg called round just before Jay's flower-arranging class ...'

'That man is a—'

'He left a letter for Agatha, which apparently contains a formal offer for the building and he asked me to contact her to tell her about it. I did try, and ... well ... I feel dreadful, but I just want to try and make a go of things at the café, make a decent profit, send at least one contribution to her cookery school project before I tell her.'

'Does this mean you've decided to stay?'

'Yes, I think it does. But I feel guilty about not telling her. What do you think I should do?'

'From what I know of Agatha, if she's given you three months to turn the café's fortunes around, then she's a woman of her word and she will give you that chance.'

'But there's only four weeks left. The café is teeming with a steady stream of customers from the time I switch round the sign in the morning to when I have to shoo the last person out at five o'clock, and yet I'm just breaking even, and that's without paying the business rates and the electricity and water bills that Agatha has already covered. There's no way the café's going to be in a position to turn a decent profit in the next month.'

'It's only April. We've got the summer season coming up – that's when the tourists and weekenders descend on Cornwall in their droves. Trust me, your business will boom! And have you thought any more about changing the café's name like Agatha suggested?'

'Actually, I have.'

'And?'

Oscar's piercing blue eyes lit up with interest as he leaned back from the table and crossed his ankle over his thigh, stretching his arms behind his head in a so-laid-back-I'm-almost-horizontal way, his soft lips curling into a smile of approval.

'I thought … well, I thought maybe The Cornish Kitchen?'

'I love it. It's perfect! In fact, I can already envision how the new signage is going to look. Would you like me to design something for you? It's sort of my area of expertise. If you want me to, that is?'

'I'd absolutely love that! Thank you so much. And just so you know, that's *not* why I asked you to come out with me today, I promise.'

Katie laughed, and if they hadn't been sitting opposite each other in a bustling seaside restaurant, she would have flung her arms around Oscar and given him an exuberant, grateful hug. As it was, she simply beamed her delight, surprised to find tears smarting at the corners of her eyes at his generosity.

'It's my pleasure. I'm sure the new name will attract even more ravenous customers keen to sample all the wonderful food Cornwall has to offer, sourced from local producers and served with a dollop of true Cornish kindness on the side. And, Katie, if you want my advice, I think you should hold off telling Agatha about Greg's offer for another couple of weeks, wait to see what happens when the new sign goes up.'

'I'm not sure ...'

'Look, Agatha more than anyone knows how important it is to follow your dreams, to do what you're most passionate about, to focus all your energy on producing a successful outcome and not to give up at the first hurdle when things don't go swimmingly from the off. She'll want you to give The Cornish Kitchen your best shot, and that means continuing to make people happy by serving the most delicious food right up until the very last minute.'

'But how do you *know* that?'

'Oh, it's just something Zoe said to me a while ago when I moved into the gallery.'

Oscar averted his eyes to catch the attention of the waiter to ask for their bill.

'How about we take a drive a little further down the coast? There're a few picturesque coves that I wouldn't mind photo-graphing for a watercolour commission I got yesterday.'

'Sounds perfect.' Katie smiled, her spirits edging up a notch as they left the restaurant and sauntered back to where they had left the Triumph Stag.

Now that she had shared her dilemma about Greg's offer with Oscar – not to mention her relief that he was on board with the new name – she felt lighter, less anxious, as though she could conquer everything, especially as she anticipated a stroll along a scenic beach with Oscar by her side.

Chapter 17

A few miles down the coast from St Ives, Oscar pulled into a hidden spot overlooking a secluded sandy beach with the endless Atlantic Ocean beyond, merging seamlessly into the pale blue of the sky, the leisurely ripple of the waves creating a soothing, hypnotic effect. Katie led the way down a steep path to the shore and plonked herself down onto a conveniently placed rock, sheltered from the breeze, the perfect place to watch the children build their sandcastles and the noisy seagulls search for a tasty bite for their lunch.

Several families were picnicking on tartan travel rugs, someone was trying to show a young boy how to fly a kite, and a couple of toddlers were searching rock pools under the watchful eye of their mother. The whole Blytonesque scene reminded Katie of her childhood, and a warm surge of nostalgia spread through her chest. It was a timely reminder that happiness could be found in the simplest of things, including a day out at the seaside.

Oscar finished taking his photographs, stored his camera away in its purpose-made rucksack, and came to sit on the rock next to Katie's where she was watching a surfing lesson taking place.

'I can totally see you on one of those surfboards.' She laughed, taking in his unruly blond hair, the frayed washed-out jeans and the pleated leather bracelet he always wore tied around his wrist.

'Looks can deceive, you know, Katie,' murmured Oscar, his eyes trained on the tiny yachts, skittering across the ocean, their sails flapping in the strengthening breeze like colourful flags.

Katie stared at Oscar, the expression on his face indecipherable and again she got the feeling that there was something, something important that he was keeping from her. But he was right; looks can, and do, deceive – hadn't she experienced that first hand? She had thought Dominic was in love with her, that she was the love of his life, just like he was hers, but it had clearly all been a show. How could he have gone through the motions of organising a wedding, and getting involved in all the tiny details that entailed, with no intention of going through with it?

She wondered at what precise moment he had decided not to come back from his stag weekend. Was it months before he flew out to Ibiza? Weeks? Days? Or had he decided when he got there, more a spur-of-the-moment decision? Tears prickled at her lashes when she thought of what she would be doing now if her life had gone according to plan and an uncomfortable lump formed in her throat.

'Are you okay?'

'Oh, erm, yes, I'm …' And to her horror, a lone tear rolled down her cheek.

'Sorry.'

'There's no need to apologise. Tell me what's upsetting you – I might be able to help. Is it the café? Are you still worried about how Agatha's going to react, because if you are, then you should just call her and tell her about Greg's offer.'

'No, it's not the café.'

'Then what?'

She sighed. She had to stop obsessing about the myriad different scenarios of when Dominic fell out of love with her, or the reasons for his change of heart, or his decision to clean out their savings account. She had to start to come to terms with what had happened and the only way to do that was by telling people, not hugging the whole traumatic interlude to herself as though it was some ugly, shame-filled secret. Maybe if she tossed it out into the open, she could set it free and eradicate the Dominic-shaped demons from her life once and for all.

'The reason I wasn't thinking straight when I mixed up the cake orders was because … was because … my fiancé had ditched me.'

'Oh, I … I'm so sorry to hear that, Katie.'

'Dominic emptied our joint bank account of every penny we'd saved to pay for the wedding reception and flew off on his stag weekend to Ibiza, and … well, he never came back. He's still there, focusing on pursuing his dream to become a professional musician.'

Now that the lid had been prised from her bottled-up emotions, she suddenly couldn't stop the words from tumbling forth.

'Do you know what the worst thing is, though? It's been over three months and he still hasn't had the decency to talk to me about why he left like he did, to explain what I did wrong, and it's the "not knowing" that's eating away inside me, burning like a glowing ember, making me feel nauseous, rejected, worthless. Sometimes I spend hours chasing question after question round my head: why did he do it? What did I do wrong? Why won't he talk to me about it?'

'You haven't spoken to him at all?'

'All I got was a two-minute phone call to tell me that the wedding was off. After that, I've only been able to speak to his best man, Iain, who, I have to tell you, is mortified that he's been left to deal with the fall-out; as indeed are Dominic's parents who have been very kind and supportive.'

'That's the most cowardly thing I've heard in a long time. Relationships break down all the time, for various reasons, but the least anyone can do is have the balls to explain their reasons, face to face.'

'You know, I tried everything to contact him for the first few days. I couldn't believe he wasn't coming back. I thought it was wedding jitters, but then I had to start cancelling the arrangements or else we'd be charged and, of course, I didn't have the money to pay for everything. Then, when I arrived in Bali, I tried to push it all to the back of my mind, and that worked to a certain extent, especially with Agatha's support, and since I got back I've had the café to concentrate on, and now I just can't face the prospect of talking to him. In fact, if I never hear or see him again, I'll be happy.'

Oscar held her gaze, clearly toying with whether or not to say his next sentence.

'You have to talk to him, Katie. It's the only way of coming to terms with what happened. It'll never be over until you do. You'll always wonder, always speculate. Even if his explanation hurts, you still have to hear it to let the feelings of rejection go.'

Katie gawped at Oscar. She knew he was talking about Dominic, but he could also be talking about someone else, someone she needed to face much more urgently than Dominic.

But first things first.

Oscar was right – she had to don her metaphorical deerstalker as soon as she got back to the café and renew her efforts to locate her runaway fiancé and ask him to tell her what had gone wrong with their relationship, as well as demanding that he return her half of the money he took out of their savings account. It would be the perfect way of making sure she kept the café.

'Thanks, Oscar. I needed to hear that.'

'You don't have to thank me. If there's one thing I've learned over the last couple of years, it's that we should face our demons, look them in the eye, challenge their veracity and then send them packing so we can live the life *we* want to live, not the one others have forced upon us.'

Oscar's voice had taken on a strident note. Katie knew there was something hidden deep in his soul that had caused him to speak so vehemently, but like her, he had his reasons for keeping it to himself. The atmosphere had switched from jolly to sombre, and she couldn't bear to dwell on her misfortune any longer.

She leapt up from the wooden bench and held out her hand to Oscar who grinned and took it. She was about to resume her consideration of the beauty of the Cornish coastline when the mischievous imp on her shoulder whispered a different scenario in her ear and so instead, she gripped his hand more tightly and began to drag him onto the beach and down towards the waves.

'Katie, what's ...'

She ignored him, breaking into a sprint, laughing as her hair flew into the air like a blonde Medusa on speed, her feet kicking up swathes of sand as she hauled a reluctant Oscar in her wake towards the point where the waves gently licked the edge of the beach.

'Hey! Stop!'

But it was too late; they were in the water and instead of stopping, Katie kept on running, continuing the momentum, splashing water over them both before letting go of his hand so she could scoop up a handful of sea to throw at him, giggling at the expression of surprise in his eyes.

'Katie, I ... Stop!!'

And, to her astonishment, she saw that Oscar's face had frozen in terror. He turned his back on her and stalked back to the shallows, back to the beach, his shoulders hunched as high as his ears, his whole demeanour screaming alarm. It took Katie a few minutes to compute what had happened, then she raced after him, only catching up with him as he reached the path leading back up to where they had left the car.

'Oscar? What's wrong?'

'Nothing,' he muttered, refusing to look her in the eye as he continued to make his way to the car park.

'But I don't understand. What just happened?'

Oscar didn't answer. His jaw had tightened as he clenched his teeth, clearly using every ounce of his willpower not to snap at her for something she had no idea about.

'Oscar?'

But he simply continued to stride away from her. When they reached the Stag, he yanked open the door and dropped down heavily into the driver's seat, draping his arms over the steering wheel and fixing his gaze on the distant horizon, his eyes narrowed, causing the ridge at the top of his nose to deepen.

Katie's stomach churned as she slid into the passenger seat beside him, bewildered by his reaction to what she had hoped would be a little impromptu fun in the sea. She had thought they were friends, that Oscar was someone she could confide in and have fun with, but it seemed that once again she had seriously misjudged the situation.

She instantly regretted cracking open the tiniest of windows into her heart, sharing her pain of being abandoned by someone she had loved, because from where she was sitting it looked like Oscar was going to be the next person in a long line of people she had thought she could trust but who had been found wanting.

Chapter 18

Silence burgeoned into all four corners of the car as Katie watched a seagull almost as big as Dotty swoop down in front of them and scoop up a discarded crust of bread, crying out in delight at its fortuitous find. Couples of all ages strolled hand-in-hand along the beach path, isolated in their own little conversation bubble, enjoying their Sunday afternoon escape from the treadmill of normal life. But as she followed Oscar's gaze out to sea, she couldn't fail to see there was a bank of dark bulbous clouds gathering and she hoped the ramblers had remembered to pack their raincoats and umbrellas.

Eventually, Oscar released his grip on the steering wheel and slumped back into his seat. When Katie saw his face, her heart gave a nip of distress at the raw agony reflected in his eyes. However, with visible effort, he managed to corral his emotions and force a false smile onto his lips.

'I'm so sorry, Katie. That was totally uncalled for – you must think I'm crazy.'

'Well …' she began, trying to inject a little humour into an awkward situation, but equally keen to offer a listening ear, just as Oscar had done for her earlier when she was talking about her broken engagement. 'What just happened, Oscar?'

'It's just that … you took me completely by surprise.'

'But what did I do?'

'Nothing, nothing. Come on, let's get back. It looks like there's a storm coming.'

Oscar twisted the key in the ignition and revved the engine, but then he switched it off again and turned in his seat to face Katie, his fingers trembling on the steering wheel. He drew in a breath and then muttered the most unexpected of words.

'I'm terrified of water.'

'You're … you're frightened of water?'

'Well, the sea. That's the first time I've been within fifty metres of the shoreline in two years and I thought I might be able to handle it, but obviously I can't. I'm really sorry, Katie, please forgive me but I just freaked out. I didn't mean to upset you. I just, well I had to get out of there.'

Bewilderment raced through Katie's brain. Oscar, a guy she had assumed was a confirmed surf addict when she had first met him, who was the absolute embodiment of a golden-tanned beach boy, was frightened of a few gentle waves? It didn't make any sense, especially as she had spent her whole life appreciating the therapeutic benefits of taking a swim in the water.

'It's okay, Oscar. Really it is, but why are you so afraid? Did someone push you in the sea when you were younger?'

It was one of the first lessons she had learned when she had started taking her swimming seriously – to *always* respect the water because it was more powerful, more unpredictable, more deadly than anything found on land, and a mere moment of inattention could lead to disaster. She knew there was a story behind Oscar's fear and she wanted to hear it so she could offer her support.

'Something happened, yes, but it's not what you think.'

Oscar's voice, usually filled with such warmth and laced with a generous helping of mischief and humour, now sounded like it was weighed down by a bucketful of sand. Instead of pushing him to reveal his troubles, Katie decided to wait, and it was a few moments before he spoke again.

'My brother, Harry, died in a jet-ski accident. I saw it happen and there was nothing I could do to help him.'

Katie's heart contracted sharply, causing her to catch her breath, followed immediately by a spasm of guilt that she had spent the last half-hour moaning about her minor relationship problems – mere blips in life's journey when compared to the loss of a much-loved sibling.

'Oh, Oscar, I'm so very sorry.'

'Harry was a real thrill-seeker. At the age of three he'd climb the highest tree in our garden with a tea towel stuffed down the back of his collar pretending to be a superhero, or Evel Knievel, and leap from the branches without an ounce of fear. Then, when he was a teenager, he moved on to rock-climbing and free-running, then at university he joined the paragliding and skydiving club. People called him an adrenalin junkie, but he just said that he was addicted to life, to squeezing every bit of excitement from every situation. What was the point of living if you stayed indoors wrapped up in cotton wool?'

'Your brother sounds like an amazing person.'

'He was – he packed more into his twenty-eight years than most people do in a whole lifetime. Two years ago, he hiked up Mount Kilimanjaro and a few days later he flew over to Arizona to kayak through the Grand Canyon. Then we went on a lads' holiday to a beach resort in Bulgaria and everyone wanted to spend an afternoon enjoying the water sports, but as I'd had too much tequila the night before, I decided to give it a miss and relax on the beach and watch instead. I must have fallen asleep and when I heard the commotion, never in my wildest dreams did I think the person they were dragging from the water was my brother. I'll never erase that image of Harry being carried onto the sand like a limp rag doll until the day I leave this earth to join him.'

Oscar couldn't go on. He lowered his forehead onto the steering wheel to take a few moments to gather his thoughts and shove them back into their darkened box. Katie placed her hand gently on his back, unable to formulate words sufficient to convey her sympathy for what he had, and was continuing, to endure.

'Two years on and I still miss him every single day. Six months after his funeral I still couldn't function properly. I was racked with guilt. Maybe if I'd stopped him from going out on the water that day, maybe if I'd been out on the water with him, I could have … I could have … Anyway, my parents handled their grief by throwing themselves into their work, leaving the house early in the morning, not returning until they were so exhausted that they fell asleep as soon as their heads hit the pillow. They never take a day off for fear their sadness will overwhelm them.'

'Was Harry an architect too?'

'Yes, a great one. Just like in every other aspect of his life, he loved pushing the boundaries of design, loved sleek lines and the use of natural products: glass, stone, marble, wood. He was much more committed to the business than I ever was. I'd always wanted to pursue a more artistic route, to try to earn my living from painting, photography, ceramics, film, rather than architecture but I didn't want to let my parents down after they'd spent so much on my education.'

Oscar paused for a beat to inhale a long strengthening breath.

'But a year after Harry's accident Mum and Dad closed the practice for a year to volunteer for a charitable organisation that was building sustainable housing in Africa. They told me to go and follow my own dreams, too, and if that meant being a starving artist in an attic in the Cornish countryside then they would support me. We'd all learned a harsh lesson, one which thankfully Harry had already known – that life is far too short to walk someone else's path.'

'What made you choose to come to Perrinby?' asked Katie, relieved to see the colour seeping back into Oscar's face.

'Oh, someone suggested it would be the perfect place to open an art gallery. She was right – I love the village. I feel at home in Cornwall and the change of scenery has helped me come to terms with what happened to Harry. Grief isn't simply one emotion; it's multiple feelings – heartbreak, guilt, denial, loneliness, anger even – and being here has taught me that we have to forgive people for leaving us, whatever the reasons. If we don't, it simply prolongs the pain and we can't move forward with our lives. You have to forgive Dominic for what he did to you, Katie. I'm sure he wasn't thinking about how his decision would impact you, just on his own desire to achieve his dreams, so you mustn't take it personally.'

It was a generous way of looking at things, and she understood why Oscar felt that way, but she just wasn't ready to consign Dominic's betrayal to ancient history. After all, she still needed to talk to him about why they couldn't have pursued his wish to be a professional musician together, after they were married.

However, she didn't want to disagree with Oscar's advice, and when she looked up from studying her fingernails, she saw he was staring at her so intently that she wondered if he could see every thought that was swirling around her brain. The intensity caused her heart to flutter, sending ripples of anticipation through her body. There was no doubt there was a connection between them, like an invisible piece of elastic that drew her towards him, and before she knew what was happening his lips were hovering inches from hers waiting for her to close the gap or move away – the choice was hers.

Her body told her everything she needed to know straight away, but her brain argued for caution. Hadn't she decided after their first kiss – the one that had caused her to reassess every kiss that had gone before – that she didn't want, or need, a new relationship? Could she really be contemplating risking her trust only for it to be snatched away again, sending her tumbling back into the abyss of devastation? She hadn't told

Oscar the full truth so he didn't know she had issues far deeper than what Dominic had done to her, which would take months of professional counselling to eradicate – something she had no intention of embarking on.

Then she thought of Harry, a man who had grabbed every opportunity with both hands and hung on with tenacity and excitement for the roller-coaster ride, never pausing to evaluate the risks, never fearing the outcome because it was the *experience* that mattered, and she really, really wanted to repeat the experience of being kissed by Oscar.

Did the rest matter?

She leaned forward and as her lips met Oscar's, sparkles of pleasure zinged out to every nerve ending, sending shock waves of exhilaration through her whole body, just as before. She closed her eyes to relish every second of the wonderful sensation: the feel of his mouth on hers, the caress of his fingertips at the nape of her neck, the pounding of her heart that she hoped he couldn't hear, the soar of her emotions as he kissed her back, softly, gently, thoroughly, and the feeling of absolute certainty that she was where she was meant to be. That everything that had gone before was merely part of a journey preparing her for what was to come.

Chapter 19

On the drive back to Perrinby, Katie's mood blossomed, as every mile they travelled she felt closer to Oscar. The mere act of sharing their respective histories, loves and losses, both joyous and traumatic, had left her with a feeling of complete calm, of gratitude that she had built a new friendship, that someone had taken the time to listen to her story and hadn't judged her, but also that she had been able to return that kindness.

But what really caused her spirits to poke their heads out of the mire of misery she had consigned them to was that no matter how devastated she was at how Dominic had terminated their engagement, how upset she was at losing the job she had loved, working for an incredible confectionery genius, nothing, nothing was as heartbreaking as the story Oscar had told her.

She *would* talk to Dominic; she would ask him to explain his actions, and even if it took her another three months to locate him, at some point it would happen and there would be people around – her mum, Cara, Agatha, Oscar perhaps – to support her through the backlash. But Oscar would never be able to talk to his brother again, never be able to ask him what had caused him to lose control of his jet ski when he did.

Again, it was a timely lesson for her to count her blessings.

Just a few months ago she thought her world had ended, but look at her now. Not only was she part of a vibrant, supportive community in the gorgeous county of Cornwall, she had also made a bunch of new friends she would never have met had she been married to Dominic. She was her own boss, too – something Dominic had scoffed at when she'd tentatively spoken of her dreams. She was free to experiment with culinary ideas and environmentally sound practices, which meant a great deal to her, and free to engage in projects that helped others, not only in Cornwall, but in Bali too.

And in addition to all this, she had made a connection with a man whose eyes were the colour of the summer sky and who had given her more in a few hours than Dominic had in two years – he had actually listened to her, and then offered his support as well as solutions. It was time to stop telling herself that this was a temporary stay in Perrinby, and to get serious. She could be happy here, she knew that, she just had to deal with a few issues and start concentrating on her future – one filled with good friends and great cake.

It was time to make her peace with the demons of her past instead of hiding from them. She was confident that she would eventually locate Dominic, find out what had gone wrong in their relationship and use the information to make changes in her life. She knew there was another issue she had to face before she would be totally at peace, but she felt confident that she could achieve that too.

And that kiss they'd just shared – wow!

A smile twisted Katie's lips as she relaxed into the seat and watched the countryside fly past her open window, letting the breeze flow over her naked forearm, and her heart giving a nip of pleasure when she saw the stone sign announcing they had arrived in the village of Perrinby. It was six o'clock and she really didn't want the day to end, so when she saw the Hope & Anchor come into view she turned to Oscar.

'Fancy a drink?'

'I'd love one.'

Oscar steered the Triumph Stag to its resting place behind the gallery and they jumped out. He had just started to flip the tarpaulin over the roof when he paused, his nose high in the air like a hungry dog catching a tantalising waft of his dinner.

'What?' Katie giggled.

'Can you smell burning?'

'Oh, I ... yes, I think it's coming from ...'

She glanced over to the brick wall that encircled the rear yard of the café where a helix of ash-grey smoke spiralled into the air.

'Oh my God! The café's on fire!'

'Quick! You get the fire extinguisher out of the boot while I try to get the gate open.'

Oscar sprinted to the paint-blistered wooden gate, whilst Katie fumbled with the lock on the Triumph Stag's boot, her heart hammering against her ribcage in panic. Just when she thought things were on an upward trajectory at last, the café was about to be burned to the ground! How was she going to explain *that* to Agatha?

She located the fire extinguisher and rushed over to join Oscar who was trying to ram the gate with his shoulder, but it refused to budge. After another fruitless shove, he changed his tactics, and in a move worthy of Jackie Chan, kicked the door from its frame.

Katie immediately raised the extinguisher, and let loose, squirting everything in front of her like a cannon at a Mediterranean foam party, determined to cover everything in sight, to keep going until the canister was empty, until a barrage of indignant screams met her ears.

'*Arr ... rr ... gh!*'

'*What the ...?*'

'Katie, is that you?' screamed Talia, covered in so much white foam that she resembled the Michelin man, her arms outstretched as she gasped for breath after the shock of the sudden dousing.

'Talia? Ryan? What are you doing here?'

And then she saw the remnants of what had been a barbecue, with burgers and sausages dripping in foam, a salad that looked like it was topped with whipped cream, and a plate of very sorry-looking bread buns. Sade was singing seductively from a CD player and the café's washing-up bowl sat on the rickety patio table, filled with ice and bottles of Ryan's preferred brand of lager. Katie's stomach performed a somersault of remorse.

'Oh, my God, I'm so sorry! I thought … we thought …'

She looked over her shoulder at Oscar, hoping that he would come to her rescue but he simply looked on, his eyes sparkling with amusement.

'I saw smoke coming from the backyard, put two and two together, added in a dollop of my current luck, and decided the café had to be on fire. Looks like I've not only ruined your supper, but a potentially romantic date night, too. Please, will you forgive me?'

Ryan, who had escaped the worst of the soaking, reached up to run his fingers through his sandy-coloured hair and scratched at his beard in bemusement. Then, his lips twitched and he grinned, reaching out to brush away a globule of foam from Talia's forehead before slinging his arm around her shoulders.

'Nothing to forgive. I've always wanted to go to one of those Ibiza foam parties – now I can say I've got wet and wild right here in Perrinby!' Ryan's eyes, the colour of liquid luck, glinted mischievously.

'I knew something like this was going to happen,' said Talia, tucking sodden tendrils of hair behind her ears and straightening her candy-striped jumpsuit that gave her the appearance of a stick of Blackpool rock.

'You did?' asked Katie, unable to keep the note of incredulity from her voice.

How on earth could anyone predict that their first date with a guy they've been lusting after for months would be rudely interrupted by a madwoman brandishing a fire extinguisher like a super-powered Nerf gun?

'Yes. Today's horoscope warned me that if I was thinking of playing with fire then I should be prepared for the consequences. I knew I should have brought my umbrella with me!'

Although the air was still warm, the last rays of light had vanished from the sky and the aroma of wet charcoal was causing Katie's eyes to prickle. She exchanged a glance with Oscar and decided it was time to bring the farce-like drama to a close.

'Come on. Let's go over to the pub. I'll buy everyone a drink.'

Chapter 20

The following two weeks were the busiest the café had ever seen and when Thursday came around Katie was grateful when Talia persuaded one of her friends, Lin – who was hoping to go to catering college in September – to help them out in the kitchen. She put the increase in custom down to getting the go-ahead for The Cornish Kitchen rebrand from Agatha – in a friendly-yet-rushed one-line email – and Oscar working flat-out to create the most stunning polished oak signage with the letters etched out and painted a gorgeous pale blue sky and clotted cream colour. It was absolutely perfect and gave the place a fresh, modern and welcoming feel.

Her conscience had gnawed away at her since receiving Agatha's brisk email and she had decided she couldn't leave it any longer to come clean about what was going on in Cornwall, despite what Oscar had said. She intended to give her friend a call first thing the following morning to tell her about Greg's visits to the café, and to read out his letter to her. She had no idea what sort of offer he had made for the building, but a tiny devil inside her prayed that Greg was like most property developers, keen to snaffle a bargain, and Agatha would find the offer far from attractive.

The foam fiasco had circulated the village grapevine and Jay had already suggested that they invite a local band along and make it a regular occurrence, introducing a little bit of the San Antonio dance scene into the Cornish countryside. But Katie had too much on her mind to add another event to The Cornish Kitchen's already packed schedule. An unexpectedly large invoice had landed on the doormat that morning and there wasn't enough cash in the till to pay it. She hoped that the pyrography event she'd organised for that night would tickle people's curiosity and turn a higher profit than the Books & Bakes evening and Jay's flower-arranging night had, but in the meantime, she needed to focus her attention on that morning's get-together – the Knit & Natter group – which would be the first she'd held in the daytime hoping it would appeal to a different clientele.

'Hey, Katie! It's only me. Thought I'd come over early to see if you needed any help setting the café up for the Knitting Ninjas this morning?'

Katie stopped rearranging the strawberry milkshake cupcakes on one of Agatha's dainty china cake stands to greet Talia, but when she turned round ready to give her the customary hug, she found herself performing an almost comedic double take.

'Erm …'

'Oh, yes, do you like it? I thought I'd dress for the occasion. What do you think?'

'I … what exactly were you aiming for?'

Katie ran her eyes over Talia's outfit, her incredulity mounting as she took in what had once been a plain black jumpsuit but which now sported miniature red, yellow and white balls of wool pierced through with mini knitting needles, tiny letters made out of felt and embroidered with what looked like speech marks and exclamation marks, and question marks, and a garland of paisley bunting draped around the neckline like an oversized collar. However, being used to Talia's eclectic taste in attire, Katie wouldn't have given this article of unique clothing a second thought if her friend hadn't also been wearing what could only be described as an extended crown made from multi-coloured pompoms and glossy green leaves.

'Frigg?'

'I, erm … what?'

'The Norse god of weaving?'

'Oh, right, okay. Great.'

'I couldn't find a god of knitting. Don't you think that's strange? Shall I fix us a coffee before everyone gets here? You look like you could do with one.'

With effort, Katie managed to wind in her slackened jaw and unfurl her forehead. She supposed she should be thankful for small mercies. When she and Talia had been brainstorming their next Cornish Kitchen event, top of Talia's list was a Naked Neon Art Class where the participants daubed themselves in luminous pastels and then turned out the lights. Katie had vetoed that on the grounds of hygiene and so, reluctantly, Talia had moved on to suggest her second choice – Quidditch sessions where everyone brought their own broom and chased around the village green after a medicine ball like a herd of demented bulls before piling into the café for a hot chocolate and a warm brownie.

After that, a morning of sedate knitting was agreed, followed by an evening of pyrography to keep Talia happy.

'Mmm, these cupcakes are amazing, Katie. You really are a genius with flavours – you know that, don't you? You're like one of those "nose" people who create exotic French perfumes, but for cake!'

'Thank you, Talia.' Katie grinned as the café's brass bell tinkled and she rushed from the kitchen to welcome their first customer of the day, smiling when she saw who it was.

'Hey, Katie, is it true you're offering lessons in fire-eating tonight, I mean like eating real fire?' asked Ryan, his eyes wide with excitement as he snatched a cupcake and jumped up to sit on one of the tables, stuffing the cake into his mouth whole.

'Sorry to disappoint you, Ryan, but no, we will not be fire-eating. Pyrography is actually fire-*writing*. Under the expert guidance of a qualified tutor, we will be using special implements to burn permanent patterns onto wooden spoons, spatulas, wooden boxes and key rings. It's a bit like engraving but with fire on wood instead of metal.'

'So it's still dangerous?'

Katie paused, then made an executive decision.

'Really dangerous. It's not for the faint-hearted.'

'Cool! Count me in. Catch you later.'

By ten o'clock, the café was thrumming with noise as sixteen very enthusiastic knitters and natterers milled around the café, drinking cappuccinos, organic teas and cordials, and sampling the various home-made cakes and desserts that were on offer before settling down to a marathon session of knitting, crocheting, embroidering and cross-stitching.

'I've got a proposition for you all,' announced Margot, a well-rounded sixty-something woman with spiked silver hair and bejewelled glasses who had commandeered the window seat. As the president of the Perrinby WI, she clearly had a knack of commanding her audience's attention because as soon as she spoke the nattering stopped immediately. 'What do you say we put our collective creative talents to good use?'

'What do you have in mind?' asked Katie, moving around the café refilling everyone's mugs with coffee and fetching slices of cranberry flapjack, apricot and almond cupcakes, and chocolate and pistachio cookies so the group didn't have to leave their knitting.

'Who's up for a session of yarn storming?'

'Oh, oh, I've heard of that!' squealed Talia who had been concentrating so hard on completing her very first attempt at crocheting a square that her whole face was screwed up into creases. 'It's also called guerrilla knitting, isn't it? Although what it's got to do with gorillas, I have no idea.'

'It's … oh, never mind.' Margot grinned, too enthusiastic about her idea to pause to unpick Talia's understanding of knitting terms. 'It's more than just a few knitted articles left around the village to make the place look pretty, it's actually recognised as a form of urban graffiti. People have covered bicycles and benches and bridges with brightly coloured yarn, so why don't we do the bandstand? It's desperately in need of a lick of paint, and this could be the answer. What do you say?'

'Yay!'

'Great idea!'

'What fun!'

'Ooo, pass me the needles.'

'Let's get started!'

Margot blushed at the excitement reverberating around the café, as she held up her hand for quiet again.

'I also think that those of us who are more proficient knitters could maybe turn our talents to more charitable aims, too. Our WI recently received a very generous donation from a wool shop in Truro of several hanks of white four-ply and I thought we could use it to knit bonnets for premature babies at the maternity unit at the Royal Cornwall hospital.'

'Fantastic idea!'

'Wonderful!'

'Count me in!'

'When we cleared out my nan's house after her funeral last week,' said a young girl with bright pink hair who had been embroidering a plain white cotton blouse with triple clefs and musical notes, 'we found bags and bags and bags filled with navy-blue, grey and cream chunky knit yarn, if anyone has any use for that I'd be happy to bring it along. It's no good for babies, though.'

'Fantastic, thanks, Jodie. Perhaps we could start Project Ivy in her honour and turn the wool into sweaters and scarves for the homeless?'

'Oh, Nan would have loved that!'

When the Knit & Natter session eventually ended – having gained another three participants who had simply called into The Cornish Kitchen for an injection of caffeine but had been so interested in what was going on they'd stayed, promising to return the following month with a length of knitted fabric for the bandstand in the most vibrant-coloured wool they could find – Katie and Talia and Lin were immediately bombarded by the lunch rush, and then the local Mummy & Me group descended, exclaiming how wonderful the new signage was.

Before Katie could take stock of how successful the morning had been, she was dashing backwards and forwards between the kitchen and the café, serving clotted cream teas with organic Earl Grey, cucumber sandwiches and vegan cupcakes. When she finally had a moment to glance at the clock, she couldn't believe it was time to switch the sign to Closed and get ready for the evening's pyrography event.

She said a quick goodbye to Lin and Talia – who promised to be back later with Ryan – and she climbed the stairs to take a quick shower and make herself presentable for the next influx of customers. Unfortunately, or fortunately depending on which way you looked at it, when she opened the door at seven o'clock there were only five people waiting on the doorstep for the fire-writing session. She called the tutor, Jason Grainger, immediately surprised when he answered on the first ring.

'Ah, Katie, I'm so glad you called. I've lost your number. Look, I'm sorry, there's been an accident involving a campervan and a tractor just outside Helston. As I'm a paramedic in my day job, I had to see if I could help, and one of the guys has a fractured femur and the farmer has concussion. The ambulance has just arrived, but there's a couple of walking wounded, so what I'm trying to say is that I won't get over to you before ten.'

'Oh, my God, how awful. Don't worry about us, Jason, we'll reschedule.'

'Great.'

And the line went dead. When she broke the news to Talia, Ryan and the newly married couple who had just fancied trying something new with their recently dumped best friend in tow, there was understanding followed by glee when Katie offered them each a parsnip and blackcurrant cupcake on the house.

When everyone had left – and she had persuaded Talia and Ryan that she didn't need any help with the clearing up – she locked the door, turned the sign back to Closed again and sank down onto the window seat. Disappointment swirled through her body, especially after that morning's runaway success, but she refused to succumb to her usual melancholy when things didn't go according to plan. She would rebook Jason for the following month, which would give her the opportunity to spread the word about the session to more people, to talk up its quirkiness and how rewarding it could be to do something different every now and again, something out of your comfort zone, out of the ordinary.

Suddenly she knew exactly what to do. For once, she ignored the detritus that surrounded her, grabbed her phone, and selected the number that she knew by heart, her spirits already rising as she anticipated hearing her friend's voice.

'Hey, Cara! How are things in the buzzing metropolis?'

'Ergh! Not brilliant, to be honest.'

'Why? What's going on?'

'Well, first of all, I've just had a date cancel on me. I was really looking forward to going ice-skating too – last time I went I was thirteen with pigtails and braces but it was lots of fun! I had visions of the two of us stumbling around the rink, clinging on to each other for dear life, or channelling our inner Torvill and Dean before re-enacting the final scene from *Bolero*!'

'Sorry, Carr, the guy doesn't know what he's missing.'

'Oh, it's fine, he probably didn't look anything like his photo, anyway.'

Katie was used to living vicariously through Cara's dating catastrophes and the two of them had spent many a night filled with Prosecco and giggles as they dissected each date for potential relationship material. However, this time, Katie thought she heard a catch in her friend's voice and she experienced a twist of concern, her own woes flying out of the window.

'Is there something else?'

'Oh, Katie, I wasn't going to say anything. You've got so much going on, I didn't want to burden you with my misfortune ...'

'Cara, tell me!'

'It's ... well, there's been rumours at the travel agency that ... that the shop's closing down and we're all going to be made redundant. Head office have been talking about it for a while; no one's booking holidays and work trips at the travel agent's any more – they're all doing it online, but it's still a huge shock. Daphne was in tears yesterday, and Gareth has already found a new job at Harrods – it's his leaving party next Friday. Oh, God, what if I can't find a new job? What will I do? How will I pay the rent?'

'You'll be fine. Worst-case scenario you can go back home to Norfolk. Anyway, haven't you always said you would love to go travelling? Maybe you could use your redundancy money, and all your travel contacts, and do just that?'

'Maybe, I don't know ...'

'Or ...'

An idea flashed into Katie's brain, but she wasn't sure whether to say anything. Cara was upset, and if nothing came of it, she would only be adding to her friend's disappointment and that was the last thing she wanted to do.

'Or what?'

'How would you feel about managing a glamping site?'

'A glamping site? What sort of a glamping site?'

'One with six cute wooden pods with arched roofs and French doors and log fires, set in an old orchard next to a wildflower meadow and a little stream. Oh, you should see them, Cara, they're like hobbit houses, except with all the mod cons like a fully fitted kitchen, a shower and flushing toilet, and there's even a picnic bench, and get this – there's also a separate tiny dogpod for people's furry friends!'

'And where is this little slice of heaven?'

'In a field right behind the café.'

'So who's managing it at the minute?'

'No one, that's the point, it's empty.'

'Sounds a bit weird. A glamping site in sunny Cornwall? It should be fully booked.'

'It belongs to Agatha, and you know she's got her hands full at the moment. Apparently, she was hoping to sort something out for the Easter holiday season, but it's obvious she's not got round to it yet.'

'Thanks, Katie, you're a good friend. I'll let you know what happens when I go into work on Monday. Anyway, how about you? How was your Knit & Natter morning?'

'It was great, lots of people came; in fact I think it was the most well-attended event so far. And guess what? We've organised a yarn bombing expedition.' Giggling, Katie explained to a fascinated Cara exactly what they had planned for the village bandstand. 'But we've also agreed to do a couple of charity projects, too – everyone's having a go at making either a tiny bonnet for the premature baby unit at the local hospital or a twiddle muff for the dementia unit, and we're meeting again next month to show off our creations.'

'Wow, it sounds like another roaring success!'

'It is, it absolutely is, but …'

'But what?'

'Well, our pyrography night didn't go ahead as planned.'

'What on earth is a pyrography night?' Cara laughed, her voice losing its edge of despondency.

'It's fire-writing. I just wanted to offer something different, but the tutor couldn't make it at the last minute. It wasn't his fault but I'll have to chalk it up as a fail rather than a success, I'm afraid.'

'It's just a blip, Katie.'

'I know, I know, don't get me wrong, I love doing these events, I love that The Cornish Kitchen is an integral part of the community, that everyone in the village has taken what I'm trying to do here to their hearts and supported me. I'm starting to see a reasonable profit, but it's nowhere near enough to cover all the bills *and* make a decent donation to Agatha's cookery school in Bali. And ...'

'And?'

'There's something else.'

'What?'

Katie told Cara about Greg's visits and how guilty she felt for not telling Agatha about them.

'Katie, can I ask you something?'

'Of course.'

'What are you doing this for?'

'What do you mean?'

'All this kindness, compassion, good karma stuff?'

'It's, well, it's just something Agatha taught me in Bali,' muttered Katie, suddenly feeling defensive. She should be used to her friend's special brand of straight-talking by now – it was what she loved her for.

'So she must have told you that karma is about more than good deeds and good food and kindness jars. It's a way of life, it's about understanding and accepting that life is a series of ups and downs and we have to rise and fall with the waves; it's about collecting moments of happiness and harmony, appreciating calm and mindfulness, celebrating the small stuff. My advice is to practise what you preach by not forgetting to factor in a few hours of relaxation.'

'You know, you might just be right.'

'I know I am. Ever since you got back from Bali, all you've been thinking about is setting up the café and making it a success. It's another one of your most endearing traits – engaging avoidance tactics when things get tough.'

'Okay, I'll take a break. On one condition.'

'What's that?'

'That you'll think seriously about what I said, about coming down here to Cornwall. There's a home for you at the café for as long as I'm here. I'm not sure how long that will be, maybe just a few weeks, but it'll be great to see you. You never know, if we can persuade Agatha to reopen the glamping site, I might be bunking in with you!'

'So you're thinking of staying even if the café closes?'

'Possibly.'

'Is there something you're not telling me? Or maybe it's *someone*?'

'No, of course not,' she said with her fingers firmly crossed behind her back, not quite ready to put her fledgling relationship with Oscar into words, and certainly not ready for the forensic cross-examination she would be subjected to by Cara if she so much as hinted at the possibility of there being a guy she was interested in. 'And you'd love it here, Carr, I know you would.'

'If everything goes pear-shaped at work, I'll think about it.'

'I'm here for you – you know that, don't you? Speak soon, eh?'

'Definitely.'

Katie smiled. 'Thanks, Cara.'

'What for?'

'For cheering me up. You always know how to make me smile.'

'What are best friends for, darling? So, now that you're brimming with positivity and optimism, you should bite the bullet; ring Agatha and read out Greg's letter to her, otherwise it'll fester and that's definitely not good for your karma.'

'I will, I promise.'

Chapter 21

When she lived in London, Sundays were Katie's favourite day of the week. After a lie-in, Dominic would usually go out for the Sunday newspapers while she rustled up brunch. Sometimes, they would go out to meet friends at the French café around the corner and stay there until teatime, eating crepes with bananas and chocolate sauce, drinking thick dark coffee, sharing a bottle of red wine or a Ricard.

That morning, as she looked out of her bedroom window overlooking the village green in Perrinby, watching the families feed the ducks, she was ambushed by a wave of loneliness. She missed her life in the capital with Dominic; she missed spending her weekdays creating ever-elaborate birthday, wedding and celebration cakes; she missed learning new skills from François, meeting their customers, hearing their stories, guiding their choices; and she missed Cara. She had made friends in Cornwall, but they didn't know her like Cara did.

Her demons began to circulate, but she had no intention of giving in to them. There was only one way she knew to send them back into the dark and dingy cervices of her brain, so she pulled on a pair of old black leggings and a Hello Kitty T-shirt that had seen better days, and headed downstairs to the café's kitchen. When she caught sight of a stray courgette and pecan cupcake left over from the previous night's abandoned class, a sharp stab of sadness shot through her chest, and she couldn't wait to reach for the antibacterial spray to start that morning's cleaning marathon.

She pushed open the door into the café and came to an immediate standstill.

'Oh my God!'

She stared at the scattered debris on the floor then raised her eyes upwards, her hand flying to her mouth when she saw the gaping hole in the ceiling.

'Nooo!'

She dropped the spray and cloth onto the nearest table and slumped down into a peppermint-green chair, dropping her head onto her forearms, fighting the surge of emotions that even a session of high-octane cleaning couldn't stem. What was she going to do? She had no money to pay for a plasterer, not to mention the other outstanding bills that were screaming for her attention.

She briefly wondered if she should admit defeat and close the café there and then, pack a bag and catch the next train to London, FedExing the key and Greg's offer letter to Agatha with a note admitting that she had failed – that would certainly be the easiest solution to her mounting problems. She would stay with Cara, look for any old job in the catering industry so she could pay her rent, and return to her previous life, minus Dominic.

Then her eyes caught on the Kindness Jar on the marble counter, filled to the brim with colourful Post-it Notes. Clearly the café's customers had taken the concept to their hearts – okay, so *one* of her ideas had been a success – and she hoped that the Post-its they had taken out had helped brighten their day in some small way.

She smiled at the thought, her spirits edging up a notch. She had just decided to choose a missive of her own when there was a heavy hammering on the front door. When she saw the familiar silhouette through the blind her first reaction was to dive under the table and hide – it was Sunday morning after all – but she knew that was ridiculous. She wiped her hands on her apron and opened the door, for once the tumble of the brass bell failing to cheer her.

'Hello, Greg. What can I do for you?'

Having learned her lesson from his previous visits, she stood her ground on the threshold, refusing to step aside to invite him into the café, making herself as tall and wide as possible and determined to make their conversation as brief as possible. Instead of the ubiquitous designer suit, in honour of Sunday morning Greg had switched to a luminous yellow sweater that wouldn't have looked out of place at the local golf club, especially as it clashed ferociously with his perma-tan.

'I thought Agatha might have called me by now about my offer.'

Greg peered at her, his eyes filled with accusation, and remorse pricked her conscience.

'Oh, well, I think the wheels of commerce and high finance might turn a little more slowly in Bali ...'

'Don't give me that! I can tell by your face that you haven't told her about my visits. You know, Katie, I didn't have you down as a someone who only cared about their own selfish interests.'

His harsh words took Katie by surprise. Was that how he saw her? Was that what she was doing?

'I ...'

'I suspected something like this would happen, so I've taken advice from my lawyer.'

Katie's stomach lunged to the ground and bounced back up again lodging somewhere between her chest and her throat. She tried to swallow, but found her throat was dry and she coughed before managing to find her voice.

'Your *lawyer*?'

'Yes, so I'm here to give you this.'

Oh God! Oh God! Oh God! Was it a court summons? Nausea threatened to overwhelm her. Why, oh why, had she listened to Oscar and Cara? She should have contacted Agatha straight away to inform her of Greg's interest. Now she'd got herself into all sorts of trouble, and what with the fallen-in ceiling and the worry about where she was going to find the money to fix it. That train up to London was looking more desirable by the minute.

'Take it please.'

'What … what is it?'

'Open it.'

The smug look on Greg's face told her all she needed to know. He had won the battle for The Cornish Kitchen, or the building it was housed in, to be more precise. Clearly he had done something amazing in his former life, before he became a property developer supremo, and this was *his* karma payback. She glanced at the envelope Greg was holding out to her, then met his gaze.

'Go on.'

She fumbled with the flap and pulled out the contents.

'It's a cheque.'

'Top marks for observation.'

She flicked her eyes back to Greg, but he simply waited, his hands shoved into the pockets of his immaculately cut black dress pants, confidence oozing from his very pores; a man used to playing the game and winning. Katie peered at the figures on the cheque and her jaw dropped.

Forty thousand pounds – Greg had handed her a cheque for forty thousand pounds!

'What's …'

'It's a ten per cent deposit for this place. If you don't pass this on to Agatha, then you'll be in a considerable amount of hot water, Katie, and we don't want that, do we?'

She could see from the look on his face that he would like nothing better than for her to be thrashing around for dear life in that hot water, but the ability to deliver a pithy riposte seemed to have deserted her.

'I'll be back here in a week and I expect Agatha to have contacted either me or my lawyer with her decision. I'm a patient man, Katie, but I won't be taken for a fool.' Greg's eyes strayed over her shoulder to the doorway leading to the kitchen corridor and the pile of plaster and hole in the ceiling. 'This place is falling down. It's in desperate need of an injection of cash. In fact, depending on what happens over the next week, I might be forced to do my civic duty and call in the health and safety inspectors. No one wants a chunk of ceiling in their date and walnut scone, do they?'

Greg laughed at his joke, then turned on his heels and strode towards his expensive car, leaving Katie staring at him speechless while her world crumbled around her ears. Forty thousand pounds; that meant that Greg had offered Agatha four hundred thousand pounds for the café and the flat above. It was a huge amount of money, especially for someone who wanted to invest in their charitable project. The cash would secure Agatha's future at her beachside café *and* the continuing viability of the cookery school for years to come.

She locked the door behind Greg and returned to her seat, tears threatening to fall. Why had she thought she could do this? Now when she got back to London, she would have another failure to contend with on her ever-lengthening list.

Fiancée – fail.

Cake decorator – fail.

Café manager – fail.

Cookery school supporter – fail.

She had no home to go to any more, and no job that had her jumping out of bed every morning with a smile on her face and a song in her heart. Maybe she should avoid London and spend some time with her mum in Crete – all safe, comfortable choices. She inhaled a deep breath, squared her shoulders and decided to treat herself to a coffee to calm her nerves as well as a slice of chocolate orange cake with the baked clementines on the top.

She had just set the kettle to boil when there was another knock at the door. She groaned. Had Greg forgotten something? A bag filled with banknotes, maybe? She blew her nose, shoved back her chair and went to take a quick peek out of the bay window, relieved to see there was no sign of the black BMW, then answered the door.

'Hi, Katie, was that Greg Forbes' car I saw screeching through the village?'

'It was.'

'Has he been here again?'

'Yes.'

'What did he want this time?'

Katie hesitated, unsure whether she would be breaching some kind of protocol if she shared their conversation with Oscar. But his gaze had already picked out the envelope she had left on the table, with the cheque next to it.

'What's that?'

Oscar strode across the café and picked up the cheque.

'Forty thousand pounds?'

'It's a lot of money, isn't it?'

'A huge amount. What's it for?'

'It's his ten per cent deposit on this place. Greg's apparently consulted a solicitor and he told me that if I don't contact Agatha now, then I'll be in some kind of trouble.'

'That's baloney!'

'Whatever it is, I think the time has come for me to give Agatha another call, don't you? She deserves to know about this. It's her decision what to do about the café, not mine, not yours, just hers. Just think about what she can do in Bali with money like that!'

'But there's no way Agatha would sell the café, Katie.'

'How do you know that, though?'

Katie caught a fleeting expression in Oscar's eyes she couldn't fathom, but it disappeared as quickly as it came.

'We don't, but she lived in this village for over thirty years. This is her home.'

'It *was* her home. Now she lives in Bali; she's happy there, and she's fulfilling her long-term dream to run a cookery school for disadvantaged teens. There's no way I want to be a part of stopping her from getting the most out of that, and I'm sure you don't either, Oscar.'

'No, of course I don't, it's just ...'

'What?'

'Nothing, you're right.'

'Is there something worrying you, Oscar?'

'No, no ... it's just that, well, The Cornish Kitchen is doing so well. You've really turned it into a vibrant part of the Perrinby community; the place thrums with customers during the day – I've even seen people queuing outside the door to partake in a slice of your famous parsnip and coriander cake, and everyone is loving the community events you ... What?'

She had already confided in Oscar that despite all the positive things he'd just listed, the café struggled to meet its bills. But, of course, he didn't know that their pyrography evening had been cancelled the previous evening or that half the ceiling was on the floor.

'It's probably for the best.'

'What do you mean?'

'The three months Agatha gave me is up in two weeks' time, and ... well, while it's true that the café is busier than I ever dreamed it would be, there's no way I'll be able to tell Agatha that the business can support itself without her continuing financial input, let alone contribute towards her cookery school's running costs. So, the project she asked me to take on might be a social success, but it's a *commercial* failure, and the sooner I come clean, the better. If I can sweeten the blow with the news of this cheque from Greg then that's great, don't you think?'

'No, I don't. Agatha gave you three months and you shouldn't give up until the very last day.'

'Oscar ...'

'Can I just say something?'

'Yes, of course.'

'When we lost Harry, I'd been dating one of his friend's sisters, Juliette, for a couple of months, but she couldn't deal with our family's grief and so we agreed to go our separate ways. I admit it was a relief; it wasn't fair on her to watch people she knew and loved suffer like we were. When I moved to Perrinby, I decided that embarking on a serious romantic relationship wasn't for me. I didn't want to fall in love with someone only to end up losing them, because I didn't want to go through even a quarter of the pain that I'd experienced losing Harry ever again.'

Oscar paused, and met Katie's eyes.

'But then I met you, with your halo of golden curls and your passion for creating quirky cakes. I love your desire to put your customers and the villagers at the forefront of everything the café does. I love that every item on the menu is made with care, that you've introduced a "pay it forward" system, and that probably without meaning to, all the activities you've organised at the café have revitalised Perrinby – even the ducks waddle around with serene smiles on their faces!'

Katie giggled, glancing out of the window to where the pond's residents were parading around the village green, as though taking part in a beauty pageant. She had to admit, the image was idyllic. When she turned back to face Oscar, he reached out and slid his palm into hers, scooting closer towards her so their knees touched and she caught a delicious waft of the cologne he favoured.

'Katie ...'

She waited, watching him as he paused to inhale a breath,

gathering his courage to say something important, something that took a tremendous effort to articulate.

'You've brought a spark of hope back into my life, something I thought had evaporated and would never return. You make me laugh, you make me eat beetroot and courgette cupcakes, you make me see the benefit of offering a dash of kindness to everyone who comes into the gallery, and you've made me realise that if something is good, it's worth fighting for. You can't give up, Katie, you can't leave!'

Katie smiled at him, delighted by his compliments about the café, at the animated way he had argued for her to continue with what she was doing there, and humbled that he credited her with sparking hope in his heart after everything he'd been through, and yet ...

'Oscar, I have to think about Agatha, I have to ...'

'No you don't. Not yet. What's two weeks between friends? It's just fourteen days, three hundred and thirty-six hours, twenty thousand one hundred and sixty minutes. It's nothing at all, and I promise to help you with the next party night, make it the best yet! Hey, why don't we organise a ceramic-painting evening – everyone loves those. I'll donate the pots and the paints, and I'll fire them in my kiln afterwards.'

'I don't know, Oscar ...'

But he wasn't listening to her; his thoughts had scooted off on a creative tangent. She shook her head as he rattled off random ideas as they came to him about different paint techniques, what colours to use and which brushes were the best and whether to use stencils and whether he had enough varnish. After five whole minutes that had required no contribution from her whatsoever, she got up from her seat to put the kettle on.

'Coffee?'

'No thanks. Actually, I think I'll pop back to the studio and check how much clay I've got. I might need to put in another order, and I'm not sure if I have enough paintbrushes. What do you think about individual artist's palettes? When we've finished making the pots, perhaps everyone could decorate them and take them home?'

Clearly Oscar's questions didn't require an answer because before she knew what was happening, he'd jumped up, grabbed her shoulders, and planted a quick kiss on her lips, sending a heavenly zap of electricity through her body.

'Oh, and I'll fix the ceiling for you, if you like. Catch you later.'

Then, beaming, he sprinted out of the door leaving only a cloud of citrus-infused aftershave behind. Katie shook her head. Her lips curled into a smile as she fixed herself a cup of chamomile tea and went back to sit on the window seat where ribbons of glorious Cornish sunshine poured through the dreamcatchers, sending dancing prisms of colour across the walls of the café.

She picked up her phone and toyed with the screen. She couldn't put off calling Agatha, despite what Oscar had said, but it looked like her final couple of weeks at the café would be filled with activity, including a painting and pottery-making class, whether she liked it or not!

Chapter 22

However, before Katie could select Agatha's number and embark on the dreaded phone call to Bali, her mobile buzzed with an incoming call. She squinted at the screen and saw it was a withheld number. Was this Greg, chasing her already, reminding her about the importance of communicating his offer? She hesitated, her finger hovering over the Reject Call button, but her conscience wouldn't let her do it.

'Hello?'

'Katie? Is that you?'

It was as though a grenade had exploded in her chest and she gasped, struggling for air as shock waves reverberated around her whole body. She hadn't heard that voice for almost five months and she questioned whether her ears were deceiving her. Once her brain had reconnected to its modem, her first reaction was to hang up and throw her phone out of the window, or into the bucket of hot soapy water she had kept on standby to wash down the tables in the café.

Her whole body trembled, her mouth was suddenly dry and every carefully constructed sentence of the speech she had rehearsed in those long, lonely hours when the sleep fairies had eluded her, flew out of her mind and she was left with a blank.

She had waited for this call for so long that now she had the chance to say everything she wanted to say, to shout, to scream, to remonstrate, she had been struck mute.

'Katie? Are you there? It's Dom.'

Was he seriously suggesting that she had forgotten what his voice sounded like? That his dulcet tones hadn't pervaded every waking moment until she had arrived in Bali and she was able to get some perspective with the help of Agatha's sage advice and counselling? Suddenly the shock abated and she was overtaken by a myriad of emotions: anger, indignation, curiosity.

'What do you want, Dom?'

'I want to talk to you.'

'You want to talk to me? After four months of avoiding every call, every email, every message via social media, every plea from your family and friends to call me?'

'Katie, I just want to explain—'

'Have you any idea how soul-destroying it is, not only to be dumped – I'm sure I would have come to terms with that eventually – but not to be afforded the respect of being told why? I was so shocked at the cruel way you handled things that I thought I would go crazy, especially when I was left to cancel everything, as well as being forced to make all those heartbreaking calls to our family and friends. You ducked out of that very well, Dom.'

'Katie—'

'Why didn't you come back, talk to me face to face, then we could have shared the burden. Instead, you made me look like a complete fool while you lived the high life in San Antonio. *Using. Our. Wedding. Savings!*'

'I'm sorry, Katie. I just well … I just sort of panicked; I think.'

'You panicked?'

'I know what I did was unforgivable, but when I got to Ibiza, I realised that this was my one chance to shoot for my dream to sing in the clubs and bars there. I had to give it a shot, Katie.'

'But we could have done that together!'

'Maybe …'

'What do you mean *maybe*?'

A note of hysteria had crept into her voice and she made a concerted effort to calm down, to corral her rampaging emotions, because she knew this was her opportunity to get to the crux of what had gone wrong with their relationship.

'It's … well, it's just that as soon as we got engaged, everything changed.'

'Like what?'

'I felt as if this massive "wedding planning" machine had swung into action and every spare moment we had was being taken up with tasting menus, decisions about invitations, wedding cars, flowers, favours and confetti with little pictures of us printed on.'

'But that's what happens when a couple is organising a wedding!'

'I know, I know, but we stopped going to gigs, I had to cancel a couple of singing engagements …'

'Singing engagements? You were booked to sing Happy Birthday at Cara's niece's fifth birthday party!'

'Yeh, but it wasn't just that …'

There was a pause and she steeled herself for what was to come. However hard it would be to listen to his character assassination, she knew she had to hear it in order to understand what had gone wrong – that was what she had been craving ever since she had realised that he wasn't coming back from his stag weekend.

'You changed too, Katie.'

'I did? How?'

'Well … it must have been all the stress, but well …'

'Dominic!'

'You were really clingy. Always wanting to come with me wherever I went, asking where I was going, who with, what time I would be back …'

'Oh, my God! That was because I loved you, Dom! I loved

174

you so much that I was marrying you, and I wanted to spend as much time with you as I could, outside of our work commitments. I wanted you to share in the decisions about our wedding day, wanted you to be part of the choices we made about every detail. I valued your input, but more than anything I adored having you by my side. It's normal for engaged couples to want to be together, Dom!'

'I felt sort of … claustrophobic.'

'Claustrophobic?'

Her heart was breaking all over again as she thought of the months leading up to their wedding when she had thought things were fine, when in actual fact, Dominic had been planning his escape.

'So that's it, is it? I was clingy so you bailed out?'

'I got cold feet. I'm sorry, Katie, truly I am. But I never fell out of love with you.'

'What?'

'That's what I'm ringing for.'

'You never …' she spluttered.

What was happening here? She felt dizzy, like she had crossed into another dimension, or she was floating on high looking down on their conversation, not taking part in the most bizarre telephone call she had ever had.

'I miss you, Katie. I know it will take a lot of grovelling on my part for you to forgive me, but I'm prepared to work as hard as I can to make it up to you if you'll give me another chance. I'm truly sorry and I know I should have handled things better than I did, but guess what, Kat? It worked!'

'What worked?'

'You'll never guess what's happened.'

'No, I don't think …'

'I've been offered a recording contract!'

'A recording contract …'

'Baz Carlton-Thomas, he's a big name in the indie music scene

175

over here, wants me to go into the studio and record an album with him! There's a decent signing fee, too, so I'll be able to pay back every penny I borrowed from our wedding fund and have quite a bit left over to cover the rent on a villa in Portinatx. Katie?'

But her brain was spinning with bewilderment, which was nothing compared to how she felt when he dropped his next bombshell into the conversation.

'Katie, I want you to come over to Ibiza. I know François fired you so you don't have a job at the moment. Never liked the guy, to be honest, and Iain says you're waitressing down in Cornwall. Come over to Ibiza and let me make it up to you. Please, Katie, say you'll give me a second chance. I screwed up big time, I know I did, but things are different now and exciting times are ahead, and before all the wedding pressure, we were good together.'

'Dom, I am not waitressing, I'm ...'

'Look, I know this has probably come as a bit of a shock—'

'Really? You think?'

'So I don't expect you to decide straight away. Don't worry about the flight, I'll pay for that and if you want to invite your mum over, then there's plenty of room, the villa's got five bedrooms, a stunning sea view, and this amazing infinity pool, there's even a gym.'

Katie tuned out; her ex-fiancé sounded like Greg and she was suddenly overcome by an overwhelming urge to laugh. She knew it was the shock, but she couldn't help it and she started to giggle.

'Katie, are you laughing?'

'No, no.' She managed to rein in her laughter.

Clingy?

Had she really been clingy?

She dredged up the painful memories of the weeks leading up to Dominic's stag weekend, scrutinising her behaviour, their conversations, and she had to admit that after two relatively stress-free years, the pressure of her pending nuptials had exposed her emotional fragility. She hadn't stopped to think how her issues, so familiar to her, could have impacted on Dominic, and now with the benefit of hindsight, she realised that instead of their engagement solidifying their commitment to each other, the stress had manifested itself in her need to ensure that she didn't lose another person she loved and whom she thought loved her.

So yes, she supposed that looking at things objectively, she had been clingy.

'I still love you, Katie. What do you say? Will you come out to Ibiza?'

'Dom, getting back together is a big decision. I …'

The sound of a door closing at the rear of the café made her pause. She leaned to her left to look down the corridor that led to the back garden, expecting to see either Talia or Zoe on the hunt for a coffee and a slice of cake, or Oscar wanting to talk about his pottery classes, but she couldn't see anyone.

'I totally get that, Kat. So, I'll say *ciao* for now and call you again tomorrow.'

And without waiting for her to reply, the line went dead. She had no idea how long she remained there in the café, revisiting every word Dominic had uttered as if it was flashing by on tickertape, and becoming more and more confused as each minute passed.

Chapter 23

Katie had been wondering what to do after she returned the keys to Agatha, but Dominic had now left her with a much bigger set of questions; questions that drowned out all the others and sent her head into a frenzy of uncertainty. Should she go to Ibiza? Should she give him a second chance? If the café wasn't going to work out, perhaps that was an option?

Then her heart elbowed its way into the argument and objected vociferously. Why was she even considering Dominic's proposal? She was a completely different person to the one he'd ditched without a backward glance or even granting her the courtesy of an explanation. Since arriving in Perrinby, she had morphed from being an ex-fiancée, heartbroken and with no job, to being the proud manager of a vibrant village café, an organiser of community activities and a delighted charity supporter. She had learned how good it felt to stand on her own two feet and drive her life forward in the direction *she* chose without anyone criticising her every move.

As she continued to mull over what Dominic had said, she realised that, perhaps inadvertently, he had presented her with the gift of self-awareness. It was as though the picture of her past had been blurred before, and now the image had come into full focus. After her sojourn in Bali, meeting Agatha – who had also reinvented her life – and then spending the last few months in Cornwall surrounded by people who knew nothing about her and yet supported her for no other reason than they wanted to, she realised that a future free of her demons was within her grasp.

It was time she practised what she preached every day to her customers at The Cornish Kitchen and moulded her own upbeat vision for the future so she could move on without the weight of the past dragging her down, and the only way to do that was to deal, once and for all, with the issues she had with her father, otherwise those same problems would continue to rear their heads every time a stressful situation arose and impact on every relationship she formed.

She made a decision.

She leapt from the window seat and scrambled up the stairs as fast as she could in search of her journal. She didn't want to delay for a moment for fear she may lose her determination – to set out, in writing, everything she had felt over the last fifteen years, every scorching, agonising emotion that had inhabited her heart since her father had walked out on her and her mum.

Why hadn't she thought of that before?

She would write everything down, using pen and paper, until there was nothing left swirling around her brain like a vortex of unspoken recrimination, then she would mail it to him in Edinburgh so he could read about her feelings of abandonment, of despondency, of inadequacy, of hurt, of anger, of bafflement that anyone could turn their backs so resolutely on their own daughter – this way, he wouldn't be able to interrupt her, or change the subject, or simply hang up because he had better things to do.

She found her journal and sat down at the kitchen table, her pen poised, anxiety gnawing at her abdomen as she chased down the words she needed to form, the sentences she needed to construct, to do justice to the years and years of internal turmoil she had experienced. She managed to scribble down a 'Dear Dad' and stopped. She couldn't do it; a myriad of random thoughts ricocheted through her brain like a flock of kamikaze lemmings and no matter how hard she tried to pin them down, she just couldn't.

Where would she start?

Her cancelled thirteenth birthday party because her mum couldn't face the curious stares from her friends' parents, her conflicting emotions when she'd been presented with a gold medal for the one hundred metre breaststroke at the county swimming championships and he wasn't there to see her joy like all the other competitors' fathers, her acute sense of loss when she grasped her A-level results to her chest as she and Cara squealed with delight that they had both got into the college course they wanted, her crushed hope when he'd demurred on walking her down the aisle on her wedding day?

And there were many other less significant milestones she had wanted to share with him, pearls of wisdom she had hoped to seek, opinions she wanted to discuss, options she wanted to explore, but each time she had reached out he'd either been too busy at work, or too immersed in his new life to even offer her the crumbs left over. No, even if she managed to get all that down on paper, there was no way she could post it.

But then she heard Oscar's voice reverberate in her ears.

What's the worst that can happen?

The worst had happened to him when he had lost his much-loved brother in an accident he had witnessed. And yet, here he was in Perrinby pursuing his dreams with a smile on his face and his hands elbow deep in oil paint and dried clay. Her father hadn't died; he'd just moved to Scotland, and, unlike Oscar, she could contact him whenever she wanted, if she had the courage, and so that was what she was going to do.

She gritted her teeth and managed to compose a first paragraph, informing him, a little formally, that she was in Cornwall, running a café, making new friends, sampling the world-famous seafood. When she turned to the crux of the issues she wanted to address, her enthusiasm stalled again and she was besieged by an almost overwhelming desire to reach for the scrubbing brush and to indulge in another marathon cleaning session in the hope that would assuage the rampaging demons she had released from their cage.

But for the first time, the reaction was fleeting.

She had to let go; had to stop carrying the heavy load of guilt around with her, had to stop allowing his abandonment to affect every aspect of her life when it was clear that he barely spared her a single thought. Her father was a stranger to her. She knew nothing about his life in Edinburgh – where he lived, where he worked, what he did with his free time – and she knew even less about Sue and her sixteen-year-old daughter, Joanne. She would have liked to get to know them, but they obviously weren't interested in getting to know her and there was nothing she could do about it. Still, she hoped the Sweet Sixteen party had been a success.

She returned to her letter and began writing again. First a paragraph, then another, and then another. A second page now, she was in full flow, the words flying from her pen, eloquent, measured, devoid of accusation, just an explanation of how she had felt growing up without a father in her life and that she wished with all her heart that it could have been any other way. She wrote for what felt like hours, but when she glanced at the clock on Agatha's ancient oven she saw it had only been thirty minutes, and yet she had produced five pages of closely formed script and had covered all the salient things she had wanted to talk to her father about but had been denied the chance.

She sat back, rubbing her hand to eradicate the cramp that had come from gripping her pen too tightly and to her surprise, her thoughts cleared, and she felt the tightness at her temples ease and the block of concrete that had pressed down on her chest for so long shift slightly, to be replaced by a feeling of …

Of what?

Relief?

Yes, of course. She had built up her issues with her father's abandonment into a mountain of Everestian proportions the scaling of which had proved to be an impossible feat, and she had carried the repercussions through into her obsession with cleanliness and hygiene, using them as a crutch whenever her mental health was fragile.

But there was something else, too.

What was it?

A certain calmness; a feeling of satisfaction that she had just done something positive for a change instead of lingering on all the negatives, that she had grasped her old 'demon' friends by the horns, looked them in the eye and told them that their time was up. No more would she allow them to control her life, her relationships, her happiness. Her father's decision to leave her mum had nothing to do with *her*; it was a decision he had taken for his own selfish reasons – which had started with having an affair with a work colleague.

Wafting the embers of hope was a futile activity, and perhaps she would do better to put her efforts into working on her forgiveness skills instead?

Marriages broke down, parents separated, all the time. Sadly, it was a fact of life. People found new partners; they moved on. Her father had made a new life in Scotland that didn't include her and probably never would. What was the point of constantly craving a relationship with someone who didn't want one with her? If she continued chasing her elusive dream, then it wouldn't only be her fiancé she drove crazy – perhaps she would do that to herself.

So, Dominic was right.

She hadn't realised it at the time, but she had been reliant on him completely for her emotional well-being instead of relying on herself. A window of clarity opened up and she understood why he'd decided not to come back from Ibiza, why he hadn't wanted to pursue his dream with her by his side. So, whilst she was on the subject of honing her forgiveness skills, maybe she should include Dominic on that list; forgive him for leaving her in the way he did, forgive him for not having the decency to call her to explain the reasons. And yet, perhaps if he *had* been honest with her before today, maybe she could have faced her demons earlier.

But then look at what she would have missed.

This whole new life she had been given – a life in which she was a valued member of the community, had made a gaggle of new friends, learned how to crochet, potentially saved a life! She had changed, really changed, and what was more, she liked the person she had become – a more rounded, empathetic, socially and environmentally aware person than she had been when Dominic had left.

She couldn't go back, only forward.

There was no way she wanted to be the Old Katie again, fixated on cleanliness and hygiene, and whilst she wouldn't exactly be throwing away the Marigolds and the antibacterial spray – she didn't want a visit from environmental services, after all – she knew that she would now be able to resist the temptation every time something went wrong. The way to deal with difficult issues was to face them head-on, to talk about them honestly and openly, to listen to friends' advice, but ultimately to make her own decisions then stride forwards with her head held high.

She couldn't control how other people acted, or reacted, or thought, nor did she want to, and she would never understand some of the decisions those closest to her made – her father's disinterest, her mother's emigration, Dominic's silence – it was up to them to choose what to do with their lives and up to her to choose what to do with hers.

And she wasn't interested in Dominic's request for a second chance. She'd noticed that he hadn't offered her a central role in his new enterprise, merely a part as a supporting actor – as an incidental escort on his journey to pursue his musical career – and the only way she could be truly happy was by following her *own* dreams with as much vigour and focus as Dominic was doing. And whilst she knew that in time she could forgive him for their broken engagement, even for the way he had handled it, she could never excuse the fact that he had emptied their joint savings account without her permission, to pursue his own agenda.

She reached out and drew her journal – a gorgeous notebook bound with Chinese silk that Cara had bought for her birthday – onto her lap. As she ran her gaze over the scribbled words for the last time, she was grabbed by an urge too powerful to resist. She ripped out the pages, all five of them, but instead of folding them neatly and going off in search of an envelope and a stamp, she continued to tear, and tear, and tear again, the whole pain-filled missive into shreds and then tossed them into the air, watching each fragment fall like a shower of snowflakes.

Almost immediately, a sensation of complete and absolute freedom descended, as though she had just emptied her mind, and body, of all the garbage that had accumulated over the years. If her father wanted to have a relationship with her, then he would contact her, seek her out, write *her* a letter, send *her* an email, give *her* a call, she wasn't going to waste any more of her time or energy chasing an elusive dream.

She stared at the words 'Dear Dad' on a confetti-sized piece of paper that had flittered down onto the table in front of her and was visited by a true light-bulb moment. Whilst her father would always bear this label, it was the people who cared for her, who loved and supported her through the good times and the challenging times who were her real family – her mum, of course, but also Cara, Agatha, Talia, Zoe, Mel, Jay, and to some extent, all her wonderful customers at The Cornish Kitchen who drank her coffee, sampled her cakes and generally brought a smile to her lips every single day since she'd arrived.

But there was one person who had done more than anyone else to make her feel truly at home in Perrinby. One special person she did want to spend her time with – a man who had shown her that when the right person was by your side, shaking the metaphorical cheerleader's pompoms, anything was possible.

Yes, abandonment by those who were supposed to love you unconditionally hurt, and it was tough to accept, but the only solution, as her mother had told her constantly, and shown her by example, was to dust herself down, count her blessings, and move on, because the alternative – never loving anyone ever again – was much, much worse.

Chapter 24

On the following Wednesday night, after saying goodbye to the last of the café's customers, Katie meandered into the kitchen to set the kettle to boil, studiously avoiding looking at the gaping hole in the corridor's ceiling. She had swept away the smattering of plaster and unless one of her customers took a wrong turn en route from the bathroom, she hoped no one would notice that the café had maintenance issues. She had just sat down with a cup of Earl Grey and a warm fig and thyme scone that passed for her evening meal, when the door burst open.

'Hi, Katie, it's me.'

Katie smiled. Who else would she be expecting to bounce in at six thirty?

'Hi, Talia. Loving the hat. Are they real bees?'

'Noooo! That would be crazy! I've made them from needle felt. Do you like them?'

'I love them, I'm just not sure having them dangle from your head on floristry wire is the safest option for when you're serving our customers with their daily coffees? And what is that yellow mat thingy you've got covering your hair?'

'Hey, I've woven this myself from organic, locally produced mole hair.'

'Mole hair?'

'Yes, who would have thought you could get hair from moles.' Katie giggled. 'I think you mean mohair.'

'Really? I've never heard of a mo. Is it some kind of cow?'

'No it's … oh, never mind. What is it anyway?'

'It's a beehive, you know, where bees live?'

'Right, of course it is.'

'Okay, so, remember I told you that I wanted to help you out with the baking for our girly pampering session tonight?'

'Yeeeees …'

Talia beamed with excitement as she reached into the oversized hessian bag hooked over her arm to extract a couple of huge Tupperware boxes, and placed them with a flourish on the table in front of Katie.

'I've made two dozen liquorice and honey cupcakes and two dozen Marmite and peppermint ones, both with cream cheese toppings, one flavoured with crushed pineapple, one flavoured with mashed parsnip, and they're all sprinkled with this amazing popping candy stuff I found on the Internet that you're going to adore! Do you think that'll be enough?'

'More than enough,' Katie assured her, fervently hoping that someone would risk their taste buds and take a leap into the culinary unknown so as not to hurt Talia's feelings. 'There's only going to be a few of us tonight. It's just a thank you from me really for all the support I've had since coming here. And I've made a lemon meringue pie and a tray of apricot and crushed almond flapjack, so I'm sure we'll be fine.'

'You can never have too much cake, Katie,' said Zoe, the next person to appear at the kitchen door, also carrying a cake tin in each hand.

'True, true,' agreed Mel, depositing a linen shopping bag on the countertop and proceeding to extract what looked like a football covered in tin foil sprouting a selection of cake pops in the shape of farmyard animals.

'Wow, they look amazing!'

'Well, I have to say that the twins and I had a wonderful afternoon making them. That one's a pink unicorn – just in case you thought it was something else.' Mel grimaced as her mother giggled.

'Yay!' cried Talia, rushing out of the kitchen to greet the café's next visitor. 'It's Ruby! Oh, I'm so excited! I've never been to a pamper night before. I'm going to get my nails done first, and then I want Katie to braid my hair so that when I wake up in the morning it'll look like mermaid hair. Do you think I should take the plunge and dye it green?'

'No, darling, I do not,' said Zoe firmly, giving her daughter a look that invited no argument.

'Hi Ruby, thanks for doing this,' said Katie, reaching out to relieve her of the huge box she was carrying so that Ruby could drag the wheelie suitcase that contained all the tools of her trade into the café. 'You've no idea how much I'm looking forward to a little bit of pampering. In fact, I can't remember the last time I treated myself to a manicure.'

'It's no problem. I love a girly night-in, especially if it involves cake and a cup of that liquorice and blackcurrant tea that I had the last time I was here. And you'll be pleased to know that I've brought a rainbow of shades of nail polish for you to choose from – just take your pick.'

As usual, Ruby had selected an outfit to match her personality: a skimpy chiffon mini-dress in a fiery orange fabric that showcased her curves to perfection. Katie's heart soared at the prospect of an evening filled with good friends and that trio of female solace – pampering, gossip and cupcakes.

'Hey! I hope you haven't started without me, darlings!' cried Jay, rushing into the café looking like he had just dashed from a Hollywood film set. Once again, he was dressed head-to-toe in black, with his mahogany quiff glued into place and his gold-rimmed sunglasses glinting in the overhead lights. His skin, too, was buffed to perfection, his eyebrows newly shaped and, of course, he smelled like a French courtesan's boudoir.

Katie had no idea why Jay thought he had any need of a pampering session, but she was happy he was there.

'Hi, Jay, welcome to The Cornish Kitchen's very first beauty night.'

'Ah, you girls are absolute saviours! I'm *soo* desperate for a manicure. Working in the floristry trade completely ruins the hands! I swear I should be buying shares in the hand-cream industry! Oh, Katie, I ran into Oscar earlier. Have you two had a lover's tiff or something?' asked Jay, a cheeky grin on his face as he took a seat in front of Ruby and spread out his fingers so Ruby could get to work straight away.

'What do you mean?' asked Katie, avoiding his gaze on the pretext of setting down a cup of his favourite peppermint tea next to him and pushing a plate of flapjack nearer so he could reach it with his free hand.

'Well, his usually cheerful charm was missing in action and he looked like he was auditioning for a part as Eeyore's younger brother!'

'Really? Well, I'm sorry to disappoint you, Jay, but that has got nothing to do with me. And, just for the record, we are most definitely *not* lovers, we're just friends.'

'Heard that one before.' Jay smirked, wiggling his eyebrows, a glint of mischief in his mahogany eyes. 'Okay, that's me done. Thank you, Ruby. Talia, *ma cherie*, it's your turn.'

'Yay!'

Talia slipped into Jay's vacated seat and held out her hands for Ruby to work her magic.

'Loving the new hat, Talia,' said Ruby, flicking one of the bees so that it bounced up and down like an alien's antennae. 'You really do have an eye for the weird and wonderful. Maybe you should think about going into business. I bet there's a market out there for the more quirky end of the millinery spectrum.'

'Oh, no, I couldn't bear to part with any of my designs; it would be like giving one of my children away.'

'Maybe you could ask your customers to grant you access rights,' suggested Jay as he took a bite out of one of Talia's Marmite and peppermint cupcakes and almost gagged, but was too polite to spit it back out.

'Do you think so? But what if they live in Newquay? Or Falmouth? *Or London*?'

Zoe rolled her eyes at her daughter and Talia got the message, narrowing her eyes at Jay's friendly teasing.

'Anyway, I can't start a business because I'm saving up to go travelling in September.'

'You are?' chorused Zoe and Mel.

'Remember, Mum? When I read you my annual horoscope in January? It said I had far to go? Well, I reckon Bali is about as far as you can go without coming back again, so that's what I'm hoping to do. When I've got enough money for the flight, I'm going to ask Agatha if I can work in her café and help out in the cookery school, just like Katie did. She's my pole model.'

'What's a pole model?' asked Jay, his lips twisting upwards.

'She means role model,' said Katie coming to Talia's aid.

'Do I? But you look nothing like a roll, Katie. I always thought that expression was a bit mean, to be honest. I mean, isn't it rude to talk about people's body shapes?'

'It doesn't … never mind.'

'Darling, if you're set on going travelling, then I'm happy to help towards the cost.'

'Me, too,' added Mel, selecting a bright scarlet nail polish and handing it over to Ruby.

'But I'm a bit worried about you going by yourself,' said Zoe, her eyes filled with a mother's anxiety for her younger daughter who was blissfully unaware of the dangers lurking in the big wide world for someone who was determined to live their life in accordance with their day's astrological predictions.

'Oh, I won't be by myself.'

The relief on Zoe's face was there for all to see.

'So who is the lucky companion?' asked Mel, giving over the hot seat to Katie while she blew on her new colourful nails.

'I'm not sure yet, but the stars said there would be someone watching over me.'

The apprehension returned to Zoe's face and, seeing her mother's expression, Mel swiftly changed the subject to avert an extended family confab in front of their friends.

'What flavour are these cupcakes again, Tal?' she asked, running her tongue along her bottom lip to collect the last crumbs.

'Liquorice and honey.' Talia smiled, delighted at her sister's interest in her culinary experiment. 'The recipe actually said golden syrup, but we didn't have any of that so I improvised. What do you think?'

'I love them! And the pineapple cream cheese topping is delicious. Katie, I think you might just have a new cupcake recipe for the café's menu board.'

'Mmm, Mel's right,' said Jay, rolling his eyes in theatrical ecstasy.

'Do you really think so?'

'Here, Katie, taste this.'

As Katie's fingers were splayed across Ruby's manicure towel, Mel fed her a bite-size piece of the cake and everyone waited with bated breath for her verdict.

'It's delicious! It's definitely going on the board.'

'You guys are the best!' declared Talia, her cheeks colouring with delight as she plonked herself down in front of Ruby to have her hair braided, chatting about mermaid hair and arguing good naturedly with her mum about having a colour change, suggesting pink if she didn't like green.

Smiling, Katie disappeared into the kitchen to replenish the teapot, and, taking a few quiet moments to herself, she sent up a missive of gratitude to the director of her own astrological chart for blessing her with such wonderful friends, friends who had no other agenda than to share an evening of chatter, relaxation and confectionery. Of course, she also counted Oscar on that list, and she couldn't forget Agatha, who, although miles away in Bali, had given her more, much more, than a certain member of her family ever had.

It was time for her to give something back beyond a few sweet treats and a manicure. Time to celebrate her decision to move forward without constantly looking over her shoulder at the catastrophe that was her past. Whatever her future held, she firmly intended to stand on her own two feet from now on, and not look to others to support her if she stumbled, and she knew exactly how she was going to do it.

'Hey, guys, I've had an idea.'

'Oh my God, quick, sound the trumpets!' cried Jay, wafting his hand in the air sending a whoosh of nail polish and industrial-strength cologne in her direction.

Katie grinned, her heart blossoming at being accepted as part of such a cheerful group of people, and her idea was just perfect to show her appreciation, but also to give something back, and hopefully, make some money for the café at last.

'It's a bank holiday this weekend so how about we have a mini fête on the village green? Everyone invited, everyone included! It's the perfect venue for the shop owners to showcase their wares.'

'Oh my God! I love it!' Ruby beamed, pausing in the process of outlining Talia's eyes with emerald green glitter. 'I could do face-painting for the children, maybe offer hair braiding, mini-facials …'

'Yay! Count me in, too!' cried Jay, jumping up from his chair, his eyes alight with enthusiasm. 'I can do a few flower-arranging demonstrations, then auction off the bouquets!'

'Great …'

'Oh, oh, oh, I know what I'm going to do!' said Talia, pogoing on the spot like Tigger's best friend. 'Mum, can I borrow your tent? The red-and-white one with the pointy roof?'

'Yes, darling, but what do you want that for?'

'And, Katie, can I borrow a couple of those gorgeous tasselled throws you brought back from Bali?'

'Of course,' said Katie, wrinkling her forehead and exchanging a puzzled glance with Zoe. 'What exactly do you have planned for them?'

'I'm going to do people's horoscopes. Oh, I can't wait! In fact, come on, Mum, I think we should get started right away. I'll start with Aries, then Taurus and maybe Gemini tonight, then tomorrow I'll do Cancer and Leo ... Oh, gosh, there's so much to do if I'm going to be ready!'

Zoe laughed, shaking her head at her daughter's excitement before turning to Katie.

'It's a wonderful idea, Katie. Maybe I could organise a stall offering pleated friendship bracelets, and I've got this lovely silver wire I use to make wedding tiaras that I could use with a box of beads to make earrings instead?'

'Sounds exactly what Perrinby needs.'

'I'll speak to Tom and Hilary at the pub, too. I'm sure they'll be happy to help with the drinks side of things, and they've got lots of Union Jack bunting left over from last summer's royal wedding. Are you going to ask Oscar to have a stall?'

'Yes, of course. Maybe he can do a children's finger-painting session.'

Ideas continued to flow, and the enthusiasm was palpable. Katie couldn't wait to tell Oscar about her ideas for the café's stall and to sit down with a glass of wine and plan the details with him, asking him to help her make sure they had all the permissions they may need, but Jay's earlier comments concerned her.

Why had he thought they'd had an argument?

But the new, improved Katie wasn't going to hang around and let a worry fester. As soon as the gang left, she intended to go straight over to his flat to ask him what was wrong. She wanted to ask him what he thought about the fête, but she also wanted to tell him about her aborted letter to her father, to thank him for his part in giving her the confidence to seize the initiative because she felt as if, at long last, a weight had been lifted from her shoulders.

However, when she finally closed the café's door at the end of the pamper session and glanced at her watch, she realised her visit to the gallery would have to be postponed until the next morning because it was after eleven o'clock.

It had been a roller-coaster sort of a day, but she was determined more than ever to put her personal trials and tribulations behind her once and for all, and to focus all her energy on other things, like organising the very first Perrinby fête, like making a success of the café, so that when she called Agatha on Saturday night to tell her about Greg's cheque, she could also report that The Cornish Kitchen was going from strength to strength and she could continue to be part of this wonderful community.

Chapter 25

The morning of the inaugural Perrinby village fête dawned with a clear blue sky and a slight nip in the air, but with the promise of a sun-filled day ahead. The dawn chorus was just tuning up for its overture when Katie leapt out of bed and flung back the curtains, her spirits high, excitement and anticipation coursing through her veins in equal measure.

She jumped in the shower, washed and rinsed her hair in tepid water – the ancient boiler was something else she needed to add to her growing maintenance list – and a wriggle of nerves invaded her chest. However, she shoved them away, refusing to allow her thoughts to linger for even one moment on her fear that The Cornish Kitchen would again make only a tiny profit or, heaven forbid, a loss, and that this could be the last event she organised in picturesque Perrinby.

Today was all about having fun, pulling together as a community, and she intended to squeeze every ounce of enjoyment out of what was going to be an amazing, joy-filled day.

She had spent the whole of the previous week baking up a storm. The minute the café closed for the day, she and Talia had retreated into the kitchen, and with the help of Zoe and Mel, had produced a veritable mountain of cupcakes – all different flavours and decorated with a kaleidoscope of colours and themes – along with scones, sweet and savoury quiches, fruit tarts, tea-loafs and a whole host of sponge cakes, her favourite being a lemon drizzle cake topped with Prosecco-flavoured buttercream and finished off with a sprinkle of Talia's beloved popping candy.

However, the pièce de résistance had to be the magnificent chocolate layer cake that she had stayed up until midnight the previous day to complete, piped with the words Katie's Cornish Kitchen in orange blossom icing and framed with miniature garlands of bunting and flags made from sugar paste and cocktail sticks.

As well as baking, Katie had put a call out to all her customers to drop in any paperbacks they had read and enjoyed, which she intended to add to the care packages she had made up – which would also include one of the cupcakes. They would be donated to the soup kitchen when the day was over. She had already decided that even if the café had to shut its doors to the paying public because she couldn't make it financially viable, that was no reason why she couldn't continue to volunteer her services, or contribute to their nightly offering with as many sweet treats as she could afford. If she took nothing else away from her time in Cornwall, she would make helping others less fortunate than herself a priority, her conscience still giving her a swift kick up the backside whenever she thought of all the cakes that François threw in the bin, that could have gone to feed hungry mouths.

However, Katie wasn't the only resident of Perrinby to have worked her socks off to produce a stall fit for a royal garden party. Ruby had spent hours watching tutorials on children's face-painting on the Internet after ordering the necessary equipment, and she was delighted to have a willing guinea pig in Talia who had been thrilled to be transformed into a glitter-bedecked unicorn complete with rainbow eye shadow, which she declared would send her Instagram feed into meltdown.

Jay had made a special early morning trip to the flower market to make sure he had enough supplies for all his demonstrations, which he intended to theme around the Cornish seaside using children's sandcastle buckets as vases, and mini picnic baskets lined with red gingham, and he'd even sourced tiny fishing nets into which he intended to slot bunches of sea holly, sea lavender and sprigs of rosemary to add fragrance. He had also bought armfuls of carnations in a myriad of colours for the 'have a go yourself' sessions he was going to run so that visitors could take an arrangement home with them.

Not to be outdone by Jay's creativity, Zoe and Mel had produced cardboard boxes covered with pretty wrapping paper and filled with everything a craft-obsessed fête attendee could wish for: squares of felt and brightly coloured fabric, reels of ribbon and lace, pots of multi-coloured beads, sequins and mini pompoms, thongs of leather and string to weave into friendship bracelets, and the silver wire to produce the promised earrings. Katie had spent a very enjoyable evening at the bridal boutique experimenting with all the accessories, producing a necklace that she was proud of but which an objective onlooker might think came from a Christmas cracker.

Tom and Hilary from the Hope & Anchor were happy to take charge of all the village's beverage needs, and their stall included a wide selection of locally produced ciders and craft ales, as well as artisan gins flavoured with rhubarb, elderflower and quince. There was even a gin flavoured with Cornish clotted cream and Katie intended to be first in line when the top was taken off that bottle! For the wine lovers, Hilary had borne the heavy burden of spending an entire afternoon at a local family-run vineyard, taste-testing their sparkling rosé made from grapes grown right there in Cornwall. She had even brought back a bottle of their own home-made brandy with her, for personal use.

Ryan, too, had taken up the challenge, becoming one of the impromptu fête's most avid supporters and declaring himself to be the village's resident mixologist, utilising the spirits he'd acquired from the pub and turning them into the most extravagant, not to mention psychedelically coloured drinks Katie had ever seen – blue curaçao, white rum and crushed pistachios anyone? Or tequila, lime juice and avocado? Or what about a fig and eucalyptus martini? Strange though these drinks sounded, Katie suspected Ryan's stall would be one of the most visited, especially when he gave them a preview of his exuberant performance, which wouldn't have looked out of place on a movie screen with Tom Cruise at his side.

Of course, Ryan had needed someone to taste-test his quirky creations and who better than Talia. The two of them had spent every night that week experimenting like a pair of visionary alchemists, diligently recording their exotic recipes in a notebook until, inevitably, the research ended in a fit of giggles, followed by a marathon session of kissing. Katie had been overjoyed when Talia had burst into the café one morning declaring to anyone who would listen that she and Ryan were now officially an item and that it was all down not to the stars this time, but to Katie who had come up with The Cornish Kitchen's concept. She had then flung her arms around its owner causing their smattering of early morning customers to burst into applause.

And Talia, too, had been working on her own contribution to the day's celebrations. With Ryan's help, she had liberated her mother's red-and-white candy-striped tent from the attic, erected it among the hobbit houses in the orchard at the back of the café, and hosed it down until the waterproof fabric glistened in the sunshine before going on to polish it until it was as good as new. Then, she had commandeered all the batik throws from the window seat in the café, along with the dreamcatchers and the long strings of crystals, which she proceeded to repurpose into an exotic necklace.

In fact, Talia's energy for Project Perrinby's last-minute village fête knew no bounds. When she wasn't waitressing in the café, or helping Katie with her mammoth bake-a-thon, or taste-testing

Ryan's cocktails, she spent every spare minute poring over her astrology charts and gathering together her extensive collection of mystic stones. She had even found the time to design a new hat, but refused to disclose the details, telling Katie that she wanted to keep it as a surprise – Katie dearly hoped it wouldn't be a shock.

Katie was filled with gratitude – in a short space of time, the whole community had come together to make the day of the fête the best it could be and, in her humble opinion, they had succeeded, and now, looking out of the café's bay window at the sun-drenched village green, it seemed the metrological gods were prepared to contribute their bit too.

She sighed; despite the hard work and the late nights, the last week had been one of the best weeks she could remember – apart from one thing.

Oscar.

The very next morning after she had proposed the Perrinby village fête, before she had wrenched open the door of the café to invite in the hungry hordes, she had skipped around to the gallery filled to bursting with excitement, even doing 'a Talia' by pogoing up and down on the spot as she waited for him to answer the door. She also secretly wondered whether she could snatch another of his heart-tingling kisses as the last one still caused ripples of pleasure to run the length of her spine whenever she allowed her thoughts to linger on it. She had never experienced such a reaction to being kissed before; a paradox of effervescent delight coupled with the most intense feeling of calm, of absolute serenity, of being where she was meant to be. She couldn't wait to hear his suggestions on how to make the fête a resounding success.

'Hi, Oscar. Guess what!'

To her surprise, instead of a wide, welcoming grin and cheeky comment about the seven a.m. visit, she'd seen a tightening at the corners of his lips and a closed expression spread across his face. Nevertheless, he had invited her in, and she had followed him into his studio at the back of the gallery where she saw he had been working on his painting of the windswept, fair-haired family on the Cornish beach.

Unable to contain her enthusiasm a moment longer, she had burst out with her news.

'We're organising a village fête! Next Saturday! We had the idea last night at the pamper party. Where were you, by the way? I thought you said you were hoping to pop in for a drink, even if you didn't get your nails done? Anyway, Ruby, Jay, Talia, Zoe and Mel, they all think it's a great idea, and they're all going to organise a stall: face-painting, flower-arranging, craft stalls, that sort of thing. Tom and Hilary are going to supply the drinks, the café will do the food, Talia's going to ask her friends from college to provide the music. So will you do something?'

There was a pause as she sought Oscar's eyes, her smile faltering when instead of voicing his usual support, he turned his back on her to switch on the kettle and busy himself with making them a coffee. When he eventually turned back round, she couldn't fail to notice the effort it took for him to force an enthusiastic expression on his face.

'Of course, what about if I take on the role of roaming caricaturist?'

'Wow, yes, that sounds fabulous. So, we need as many people as possible to help with the setting up. Ryan has said his parents can supply all the stalls and the tablecloths – apparently, they still have all the gear from a street party they had last year, so that's sorted. Do you think you could design a poster and disperse it far and wide? Talia has said she'll put a couple up in the college and the high school, and we can do a social media splurge. Oh, Oscar, I really hope this will drum up lots of business for everyone in the village.'

'It's a great idea, Katie. I'll do everything I can to help, but sorry, you'll have to excuse me. I've got a commission I need to finish for tomorrow.'

For the first time since she had met Oscar, Katie felt as though she was being dismissed, but she knew that wouldn't be the case. She understood how stressful deadlines were after being in the cake-making business with François as her boss, so she swallowed down her coffee, and leaned forward to place a quick kiss on his cheek.

'Thank you, Oscar.'

'Welcome,' he replied, somewhat stiffly.

And, as promised, Oscar had been there every day with the rest of the villagers as they came together to get everything ready, even creating the most fabulous poster, which couldn't fail to pique the interest of even the most reluctant of fête goers to pop along and sample their wares. However, whilst she understood completely how hard it was to run a business during the day and get stuck in with the preparations by night, she had still found it odd that they hadn't been able to carve out a single moment of alone time, not even one.

Now, the Old Katie would have pondered on that, would have read all sorts of negative subtexts into the situation, such as he'd lost interest in her or she had somehow offended him, but the New Katie refused to go there. Instead, she simply focused on the task ahead, a huge one by anyone's standards, plastered a smile on her face and gave him a cheery wave whenever she saw him helping the others, and shelved her desire to talk to him about what was on his mind until the fête was over. She had missed his company, though, missed their easy camaraderie, and regretted the fact that she hadn't had the chance to tell him about her aborted letter to her father, how cathartic the process had been, as well as what had prompted it.

A sharp tinkle of the door chime brought her thoughts zooming back to the present. She tied her hair back with one of Talia's mermaid bands, and she rushed down the stairs, grabbing one of the new Cornish Kitchen aprons she'd invested in when her ex-landlord in London had, somewhat surprisingly, returned her deposit in full, from the back of the kitchen door before stepping into the café to give Talia a warm welcoming hug.

'Hi, Katie! Guess what?'

'What?' Katie grinned when she saw the excitement on her young friend's face.

'I've read our horoscopes in three different magazines and on ten different Internet forums, and apparently today is going to be an auspicious day. I had to look up what that meant but I'm over the moon! I don't mind admitting that I had a bit of a panic when I thought it said suspicious.'

'It certainly is an auspicious day, Talia,' agreed Katie, handing her one of her favourite carrot and walnut smoothies made with almond milk to kick-start what she knew would be a very long and tiring, but exhilarating and hopefully successful, day.

'Mmm, delicious, you make *the* best smoothies! Okay, so, are you ready to be amazed?'

Katie wasn't in the least bit surprised to feel her stomach give an uncomfortable lurch, but she rallied, plastered a smile on her face and said, 'I am.'

'Close your eyes.'

Oh, God!

'Right, they're closed.'

She heard a brief rustling sound and then: 'Okay, now ... open them!'

'What am I ...'

'Ta-dah! What do you think?'

Turning her involuntary guffaw into a throat-clearing exercise, Katie gazed in utter amazement at Talia's new hat; no, 'hat' was the wrong word. Headpiece? Turban? Sartorial architecture? Whatever it was, it was beyond amazing, far, far, *far* beyond amazing, in fact almost as far as a galaxy far, far away!

'That's just so ... stunning!'

'I knew you'd like it.' Talia beamed, delighted at Katie's reaction to the multi-sized, multi-coloured spheres bounced on wires like satellites around her head – which was covered in a bright yellow-gold tightly fitted cap. 'It's the solar system! Look, this is Venus, this is Mars, and this is Pluto. Did you know that some crazy guy thinks that Pluto isn't a planet?'

'Yes, I had …'

'Do you think anyone will notice that Jupiter is not to scale?'

'No, I … why?'

'Well, I decided to make it much bigger because it is the planet of good luck and I thought we could do with as much luck as possible to make sure the fête goes well – and look, it's worked!'

'Talia, the fête hasn't started yet.'

'The weather, I mean the weather! The sun is shining!'

Katie couldn't help but grin at her friend who had probably thought about more aspects of the Perrinby village fête than all the villagers put together, and her heart ballooned at her good fortune in being sent such a force of goodwill and positivity, even if she did have a quirky taste in hats.

'It certainly is, and I for one will be eternally grateful to you, Talia. Now, come on, let's get these cakes over to our stall on the village green and then see if we can help anyone with theirs.'

'Okay, but hang on while I hide my hat. I want it to be a surprise!'

Talia carefully returned her precious creation to its bag and then disappeared into the kitchen to collect Agatha's old china cake stands that she had decorated earlier with tiny garlands of floral bunting, whilst Katie carried the huge square chocolate cake smothered with chocolate ganache and decorated with miniature sugar paste figures of everyone who was manning a stall that day.

They had taken only two steps towards the door when it burst open, the brass chimes jangling ferociously in objection.

'Miss Katherine Campbell?' asked the jolly-faced postman, his wispy white hair floating high in the breeze as he stepped over the threshold waving a large white envelope.

'Yes, that's me.' Katie smiled, putting down the cake to take the envelope from him.

'Sorry, this one's to sign for.'

'Oh, okay.'

'Recorded delivery.'

'No problem. Are you coming to the fête this afternoon?'

'Wild horses wouldn't keep me away. I got up extra early this morning so I could get my round done in plenty of time – and a slice of that chocolate cake you've got there has definitely got my name on it!'

Katie scribbled her signature on the postman's proffered device and he handed the letter over.

'Thank you,' she mumbled, peering at the postmark.

Grange & Harlow, Solicitors & Commissioners for Oaths.

The words sent her stomach plunging southwards. Greg again! But she didn't have the time to think about his mission to turn the Cornish village into an extension of Knightsbridge, so she quickly shoved the envelope under one of the cushions on the window seat, picked up the chocolate cake, and marched out to the village green where she placed it in pride of place on The Cornish Kitchen's stall overlooking the duck pond.

Chapter 26

'Hello? Hello? Can everyone hear me?' shouted Jay as he tested out the microphone.

'Yes!'

'Of course we can.'

'Loud and clear.'

'Get on with it.'

'Okay, I'd like to welcome you all to the inaugural Perrinby village fête!' continued Jay, beaming with delight at being given the honour of cutting the ribbon to signal the official opening of that afternoon's celebrations. 'I hope you have a *bootylicious* time here, and please do make sure that you visit every single stall, especially mine! So, without further ado, I declare this party open!'

With a flourish worthy of launching a cruise liner, Jay brandished a huge pair of floristry scissors and cut the bright pink ribbon to a polite smattering of applause before the throngs that had gathered rushed off to their favourite table like a herd of ravenous wildebeests.

Within minutes the whole of the village green thrummed with chatter as the visitors, from residents of the surrounding villages, to the members of the local WI and volunteers at the soup kitchen, from holidaymakers and their families to a gang of teenagers who had come along to support the band's first open-air gig in the bandstand. Katie was also thrilled to see a contingent from Edgemont Manor, led by the indomitable Hector.

'Hellooo, hellooo!'

'Hi, Hector, it's good to see you again.'

'And you, my dear Katie, and you. However, I'm afraid I'm the reluctant bearer of some very sad news.' Hector paused, his forehead creasing with distress. 'It is with a heavy heart and a great deal of sorrow that I have to inform you of the recent passing of Dorothy Bairstow, the old lady you rescued when you paid us a visit last month.'

'Oh, no, Hector, I'm so sorry to hear that.'

Katie stepped out from behind her stall to give Hector a huge hug, unsurprised to see tears sparkling at the corners of his soft brown eyes. She knew he viewed every single one of the residents at Edgemont Manor as part of his extended family and so he was bound to feel the pain of Dorothy's sad demise.

'Peacefully in her sleep – just as she wanted. She's with her Arthur now, bless her. Anyway, life goes on, doesn't it? And how better to celebrate all the good things it has to offer than partaking in one of those exuberantly decorated cakes, and I'll relieve you of one of those delicious looking scones too, if I may?'

'Certainly!'

Katie grinned and handed Hector one of the unicorn cupcakes that Talia had insisted they add to their menu, the requested scone, and added a slice of The Cornish Kitchen's chocolate cake, which brought a smile back to his face.

'You are an absolute darling.' He beamed, before shouting a cheery greeting to Jay and trundling along to chat to him about all things floral and tennis-related.

'Hey, Katie, why don't I man the stall for a bit while you take a tour?' suggested Mel, already reaching for the spare Cornish

Kitchen apron. 'Maybe you can ask Talia to tell you your horoscope.'

'Oh, she's already told me that all Leos far and wide are going to have an auspicious day.' She giggled.

'Could have told you that myself,' muttered Mel as she shooed Katie away towards Ruby's stall where she had just finished painting another glittery rainbow on the face of a curly haired five-year-old.

'Want me to braid your hair, Katie?'

'Is it that bad?' She laughed.

'Well, I had hoped that you'd pay at least one visit to the salon!'

'I know, I know, I just haven't had a minute to indulge in a new haircut. But you know what? I think I like it better like this, longer, more loose and natural.'

'I love it, but maybe just a trim, eh?'

'Okay, okay, will next week do?' She laughed, taking the hint.

'I'll hold you to it.'

Katie continued her stroll around the green, her thoughts drifting. What she had said to Ruby was true. When she'd lived in London, she had made a concerted effort to keep her curls under control with expensive cuts and styling products so that she didn't end up looking like she'd been dragged through a hedge on the back of a Chelsea tractor. But here in Cornwall she didn't feel judged by her appearance, and while she always made sure her hair was tied back when she was working in the kitchen, she didn't feel the same pressure to keep it short and elegantly styled – something else to add to her list of revelations.

'Hey, Katie, can I interest you in a Cornish Conundrum?'

Katie laughed at the apt moniker Ryan had given to his signature cocktail. She approached his stall, crammed with bottles of liquor in every colour of the rainbow; a stall that was proving even more popular than the Hope & Anchor's beer and wine stall. She smiled at the boyish enthusiasm radiating from his every pore as he threw his silver shaker in the air like a professional juggler.

'What exactly *is* a Cornish Conundrum?'

'Well, I couldn't decide whether this organic elderflower cordial would go better with Vodka, gin or white rum.'

'So which did you choose in the end?'

'I went with all three, with a handful of crushed mint leaves. Here, have a try.'

There was such fervour in Ryan's eyes that Katie didn't feel she could refuse to at least taste his unique, and most likely *extremely* potent, concoction, but she made sure she took just the smallest of sips because she had no intention of letting the rest of the day pass by in an alcohol-fuelled blur. She wanted to remember every golden moment for when she was sitting in rain-soaked London dreaming of the sunshine-filled days she had spent in Cornwall.

'Mmmm, that's …' She coughed before croaking, 'Delicious!'

'Great! You know, I think this one is definitely going on my list for when I offer my services as a mixologist in the bars and restaurants of the wider world this summer – Ibiza, Corfu, Koh Samui, maybe even Bali! What do you think?'

'Sounds like a plan,' agreed Katie, smiling at the excitement on Ryan's freckled face. 'By the way, I don't suppose you've seen Oscar anywhere, have you?'

'He was over by the bandstand last I saw him. Hey, have you two had a fall-out?'

'Not as far as I know.'

However, for Ryan of all people to ask her that question she now knew for sure that the cooling of their friendship wasn't a figment of her imagination. What had happened? she wondered. Had she done something wrong? Why had their relationship hit the rocks at the same time she had been thinking about opening up to him about her feelings?

Katie was about to make a beeline for Talia's astrology tent, now that the queue had finally disappeared, when she paused. It was one thing *telling* herself that she had changed, that she now had a handle on her emotions, that she could move on with a clear head and with optimism for the new path she would travel, it was another thing altogether to actually put those good intentions into practice – and that was exactly what she was going to do.

She changed direction and made her way towards the bandstand in search of Oscar. He had been acting strangely towards her all week – she wanted to know why, and the only way she was going to get that answer was by asking him straight out. Right now.

She smiled at the eclectic group of musicians who were clearly having the time of their lives playing their instruments in public, especially as a bunch of friends holding empty cocktail glasses were bopping away to their tunes.

But Oscar was nowhere to be seen.

She was about to head towards the gallery when she saw him chatting to Hector by the duck pond and switched direction again, grateful when Hector melted away after giving her another warm hug and congratulating her on organising such a grand afternoon in such a short space of time.

'Hi, Katie, how's the café's stall doing?' asked Oscar, smiling at her – except his eyes did not quite meet hers and she felt an uncomfortable tightening in her stomach.

'It's doing really well,' she said, striving for normality, but she knew her smile looked like something the Joker might wear. 'Mel's in charge so I don't think there'll be much cake left by the time I get back.'

'That's great.'

Oscar stuck his hands in the front pockets of his frayed jeans and shifted awkwardly from one foot to the other. His behaviour was so out of character for him that she was even more determined to get to the bottom of what was going on. Oscar was usually so laid-back he was almost horizontal, but the way his gaze slid away from hers as though he couldn't wait to escape from her company, set her alarm bells ringing.

'Okay, tell me what's going on,' she blurted, heat rushing to her cheeks as she saw Oscar almost do a double take at her directness.

'Nothing's wrong. What do you mean?'

'What I mean is that you have been avoiding me all week. Ever since we announced the fête, in fact. What's wrong? Don't you think this was a good idea?'

'No, no, no, it's not that ...'

'So it *is* something. What?'

Oscar combed his fingers through his hair, causing it to stand up in random tufts, his dark blue eyes filled with indecision, then she saw his shoulders droop in resignation and he let out a long sigh.

'Oscar?'

He reached out, took her hand in his, and guided her towards the gallery where he shut the door, turned the sign to Closed, and ushered her towards the studio at the back.

'Hey, you've finished the painting!'

Katie stared at the glorious scene of the young family frolicking on the white sandy beach with the waves lapping the sand and the sky stretching all the way to infinity and beyond, the two little boys scampering after each other, their eyes alight with joy as their proud parents looked on ... and suddenly she knew.

'Oscar ...'

She turned to look at him and instantly she realised she was right. And there was that same flicker of sadness dashing across his face, almost imperceptible, but nevertheless still there.

'That's you, isn't it? That's your family?'

'Yes.'

Once again, Oscar chose to busy himself with making them a coffee to hide the pain she knew he was experiencing. She stared at the masterpiece created in watercolour, certain that every detail, every brushstroke, contained a piece of his heart and soul.

'It's beautiful, Oscar, truly beautiful.'

Oscar nodded absently as he handed Katie her coffee and

came to stand at her side, hugging his paint-splattered mug in the palms of his hands.

'It's for my parents' thirtieth wedding anniversary next week. I'm sorry I've been a little preoccupied this week, but well, I needed to finish it.'

'That's fine, Oscar, really it is.'

Katie took a step towards him. She laid her hand on his arm to offer her understanding and support for what must have been an emotional commission, but when she sought his eyes they still contained a guarded look, and she didn't have to be a mind-reader to know there was something else going on. Her head was telling her to leave it, but her heart refused to listen, so she inhaled a breath and pressed on.

'And?'

'What do you mean?'

'What else?'

Oscar hesitated and she knew she had guessed right. There was something he wasn't telling her, and she intended to get to the bottom of it. No more would she walk away without getting the answers she deserved; the answers to all the questions that swirled around her head, because without answers the questions multiplied and ballooned into great big issues that caused her demons to dance with glee.

'I know there's something else, Oscar, and I'm not leaving this gallery until you tell me what it is.'

She plonked herself down on a wooden stool covered in hardened splodges of clay and waited, taking the occasional sip of her black coffee. Silence expanded and all she could hear was the faint sound of music from the band, accompanied by shrieks of children's laughter and the clock on the wall ticking the time away. She hoped Mel would forgive her for not returning to her stall after her allotted thirty minutes, but even if she had to stay at the gallery until midnight, she was going to find out what was bothering Oscar.

'Oscar?'

'I overheard your phone call. Sorry.'

'What phone call?'

And then she realised and everything fell into place.

'You mean with Dominic?'

'Yes. I wanted to give you the space to decide whether to take him up on his offer to get back together. I assume he's asked you to go over to Ibiza?'

'Yes, he did.'

'Well, that's good news. I hope ...'

'No, it's not good news, not good news at all. I have absolutely no intention of going to Ibiza or of reconciling with Dominic. Our relationship would never work because I'm a completely different person to the one he ran out on all those months ago, and what's more, I don't love him, haven't for a while. However, I do have *one* thing to thank him for.'

'You do?'

'Yes, I know it took a great deal of courage for him to make that call after what he'd done. It would have been so much easier for him to just close the door on that Chapter of his life, on our failed engagement, to put it down to experience and move on. But he didn't, he chose, albeit belatedly, to contact me so he could explain why our relationship had ended, to get everything out in the open, to listen to what I had to say, whatever that would be, and that made me think that if Dominic could do it, then so could I. So I ...'

Katie paused, tears gathering along her lashes but she whisked them away, not wanting to lose control of her emotions. Now it was Oscar's turn to step forward to place his hand on her arm, and this time she saw he had no difficulty in holding her gaze, and despite her heart pounding away at her ribcage as though it was auditioning for a Japanese Taiko competition, she smiled with relief.

'So you?' Oscar prompted, his forehead creasing in confusion.

'I told you that my parents separated when I was twelve, but what I didn't tell you was that my father has preferred to have as little involvement as possible in my life ever since. I've rung him several times over the last few years, but the calls always left me feeling even more despondent, even more worthless. So I decided ... I decided to write him a letter instead, well, more of a thesis really.'

Oscar nodded but remained silent, not wanting to interrupt her.

'I wrote down everything and anything that came into my head: all the pain and the sorrow of losing him, the constant wondering why he had never stayed in touch, whether it was something I had done wrong, how I'd strived to achieve something amazing like winning a gold medal at swimming so that maybe he would come back to congratulate me, how devastated I was when he refused to walk me down the aisle, or comfort me when Dominic left ... Everything, every tiny detail, every seemingly insignificant event that had torn right through my heart, I poured it all out.'

'Oh, Katie, I had no idea. Why didn't you talk to me about this?'

'That's what I should have done a long time ago, maybe with Cara, maybe with my mum, maybe with Agatha, but it took coming here, opening the café, meeting a bunch of new friends who know nothing about my history, nothing about what had happened and who I thought I was, to make me realise that I deserve more than a few crumbs of my father's attention. When I finished writing everything down, I realised that if he chose to live his life without his daughter in it, then he's not worthy of any more of my attention.'

Her emotions were calming now, her heart rate slowing to a gentle trot as she worked her way through her scattered thoughts, the window of understanding opening another inch wider.

'Katie, I ...'

'That's the gift you gave me, Oscar. I learned how important it is to stand on my own two feet, instead of seeking out the crutch of a less-than-perfect relationship or at the bottom of a bleach bottle, and to face things head-on. Since arriving here, I've met people who are struggling with issues far worse than mine, and have bravely stepped up and challenged them. And that's what I did, and as soon as I scribbled the final word on that letter, the terrible weight I've been carrying around for as long as I can remembered dissipated.'

'So, do you need a stamp?' asked Oscar, his eyes sparkling at her achievement.

'But that's the point, really. I don't need to send the letter to my father. What good would it do? None; in fact, it would probably push him further away, solidify his view that he was justified in moving on with his life without me in it. It's me who needs to change, Oscar; it's me who needs to accept that I can't control what other people decide to do even if their actions cut to the very core of my heart. I signed my name at the bottom and then ...'

'And then what?'

'I tore it into tiny pieces, tossed them into the air like confetti at a wedding, and the sense of freedom that followed was amazing. I feel as though I've been released from the shackles of my own making, like a concrete block has been lifted from my chest, freeing me to live my life for *me*, the new Katie, the real Katie, the one who smiles when she wakes up in the morning, the one who loves baking cakes and decorating them, the one who loves Prosecco and gossiping with her friends, and ... well, like I said before, the person I have to thank is you.'

She raised her eyes from where she'd been scrutinising her palms and saw that Oscar's lips were inches from hers, but, much as she'd like to revisit that mind-blowing bolt of lightning she'd been dreaming of since their very first kiss, she hadn't finished yet; there was still more to say.

'I intend to call Dominic first thing tomorrow morning and

tell him that I'm not going to Ibiza and that it's over between us, for good. But I'm also going to thank him for helping me, in his own weird way, to see the light.'

'That's very generous of you, Katie.'

'Holding a grudge would hurt me more than it would hurt Dom.'

'That's one way of looking at it.' Oscar smiled, slipping his hand into Katie's and giving it a squeeze, before casting a quick glance out of the window. 'I think we should get back to the fête before they send out a search party. In fact, look, I think they're starting to wrap up.'

'Hang on, there's something I want to do first.'

Oscar paused, then smiled, understanding her meaning.

'Me too.'

And when his lips touched hers, everything she had just talked about melted away and she abandoned herself to the delicious fizz of pleasure that coursed through her body, followed by a wave of absolute calm and contentment, of certainty that this was what was meant to be. Oscar continued to kissed her, softly, gently at first, caressing her cheek and the back of her neck with his thumb, lacing his fingers through her curls, then becoming much more serious, ardent even, until she pulled away breathless, joy radiating to every corner of her body.

It was a few more minutes before they left the gallery, arm-in-arm, to seal their new relationship with one of Ryan's finest cocktail concoctions, which he had fittingly labelled The Cornish Celebration in their honour!

Chapter 27

'Well, that went really well!' declared Oscar, plonking himself down on The Cornish Kitchen's window seat. 'I vote that we make the Perrinby village fête an annual thing, what do you think?'

'Absolutely!' agreed Zoe, swiping his feet from a chair so she could sit beside him.

'I think we should do one every month!' said Jay as he deposited a tray laden with cups and saucers and a huge brown teapot onto the table in front of them while Katie added a plate of the last few cookies in the whole of the café, probably the whole of Perrinby.

'God, no way am I doing that every month! I'm exhausted!'

Katie glanced out of the bay window overlooking the now returned-to-normal village green, bathed in the soft amber glow of the setting sun, marvelling at how a passing stranger would never know there had been a party at all. As soon as the last of their visitors had left for their holiday homes and glamping sites, a human machine had swung into action with practised efficiency. Stalls were cleared, tables were dismantled, litter was picked, and only the bunting framing the Hope & Anchor remained as a nod to the fact that there had been a celebration that day.

'Hey, where's Talia? I thought she would be here regaling

us about how her astrological predictions were spot-on,' said Oscar, turning in his seat to peer out of the window through the gathering shadow of dusk towards the pub.

'Actually, now I come to think about it, I haven't seen her for a while either,' said Zoe, a flicker of concern darting across her face. 'I'll just send her a quick text.'

'I hope she's okay,' said Katie, her heart quickening.

She too had expected Talia to be right there with them, filled with excited chatter about her day, and with maybe a few comedic anecdotes thrown in for good measure. It just didn't feel right to be sitting there, enjoying a cup of tea and a well-earned rest, chewing over the day's events without her cheerful face in their midst.

However, Katie had something else apart from Talia's unusual absence on her mind, so while the others gossiped about a number of things, she grabbed the teapot on the pretext of refilling it, and made her way to the kitchen. As soon as the door swung closed behind her, she opened The Cornish Kitchen stall's takings tin – a colourful metal biscuit box from the royal wedding – and began counting out the cash they had taken that day. As she tallied up the notes and coins, she was happy to see that she had made a decent profit for the café, that all her hard work had paid off – it was a wonderful feeling.

However, the fact still remained that there was still not enough to send over to Agatha so she could expand her beloved cookery school and take on more students. If Katie were honest, and there was no point in being otherwise, she knew that the most prudent course of action for Agatha was to sell the café and the apartment to Greg, or someone like him, which would release the funds she needed to invest in her Balinese project. It was the most sensible option if she was going to have any chance of securing her future on the 'Island of the Gods', and that of her community enterprise.

Katie realised that it was time to put Agatha first.

A wave of desolation washed over her. She was devastated about losing the café after everything she, and everyone else in Perrinby, had put into it, but what upset her the most was the fact that Agatha had put so much trust in her, had been one of the only people who believed in her at a time when she was at rock bottom, and she had let her down. There was no more money – every penny of her savings and her returned deposit was gone – and if the café couldn't support itself, then there was no alternative but to sell it, and sell it quickly so that Agatha didn't lose any more of her divorce settlement. Katie didn't want to put the future of the café in Bali at risk, or the cookery school.

She knew she had apologies to make; even though she *had* tried to contact Agatha several times, always getting her voicemail, she still hadn't actually told her about Greg's offer or about the cheque he had left, and she couldn't in good conscience wait any longer. This time, if she couldn't reach Agatha on the phone, she would call Jallie – one of the friends she had made who ran the local hostel in Sanur – and ask her to pop round to the Beachside Café to tell Agatha to ring her immediately, then she would send Agatha a detailed email, covering every visit made to the café by Greg.

Decision made, Katie felt a little better. She rinsed the teapot with hot water, popped in a handful of tea bags and was about to return to the café when she heard a faint mewling sound coming from the back garden. She leaned over the sink to peer through the window, but twilight was well into its second act and as there were no street lights at the rear of the café she couldn't see anything.

Just as she pulled back, she caught a flicker of movement to her left and decided to investigate, her heart jumping into her mouth as she pushed open the back door and was presented with a pale, ghost-like figure crouched on the bottom step, her head lowered onto her forearms, shoulders shaking.

'Oh my God! Talia, what's wrong? Why are you sitting out here?'

Katie rushed forward and dropped down onto the step next to Talia, draping her arm around the girl's shoulders as they heaved with a cacophony of sobs. Her crazy planet hat had been discarded at her feet and the Balinese shawl hung loose around her arms warding off the nip in the air now that the sun had finally disappeared over the horizon, and yet she still trembled. When Talia eventually turned to face her, a spasm of shock reverberated through Katie's chest at the sight of her puffy, red-rimmed eyes and tear-streaked cheeks – clearly Talia had been crying for some time.

'Talia, please, tell me what's wrong.'

Talia wiped her eyes with the end of her sleeve and forced a weak smile on her face as Katie reached out to lace her fingers through hers, squeezing her hand to indicate her support.

'Please, Talia.'

'It's Ryan.'

'What about him?'

'He's … I …'

For a moment, she faltered, but then cleared her throat, inhaled a deep breath and met Katie's gaze.

'I saw him with someone else.'

'You did? When?'

'This afternoon, in the car park at the back of the pub.'

'Are you sure?'

Talia nodded, her whole body slumped like a puppet clipped of its strings and Katie's heart went out to her, to this young girl who had given her so much, always with a smile on her face; so full of life, full of optimism, focused on the future instead of the past. It hurt to see her so down-hearted, so defeated. But Katie couldn't believe that Ryan would be seeing someone else. So, because of her recent personal experience, and for Talia's peace of mind, she had to make sure there was no misunderstanding.

'What exactly did you see?'

'I saw him with her. Kissing.'

'Kissing?'

'Well, not kissing exactly, but hugging.'

'Who was it?'

'I don't know. I've never seen her before.'

'What did she look like?'

'Well …'

'Talia?'

'I didn't get a good look because I was so upset that I just turned straight round and ran back to hide here in the café until I heard you and Mum coming, and then I came out here to the garden. Sorry I wasn't around to help with the tidying up, Katie, but I just couldn't face everyone. Oh God, what am I going to do? My chart didn't say anything about this, not one thing.'

'Talia, I—'

'But it did say I was going on a long journey. I thought that was about me wanting to go travelling, but do you think it means a sort of emotional journey – like to hell and back?'

'No, I do not think that.'

'Well, at least I won't have to hang around here watching him fall in love with someone else.'

'What do you mean?'

'I've emailed Agatha, just a couple of minutes ago, to ask her if I could go over to help her out at the Beachside Café and her cookery school – like you did – and guess what?'

'What?'

'She said yes!'

'You got a reply straight back?' said Katie, incredulously, temporarily diverted from Talia's pain-filled woes.

'Yes …'

'But I've been trying to call her, left voicemails …'

'Oh, she's been away, something about a silent yoga retreat? No phones, no social media, no Wi-Fi, that sort of thing?'

'Ah, that explains …'

'I'm so sorry, Katie, but I'm sure you'll find another waitress who's much better than I am.'

'I doubt that very much, Talia. There are no waitresses in the whole of Cornwall better suited to working at The Cornish Kitchen than you are. But if you want to travel, to see some of the world, then that's great, and you'll absolutely love Bali – it's an amazing place, so vibrant, so full of life. But I won't let you go until you've talked to Ryan and asked him what's going on.'

'Oh, no, I can't do that.'

'You can and you will, and there's no time like the present.'

'No, really, Katie …'

But Katie had no intention of allowing Talia to suffer the same long, lonely nights of meandering through the labyrinths of always wondering, of building up increasingly miserable scenarios of what was, or could, or must be going on that ushered her ever closer towards the precipice of her sanity.

Talia did not deserve that.

So she scrolled through the contacts on her phone and sent Ryan a text asking him to come over to the café, and within what seemed like seconds he was hammering on the back gate and Talia's eyes were widening with panic. Katie patted her arm then went to let him in.

'Just talk to him; ask him what's going on. I'll be in the café if you need me.'

And she left them to talk, sending up a fervent message to the director of Talia's astrological charts that she hoped she had done the right thing – and that now it was over to her.

Chapter 28

'Where've you been? Everyone's left,' said Oscar as he met her in the corridor on her way back into the café.

'Oh, Talia and Ryan are outside. There's been some sort of misunderstanding and they're talking it through. They could be there for a while.'

Katie met Oscar's gaze, his blue eyes filled with curiosity, and she made a decision. Talia wasn't the only one who needed to talk, needed to be completely honest about their future. It was time she told Agatha about the café's finances.

'Oscar, about the café …'

'Actually, there's something I need to talk to you about, too.'

'Really?' said Katie, following him back to the window seat, pouring herself a mug of her favourite Earl Grey tea and curling her feet under her bottom as she settled onto the cushions. 'I think I'd better go first.'

'Katie—'

'I've added up the money we took at the fête today and we've done really well, but even if the café continues to go from strength to strength, it'll still be months before I'll be able to send even a decent donation to Agatha's Bali project. It's time to accept that. I feel terrible that I haven't kept her up to date with what's been happening here, and even worse that I haven't told her about Greg's offer – she has a right to know, Oscar, and I happen to think that the sensible solution is for her to accept it.'

'Katie—'

'It's the middle of the night over there now, but I'm going to call her first thing in the morning and this time if the call goes to voicemail, I'm going to get Talia onto it. Would you believe that she emailed Agatha just over an hour ago and heard straight back? I'm going to tell her that I'll close the café next week and post the keys back to her, or, depending on what happens with Talia and Ryan, Talia could deliver them in person.'

'What do you mean?'

'Talia has just handed in her notice at the café – perfect timing! – and she's going travelling. Her first stop is going to be a stint at Agatha's Beachside Café. I hope she'll tell Agatha how hard we've both worked to make the café profitable and that we couldn't have done anything more, that it was just impossible to make a profit, but it's better to admit defeat before the business plunges into debt, don't you think?'

'Yes, I do, but—'

'I feel awful. I've let Agatha down, wasted money that could have been better spent on her cookery school.' Katie paused to gulp down on her rising emotions, suddenly determined to put a positive spin on her three-month stay in Perrinby. 'But I've enjoyed every minute of my time here. Everyone has been so welcoming and kind and I've learned so much, not just about running a café and organising events, but about myself, too.'

'So what are you going to do?'

For all the emotional trauma that was swirling around in her body, making her feel light-headed and breathless, she couldn't help smiling when she saw the panic on Oscar's face. She knew for sure that he was as upset and disappointed as she was that the café hadn't succeeded, but once again she found herself at a crossroads in her life's journey as she contemplated what fate had in store for her next.

There was one thing she knew for certain, though. She would not be leaving Cornwall, not leaving this kind, generous, thoughtful man sitting next to her in the now-dark café, his piercing blue eyes filled with affection, and maybe something else.

'I'm not sure, but my home is here now, so I'll look for a job in one of the hotels on the coast, or maybe even start my own freelance cake-decorating business – only human customers though, not dogs!' She laughed, trying to make light of the situation, of the fact that she wouldn't only be saying goodbye to her dream business venture, but also her home. However, she hadn't fooled Oscar.

'Look, Katie, whatever you decide, I want you to know that I'll be here for you. There's a spare room waiting for you at the gallery next door, but before we go any further, there's something I've got to—'

'Oh my God, I completely forgot!'

'What now?' sighed Oscar, a smidgeon of irritation creeping into his voice.

Katie leapt up from her seat and lifted the satsuma-coloured cushion she had been sitting on to extract the envelope she had signed for just before the fête got under way.

'What's that?'

'The postman delivered it this morning. It's a letter from Greg's solicitors and I couldn't face opening it while we were getting ready for the fête. I didn't want anything to spoil the day and I thought, well, I thought that if by some miracle we made a huge profit, then maybe … well, never mind.'

She stared at the large white envelope in her hand, expecting it to grow horns or instantaneously combust into flames.

'Are you going to open it?' asked Oscar, scooting in closer to take her hand and give it a supportive squeeze.

'I suppose so.'

'Whatever it says we'll deal with it together.'

Katie smiled, finally at peace with who she was, who she trusted, and most important of all, who she loved. She knew she could rely on Oscar to support her through the next few weeks as she explored the next few Chapters of her life, but even if he wasn't there, she knew she would handle whatever life threw at her on her own. She was no longer the 'clingy', anxiety-laden woman who had arrived in Perrinby with her problems weighing heavily on her shoulders, but was a happy, relaxed, optimistic person who looked to the future with her heart filled with hope, with excitement brimming for what her uncertain future might hold.

And yet, while she undoubtedly had a great number of people to thank for bringing her to this place, she knew a huge part of her transformation had been down to the influence of what she and she alone had created at The Cornish Kitchen, because the little café had given her so much more than somewhere to lay her head and to work on slaying her demons – it had given her hope and faith in the future. Whatever Greg's solicitors were writing to her about, she knew she would face it head-on and deal with it, so she slid her finger along the flap, then paused before removing the correspondence.

'Are you okay?' asked Oscar, his eyes creasing in concern.

'I'm fine – actually I'm more than fine. But before I read this, I just wanted to thank you, Oscar.'

'Thank me? Why?'

'For showing me how to deal with whatever life throws in my path with integrity, perseverance, and most of all gratitude. Life has its challenges, some pleasurable, some not, but it's so much better than the alternative.'

Oscar grinned, then leaned forward to place a gentle kiss on her lips, which quickly morphed into something much more passionate that told Katie everything she needed to know about the way he felt about her and sent a great whoosh of confidence through her veins. She didn't have to do this alone; she'd have Oscar by her side every step of the way, and her heart soared. She whipped out the solicitor's letter, and turned it round so they could read it together, her jaw dropping further and further with every sentence she read.

'Oh … my … God …'

'Oh, my God!'

'It's not from Greg's solicitors.'

As she came to the end of the missive, Katie's eyes filled with tears and once again she was reminded of the true meaning of karma – how one good turn deserved another, or yin and yang, or what goes around comes around.

'I can't actually believe what I've just read!' she managed to mutter as the tears trickled down her cheeks. 'With everything that's been going on, I forgot to tell you that I saw Hector at the fête and that he told me Dorothy had sadly passed away, but never in my wildest dreams did I expect … I mean … it's so … so generous, so kind, so incredibly thoughtful of her. Thirty thousand pounds! It's just … it's too much … it's …'

'It's: *a gift to ensure that the little café in Perrinby continues to serve the community for years to come*,' quoted Oscar, pointing to the paragraph in the lawyers' letter that explained the reason behind the surprise bequest that Dorothy had made in gratitude to Katie for ensuring that she hadn't ended her long and happy life on the cold hard floor of the manor's summerhouse.

'She was a nippy, you know,' murmured Katie, still trying to take in what had happened. 'Loved working in the Lyons tea rooms. In fact, she met her husband Arthur there. I think that was why we connected so quickly. She wanted to come and visit the café, wanted to see what we were doing here, sample some of the cakes, join in with the gossip, but I guess, well, she didn't quite make it.'

Katie's heart gave a squeeze of sadness that she hadn't been able to show off the café to Dorothy, hadn't been able to offer her one of her fig and walnut scones or a slice of her lemon curd tart, but the sadness was mingled with affection for the old lady and her kindness, with overwhelming gratitude for the lifeline she had thrown, not just to Katie herself, but to the whole community of Perrinby so they would be able to enjoy their village café for a few more months.

And maybe, just maybe, they would be able to make a bigger profit over the summer months as the visitor numbers to Cornwall increased and the word of their community events spread, and she added more to the list. Perhaps Jay would lead a pumpkin-carving session, or Ruby would demonstrate Hallowe'en manicures, or Zoe would offer Christmas bauble-making classes, all of them accompanied by oodles of Cornish Kitchen cake and lots of tea and coffee.

But those plans were for later.

The only thing she wanted to do now was sink into Oscar's waiting embrace, where she would have happily stayed all night if they hadn't been so rudely interrupted by an ear-splitting screech of joy from the direction of the café's kitchen.

Chapter 29

'Katie! Oscar! Guess what!'

Katie laughed, reluctantly pulling out of Oscar's arms and exchanging an eye roll with him as he hooked his arm around her shoulders and they both waited for Talia to tell them the details of another one of her crazy plans. What would it be this time? Launching an alternative millinery empire, studying for a degree in astronomy, being the first Cornish woman to travel into space?

Katie was overwhelmed with relief to see Ryan standing by Talia's side, beaming as he curled his arm around her waist and pulled her closer. There would be time to ask Talia for an explanation of the upsetting scene she had glimpsed in the pub's car park later. Now, all she wanted to know was why Talia was so excited she was doing an excellent impersonation of Tigger on speed.

'Come on, then. Spill the news! Don't keep us in suspense.' She giggled as she snuggled into Oscar, loving the sensation of security and calm that seeped through her veins as she felt the warmth of his body and the inhaled fragrance of his lemony cologne.

'We're going to Bali together!'

'Wow, really? That's fabulous news!'

Talia flicked a quick glance at Katie before saying, 'Ryan's cousin, Greta, is visiting from Australia, actually arrived this afternoon ...'

Ah, thought Katie, a smile spreading across her lips as she nodded an acknowledgement of the message Talia had surreptitiously sent her, hoping that she had silently indicated that her secret was safe with her.

'And she's offered Ryan a part-time job at her restaurant in Adelaide in September, so we're going to backpack over there together, stopping off in Bali to work at Agatha's café and cookery school to brush upon our skills before heading over to Oz. Isn't that just ... well, just absolutely incredible?'

'It certainly is.' Katie grinned, leaping out of her seat to hug Talia, then Ryan.

'I've always wanted to go to Australia and now I get to go with Ryan and it's a ... well, it's a dream come true, isn't it, Ryan?'

And without warning, Talia flung her arms around a somewhat shell-shocked Ryan.

'Awesome,' was all he managed to say, but Katie could tell he was just as excited about what the future could hold as Talia was.

Katie turned to smile at Oscar, but an electric shock zapped through her chest when she saw the frozen expression on his face.

'Oscar? Is there something wrong?'

'Oh, erm, no, nothing. That's fabulous news, Talia, Ryan.'

But it was clear something was amiss and Talia and Ryan picked up on it immediately, quickly stepping forward to say their goodbyes, then leaving the café to give Katie and Oscar some space to work it out. As the door chime stopped tinkling, Katie sat back down on the heavily embroidered cushions, crossed her legs, and turned to face Oscar.

'Come on, tell me.'

'Well, I know I should have told you this before, and believe me, I did intend to, but well, I ...'

'Oscar?'

'When I tell you, I want you to know that I never meant to keep this a secret from you. Well, I might have done at the start because ... well ...'

'Oscar!'

'As you know, when Harry died, I went into meltdown. I questioned everything; what if I'd gone out with him that day, what if I had stopped him from going, why him and not me, what was the point of going on without Harry in my life? All the usual questions everyone asks when they lose ...'

Oscar paused to gulp back a surge of emotion.

'When they lose their amazing, talented, happy-go-lucky little brother. I went off the rails. I refused to continue working for my parents' firm. I started staying out late, not coming home, getting sucked in with the wrong crowd, generally spiralling downhill until ...'

'Until what?' Katie urged, taking hold of Oscar's trembling hand, trying to transfer some of her own strength into his veins so he could reach the end of his confession in the knowledge that whatever he had to say, it would never change the way she felt about him. She would still love him, still be by his side cheering him on in everything he chose to do.

'My parents couldn't get through to me, so my aunt stepped in. I'm ashamed to admit that if she hadn't, I would not be in such a good place right now.'

Oscar paused again, his thoughts clearly dwelling on that painful time in the past when he had been enveloped in such a dense fog of grief that he hadn't been able to find a way out without help. Eventually, he forced himself to tune back into the present.

'My aunt knew that it had always been my dream to paint, that whenever I had a brush in my hand I entered a completely different world; a world where I could escape the pain of reality and create anything I wanted. So, she set me up with the gallery and studio in the hope that a fresh start would deliver more focus, lead me in a different direction, well away from the turbulent, chaotic lifestyle that I was leading in London to the tranquillity of the Cornish countryside. And it worked, and I have her to thank for saving me, for saving my life, and for showing me the path to a new future. She's a truly wonderful person.'

Once again, Oscar hesitated, fiddling with one of Zoe's leather friendship bracelets on his wrist until he met Katie's gaze.

'But then you know that.'

'I do?' She scrunched up her nose in confusion and bewilderment.

'I'm sorry, Katie.'

'What for? I don't understand.'

'Agatha doesn't just own the café and the orchard at the back with the wooden holiday pods; she owns the whole building, including the gallery and the studio, where her only nephew lives, works and has found solace, and – because she has no children of her own – a place she had promised as we grew up, that one day would belong to Harry and me, except fate intervened and it didn't work out that way, and well, you know ...'

For a few moments Katie was at a loss to comprehend the words coming from Oscar's lips, and then, suddenly, the truth rushed at her like an express train.

'Agatha is ... Agatha's your aunt?'

'Yes. I should have told you, Katie, I know that, but I realised fairly quickly that she hadn't mentioned we were related when you were in Bali, had chosen not to confide that piece of information, and I didn't want to ... well, I thought there must have been a reason she didn't tell you, a reason why she'd sent you here, but I had no idea what that was.'

'Me neither,' murmured Katie.

'She's crafty, is my Aunt Agatha, always has been. I've tried to call her, lots of times, just like you have, but I came to the conclusion that she must be avoiding my calls, and yours, so she didn't have to explain why she'd kept our family connection a secret …'

'She wasn't avoiding our calls, Oscar. According to Talia, she's been on a silent yoga retreat in Ubud; no phones, no emails, no contact with the hustle and bustle of the outside world, no difficult conversations about property developers with deep pockets …'

'Ah, that makes sense.' Oscar nodded, lifting his gaze to meet Katie's, his expression turning more serious. 'That's absolutely the sort of thing my aunt does – self-care she calls it. And now, when I do get to speak to her at last, I can tell her that whatever her reasons for sending you here, she was spot-on because you, Katie Campbell, are the envoy of Balinese karma.'

'I am?'

'Not only have you breathed new life into Agatha's abandoned café, you've been the catalyst to revitalising our little community, and it looks like you've single-handedly saved it from the clutches of Greg Forbes. But best of all, you've brought a spark of joy into the life of her beleaguered nephew, something I never thought possible, and I need to thank her for her foresight, for her certainty that no matter what happens there's always hope, always the potential for happiness.'

Oscar's lips hovered next to Katie's and she quickly closed the gap, sinking into the blissful sensation of being in his arms, of feeling safe, secure, loved, of experiencing that same spark of joy that Oscar had spoken of, and which Agatha had also counselled her to find. So, when she at last pulled out of his embrace, tears sparkling along her lashes, she was determined to say the words that had been on her lips all day. Now was the perfect time – now that she was staying in Perrinby for the foreseeable future – but Oscar got there first.

'I love you, Katie.'

'I love you too, Oscar.' She grinned.

'I can't wait to call Agatha! I wonder what she'll say?'

232

Katie settled back against Oscar's chest, her thoughts scooting off to the wonderful, thoughtful, compassionate woman she'd had the good fortune to encounter at that picturesque beachside café overlooking the Indian Ocean six thousand miles away; to the cookery school next door, which every day hummed with the sound of cheerful voices as Agatha gently guided new hands in the art of creating culinary masterpieces; to how, despite the difficulties her own life had thrown in her path, she had managed to rise above self-pity and regret to focus on all the good things that could be found in every corner of the world if you only took the time to look.

Agatha had not only offered her grief-stricken nephew the chance of a new start, an opportunity to work his way through the sudden and devastating loss of his brother via his painting, but she had done the same for her, a complete stranger, in the certain knowledge that good fortune would prevail, not just for Katie herself, but for the whole community of Perrinby that she had left behind and which had meant so much to her.

Katie's heart flooded with gratitude for Agatha's kindness and as she met Oscar's eyes, that thankfulness morphed into overwhelming love for what Agatha had given her – not just The Cornish Kitchen, but someone she could love with all her heart and soul and who loved her back.

A generous gift indeed.

THE END

The Cornish Kitchen's Recipes

Katie's Rhubarb & Custard Cupcakes

Ingredients
For the cupcakes:
225g softened butter
225g caster sugar
4 eggs
225g self-raising flour
1 tsp baking powder
2 tbsp milk
For the filling and topping:
400g rhubarb, washed & chopped into pieces
50g sugar
One piece of stem ginger, chopped
200g softened unsalted butter
375g icing sugar, sifted
75g custard powder
1 tsp vanilla essence
50ml milk
Small pot of ready-made custard
Red food colouring

Method
1. Place the rhubarb on a baking tray, sprinkle with the sugar, stem ginger and three tablespoons of water, then wrap in foil and bake in the oven 180°C/160°C fan/Gas mark 4 for 15–20

mins. Remove and leave to cool, then drain the compote through a sieve, allowing the juices to collect into a saucepan and then simmer until reduced by half.

2. In a mixing bowl, beat the 225g butter and caster sugar together until pale yellow in colour, then add the eggs, one by one with a little flour. Fold in the remaining flour, baking powder, and finally add the milk. Divide between 18 muffin cases, then bake in the oven for 15–18 mins at 200°C/180°C fan/Gas mark 6 until golden and springy to the touch. Leave to cool.

3. For the buttercream icing, combine the butter, icing sugar, custard powder and vanilla essence, adding the milk carefully until the correct consistency is achieved.

4. When the cakes are cool, use an apple corer make a hole in the centre of each one and fill to halfway with the rhubarb compote and then fill to the top from the pot of ready-made custard. Next, draw stripes of red food colouring onto the inside of a piping bag, fill it with the buttercream and then pipe each cupcake with generous swirls. Drizzle the rhubarb syrup to taste.

Enjoy with elderflower cordial or a fruit tea of your choice.

Talia's Liquorice & Honey Cupcakes

Ingredients
For the cupcakes:
225g softened butter
200g caster sugar
4 eggs
225g self-raising flour
1 tsp baking powder
3 tbsp runny honey

2 tbsp milk
For the icing:
150g softened butter
300g sifted icing sugar
1–2 tsp liquorice essence
2 tbsp milk
Black food colouring (optional)
Popping candy

Method

1. In a mixing bowl, beat the butter and sugar together until pale yellow in colour, then add the eggs, one by one with a little flour. Fold in the remaining flour, baking powder, and add the honey and finally the milk. Divide between 18 muffin cases, then bake in the oven for 15 mins at 200°C/180°C fan/ Gas mark 6.
2. For the buttercream icing, combine the butter and icing sugar, then add the liquorice essence, using ½ teaspoons depending on taste. Add the milk. Add a drop of black food colouring if desired. Wait until the cakes are cooled and then pipe the buttercream in swirls and sprinkle with popping candy.

Enjoy with a cup of Earl Grey tea.

Enjoyed *Katie's Cornish Kitchen?*
Read more feel-good books from Rosie
Chambers ...

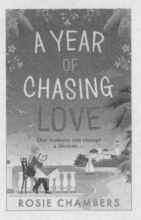

One moment can change a lifetime ...

The last thing top divorce lawyer Olivia Hamilton ever
expected was to be served her *own* divorce papers! To escape
her marriage troubles, she agrees to go on a year-long trip to
find the ultimate guide to love.

Travelling the world, surrounded by stories of love and
happiness, it's not long before her thoughts turn to Nathan,
her soon-to-be ex-husband, and she starts to take note
of her own lessons in love.

But with Nathan over a thousand miles away,
will it be too late?

Keep reading for the first chapter

Prologue

'There's a guy in reception asking to see you, Olivia.'

'Did you ask him to make an appointment?'

'I did, but he said he'd wait for as long as it took for you to see him.'

Olivia sighed. As a divorce lawyer she often had clients calling into the office, hoping to see her straight away, desperate for someone to listen to their story. Usually she didn't mind, and if she didn't have a prior engagement, she'd try her best to accommodate them in her crammed-to-bursting diary. After all, she knew how hard it was to take those first steps to visit a solicitor, never mind rustling up the courage to divulge the most heart-breaking details of your failed marriage to a complete stranger.

'Okay, no problem. I'll squeeze him in before I see Mrs Coulson at eleven thirty.'

'Shall I show him up to your office?'

'No, no, it's okay. I need a coffee so I'll come downstairs with you. You never know, I might be able to persuade him to make an appointment.'

Olivia pinned a professional smile on her face and followed Katrina down the corridor, giggling at the clickety-clack of their stilettos on the polished wood flooring. Little did she know that would be the last time she would laugh for a long time, because as soon as she stepped into the reception area, a crumple-faced man leapt out of his seat, reached into the pocket of his grubby raincoat, and extracted a large manila envelope which, incongruously, he then waved in the air. The glee reflected in his hard, ball-bearing eyes was the absolute antithesis of the bewildered confusion that was racing through her veins.

'Mrs Fitzgerald?'

'Yes?' Very few people outside her circle of friends knew her married name. Alarm bells started to ring, and she exchanged a quick glance with Katrina who was staring at the man with patent dislike. 'What can I do for you, Mr ...?'

In order to elongate the drama, the man took a few moments to survey the elegant, marble-walled foyer of Edwards & Co, Solicitors and Commissioners for Oaths – already devoid of its Christmas decorations despite twelfth night being the following day – deriving obvious pleasure from the perplexed expressions on the faces of his audience. A tickle of recognition began to agitate at the edges of Olivia's memory; the dishevelled attire, the ill-disguised porcine proportions, the whiff of stale nicotine. Where had she seen him before?

'Just leave the papers and get out!' snapped Katrina, the first of her colleagues to step forward to break the freeze-frame image.

Without further ado, the envelope was thrust into Olivia's hands and the process server ambled towards the smoked-glass elevator, a grin on his face and an air of satisfaction following in his wake. As the doors slid shut behind him, the burble of conversation magnified. No one needed a Private Detective badge to work out that what had just transpired had come as a complete shock to Olivia.

'Come on,' said Katrina. 'I think some privacy is—'

'Hey, I know that guy!' announced Miles, a fellow divorce lawyer and Olivia's least favourite colleague. 'That was Jack Leyland, Ralph Carlton's personal lackey – does all his dirty work for him. What was he doing here, though? I thought we instructed that ballet-shoed princess, Heidi Fowler, to deliver all our court documents, not that piranha. Although, I've always said that Jack does have his uses. Are we changing our approach at last?'

Ralph Carlton was renowned throughout the legal profession as the go-to rottweiler in the field of matrimonial litigation, which could only mean one thing. Olivia's stomach gave a pain-filled lurch and a curl of nausea began its assiduous journey around her chest.

Oh God, surely not!

'No, Miles, we …' she muttered, desperately trying to reconnect her brain to its modem.

'Because I have to tell you, all this conciliatory, non-confrontational malarkey is starting to scratch at my balls. We need to get a lot tougher in our negotiations, especially after that article about you being London's Top Divorce Lawyer appeared in the local rag. Ridiculous accolade, if you ask me – just because you've achieved the questionable milestone of having handled five hundred divorces doesn't mean that—'

'Shut up, Miles. Haven't you got secretaries to harass?' said Katrina mildly, taking charge of the situation and guiding Olivia out of the reception and back down the corridor to her corner office.

By now, panic was beginning to ricochet around Olivia's body, her throat had contracted around what felt like a prickly pear, and she felt light-headed. She collapsed onto the overstuffed leather sofa she used to interview the more emotional clients who sought her advice and slowly slid the paperwork out of the envelope as if it contained a poisoned pen letter – the effect it caused was almost as bad.

Because London's Top Divorce Lawyer had just been served with her very own divorce petition.

Chapter 1

'I didn't think he'd do it, Kat.'

Olivia sunk into the 'sympathy couch' and met her friend's
eyes, her fingers trembling on the rectangular missive of tragedy.
The shock of the public ambush had begun to thaw but the
horror remained, settling just below where her heart hammered
out a symphony of sorrow against her ribcage. Nausea lingered
at the back of her throat, constricting the flow of oxygen, and
the threat of tears blurred her vision.

'I know, Liv, I know,' murmured Katrina, patting her hand
and offering her a tissue.

Olivia accepted, dabbed the corners of her eyes and started
to peruse the documents.

'Oh, my God, no! I don't believe it.'

'What?'

'Nathan's cited Unreasonable Behaviour! Listen to this! *The
Respondent is a workaholic, often spending in excess of eighteen
hours a day at her office, refusing to accept, and dismissing the
importance of, her responsibilities to their relationship. Many holidays and weekends away have been cancelled or cut short due to
the tenacity with which the Respondent pursues her career.*'

'Oh, Liv, I'm so sorry ...'

'And what about this: *The Respondent has persistently neglected the Petitioner and their extended family and friends despite numerous attempts by the Petitioner to rectify their growing estrangement.* And this: *Since the inception of their partnership, the Petitioner has made clear to the Respondent his desire to start a family but* ... Oh my God, no, no, no, no ...'

The anguish churning through her veins threatened to overwhelm her as she continued to read the painful litany of accusations, and the stark truth of what lay at the crux of their problems was revealed.

'*But the Respondent refuses to contemplate the proposal, continually deflecting the Petitioner's heartfelt pleas to participate in a rational and intelligent conversation, citing the importance of her career over the creation of a family.*'

Olivia raised her eyes to meet Katrina's and the sympathy scrawled across her friend's face almost caused her to crumble completely. She swallowed down hard, inhaled a steadying breath and made an attempt to corral her rampaging emotions. She had to admit she was acutely aware of Nathan's desire to start a family. At his lavish fortieth birthday party at The Dorchester just before Christmas, she'd witnessed for herself the hunger in his heart as he had hugged each one of Katrina and Will's three young children in turn when they presented him with a selection of home-made birthday cards covered in dried pasta and sequins. But reading about his rejected yearning for fatherhood as a ground for her 'unreasonable behaviour' in bold, black typescript, well, it shocked her to the core.

'Look, Liv, these things always sound worse when they're written down.'

'We always say that to our clients, don't we? Well, let me tell you now, for the record, those words are no consolation. I promise that from now on, I won't be caught trotting out that old chestnut again.'

'And you know what? I'm absolutely certain this is all Ralph

Carlton's doing – he's the ultimate exploiter of human misery! No wonder you had no advance warning – it's his trademark.'

Olivia thought of the undisguised triumph in the process server's eyes. The knowledge that he would, at that very moment, be scurrying back to his employer to recount every painful detail, caused her cheeks to flood with warmth. Then, her mind switched to the headlines that had been splashed across the local newspaper the previous month. The story had also been picked up by the *Law Society Gazette*, as part of their end-of-year round-up of news, which had ensured maximum publicity for the article celebrating the debatable accomplishment of her five hundredth divorce.

She had squirmed at the label the tabloid had bestowed on her – '*London's Top Divorce Lawyer*'. She knew the dubious badge of honour would rile many of her peers but especially Ralph Carlton who had grabbed that self-styled accolade for himself years before. In fact, she wouldn't put it past him to casually leak the little gem that that same 'Top Divorce Lawyer' had joined the exclusive club no one wanted a golden pass for. She knew any gossip would spread like red wine on a cream carpet, and even if Ralph didn't breach the code of ethics on client confidentiality, she had no difficulty in remembering Miles's fascinated attention in the foyer and he was one of the biggest gossips she knew.

'Liv, everyone knows Ralph Carlton is a rabid vulture who feasts on the bones of broken relationships. I can totally picture him now, grinning away on his dung-splattered perch as he drafted those awful allegations. Nathan would never say any of those things.'

'But, sadly, not one of them is untrue. I *do* neglect Nathan, and our family and friends! I *do* work all waking hours here at my desk – my personal life is just one of the casualties I left in my wake when I chose the marbled entrance hall of Edwards & Co twelve years ago. I *do* cancel our date nights and I *do* miss important landmark birthdays. Remember Nathan's mother's sixtieth?'

Olivia grimaced with shame as she recalled the expression of displeasure on her mother-in-law's over-powdered face when she'd dashed into The Music Room at The Ritz an hour after the word 'Surprise!' had been hollered.

'Yes, maybe, but Nathan works just as hard as you do. *And* he's away from home more often than you are.'

Loyalty drew an indignant expression on Katrina's olive-toned features, but no amount of heartfelt empathy could distract Olivia now that she was on a roll of rigorous self-analysis and recrimination.

'*And* remember those VIP, rarer-than-gold-dust tickets Nathan landed for the opening night of *Waitress* at the Adelphi Theatre last year? How I'd been banging on about going to see the show for ages? But it was Hollie who ended up going as his "plus-one" – his wife's best friend instead of his neglectful wife! And I've lost count of how many "must-have" restaurant reservations we've cancelled.'

'But, Liv—'

'*And* the one about the missed holidays is true. In the seven years since our honeymoon, we've managed a weekend trip to Blackpool to watch Rachel and Denise dance at the Winter Gardens, and a flying visit to Edinburgh to see his brother, Dan, get married. But, if I recall correctly, even on that occasion I insisted we caught the first flight back to London so we could be at our desks at the crack of dawn on Monday morning. In fact—' she loathed the squirm of guilt that wriggled through her abdomen '—I have to confess that I actually popped into the office on the way back from Heathrow.'

'Olivia—'

'*And* Nathan has tried to talk to me about starting a family. That one's true, too. It's just I'm not ready to give up on my career for a pile of dirty laundry and cracked nipples. Miles would almost certainly muscle in on my caseload and he'd ruin everything I've been building these last few years with his attitude of bulldog rather than guide dog! I can't give it all up to swan off and have a family. I just can't!'

'Life doesn't end when you have kids, you know.' Katrina smiled, sweeping her long mahogany hair over her shoulder, her eyes softening at the mention of children.

But Olivia had all the evidence of the impact of motherhood right in front of her eyes. Katrina possessed a first-class honours degree in law from Durham University, Olivia's own college where *she* had only managed a 2:1. In fact, if Olivia were brutally honest with herself – and what better time than now – she would have to admit that Katrina was a better lawyer than she was. Nevertheless, her friend was content with her position as paralegal at Edwards & Co in return for flexible, part-time hours so she could put her expanding family's needs first. *'Date nights, not late nights'* was Katrina's mantra.

'Nathan is ambitious, too,' insisted Katrina, coming to sit next to Olivia on the couch. 'Wasn't he in Paris for a month before his birthday, and isn't he about to start a six-month secondment to Singapore next week?'

Olivia acknowledged the veracity of Katrina's argument but didn't mention the qualifying mitigation that Nathan had pleaded with her to fly over to Paris for a pre-Christmas weekend whilst he was there, all expenses paid. The 'City of Romance' held a special place in both their hearts as the French capital was where they'd honeymooned, and yet despite this, Olivia had been unable to drag herself away from her precious clients, or her volunteer work at the local homeless shelter at their busiest time of the year.

However, she knew it was her refusal to contemplate a sabbatical from work to travel with him to Singapore that had provided Nathan with the impetus to end their marriage – the first step of which she held in her ice-cold hands. She cringed as she recalled the disappointment and hurt that she'd seen etched on his handsome features as he had begged her to start the new year by seizing the opportunity to mend their flagging relationship.

'How can he expect me to ditch my career and go chasing after him halfway around the world?' she pleaded, twirling a strand of her toffee-coloured hair absent-mindedly around her fingertip, but she could see from Katrina's hesitancy that her chosen line of advocacy was weak.

'He only wanted you to take a couple of weeks off, help him to settle in, spend some quality time together – not resign your partnership at Edwards & Co.'

'But my clients depend on me!'

'Your clients would've managed without you, Liv. Miles might be a pain in the butt and profess a different approach to marriage breakdown than you, but he's a good enough lawyer.'

'But I loathe the way Miles and Ralph Carlton do business, racking up the acrimony with twisted truths and spurious allegations.' She brandished the envelope in her hand as evidence. 'Inciting the parties to fight over their pepper pots and garden gnomes so that their legal fees are exorbitant and the money cascades into the lawyers' coffers.'

Olivia knew that the majority of her clients were involuntary refugees from the countless matrimonial conflicts waging across London and the Home Counties. They chose to consult her because she took an interest in their emotional wellbeing as well as the paperwork. She listened to their grievances, smoothed over the thorny issues of contact with the children and dividing the joint assets, offered pragmatic solutions as well as the astute application of legal principles. An involuntary smile twitched her lips as she recalled the ridiculously childish correspondence she had been forced to discuss only yesterday with Martha Grainger, the CEO of an ethical jewellery company, when Ralph's client, Martha's ex-husband, had demanded shared access to their allotment of chickens.

Would she and Nathan descend into the quagmire of such pettiness?

Her emotions crashed again. It was the new year, a time for looking forward and making resolutions, and she was getting divorced! All the sadness, the verbal spats, the possessiveness, the obstructiveness and the squabbling that she dealt with on a daily basis would be lurking for her own indulgence as the dissolution of her marriage travelled through the divorce court.

Then an added horror poked its nose above the parapet. Was Nathan involved with someone else? She shoved that pernicious thought deep into the crevices of her mind. If Nathan was anything at all, he was an honest and straightforward guy, favouring the communication of difficult issues in a balanced, non-confrontational way, but he had been pushing against an immoveable concrete barrier the previous year when wanting to talk seriously about their future. Whenever they were at home together in their pristine apartment overlooking the River Thames, she was usually so exhausted that any conversation beyond what was for dinner was too taxing to contemplate. No, she knew Nathan would not be dating anyone else.

There would be no vitriol or salacious accusations for the Fitzgeralds. Whilst she was mortified at the way the divorce papers had been delivered, and revolted at his choice of legal representative, after the initial shock and disbelief had dissipated, she had to admit the commencement of the divorce process had not come as a surprise. If there was ever a good time to end a marriage, then this was it: a new year, a fresh start, *and* whilst Nathan was away in Singapore – leaving her alone in London to sort out their apartment without the added awkwardness of living together under the same roof.

A mantle of loneliness draped its folds around her body and settled heavily across her shoulders. The delivery of that simple brown envelope meant her destiny was now shrouded in a veil of ambiguity.

'You're due loads of leave, Liv. Why don't you take a trip to see your parents in Yorkshire?'

'I can't go to Yorkshire, Kat.'

Olivia pushed herself out of the depths of the sofa, straightened her charcoal-grey pencil skirt and strode over to her desk. She shoved the offending documents into her bottom drawer and turned to look out of the window. From the twelfth floor, the view over the angular rooftops of the City of London was awe-inspiring but one which she seldom noticed, much less appreciated. A shaft of early January sunshine had the audacity to bathe the room with its wintry light, and she managed a brittle smile at the irony – surely there should be a cacophonous thunderstorm raging and rain lashing against the windowpanes?

Except this wasn't a nightmare, or a horror film; it was reality and she had to deal with it.

'I suppose I'd better inform Henry of my impending singlehood.'

Chapter 2

'I'm extremely saddened to hear your news, Olivia. Nathan is not only an intelligent and competent corporate lawyer but a decent, considerate man. Jean and I were delighted when we heard he was being promoted to Lead Counsel at Delmatrix Pharmaceuticals at their Singapore office. You youngsters today have so many opportunities.'

Olivia squirmed a little under the steely pewter gaze of Henry Edwards, the senior partner of Edwards & Co, feeling dwarfed by the gravity of the situation she found herself in, and the wing-backed leather chair facing his gargantuan desk that wouldn't have looked out of place in a Gentleman's Club. However, after being his business partner for almost ten years, she knew whatever pearls of wisdom he was about to dispense, they would be judiciously selected and carefully delivered.

'Olivia, it's time I spoke frankly with you. Jean and I are worried about your health. It's apparent to even the most casual of onlookers that you're not sleeping well. And when did you last enjoy a decent meal – and I do *not* mean those psychedelic cocktails that you, Hollie and Matteo devour with such gusto? You need to take a break from the legal grindstone, especially after this life-changing event.'

'Henry, I—'

'No, please, just listen.'

Henry ran his arthritic fingers through his thick, ash-coloured hair, for the first time displaying a hint of reticence, clearly somewhat uncomfortable with treading the line between showing concern for his younger partner's obsessive work patterns and invading her privacy.

'I know you're not going to like me saying this, but I miss the spirited, rosy-cheeked woman of twenty-nine I met ten years ago; eager, ambitious, brimming with energy and enthusiasm for the law. It hurts me to see how much that young lawyer has transformed into the frazzled, exhausted, stressed-out person who sits before me now and I truly regret not noticing sooner.'

'Henry, I'm not—'

'Please, Olivia, hear me out. For the first time, Jean and I have made a few New Year's resolutions and if all goes according to plan, this time next year we'll be boarding a luxury liner for a round-the-world cruise. Life is short, and every day becomes more precious as the age of seventy is waiting in the wings to ambush us. Jean deserves the indulgence of her long-held dream, and to that end I've reserved a Princess Grill Stateroom on the *Queen Elizabeth*.'

Olivia smiled. She was delighted that Jean had got her own way at last. She knew the division of labour in the Edwards marriage was considered old-fashioned; Jean, giving up her career as a midwife to devote her gentle-but-firm skills to steering their two beloved daughters through life's challenges – both of whom had chosen to follow their mother's footsteps into medicine – whilst Henry performed the role of breadwinner and doting father. She was about to congratulate him on his decision, but Henry had already launched into the next part of his submission.

'I struggled to recall the precise nature of the clause in our partnership agreement pertaining to the taking of sabbaticals, so I took the liberty of checking. After ten years of service, all

Edwards & Co partners, including you, Olivia my dear, qualify for a ten-month sabbatical at half their monthly drawings.'

'I qualify? I thought it was you and Jean who were planning to take the world by storm?'

The switch in focus caused a twist of anxiety to whip through Olivia's veins and she dug her fingernails into her palms to prevent herself from reaching up to fiddle with an escaped tendril of hair to alleviate the unease that had settled in her gut. What was going on? She didn't have to wait long to find out.

'Take a break, Olivia. Spend some time away from the crazy, soul-destroying world of divorce and relationship breakdown, of clients squabbling over meaningless possessions, of financial skul-duggery and underhand espionage. Do you know, I even heard the other day that a lawyer had plundered the depths of decency by removing the dustbin from a spouse's back garden? I mean, what is the legal profession coming to? How you and Katrina remain sane is a constant worry to Lewis, James and I.'

Henry expelled a sigh filled with incredulity, and not a little relief, that his chosen legal specialism was commercial property litigation and tax management and not the cut-and-thrust of verbal jousting prevalent in the field of matrimonial litigation. However, his words had sent Olivia's thoughts reeling and it took her a few seconds to catch up, her throat dry when she spoke.

'Henry, I really can't take time off at the moment …'

'I'm not saying you won't be missed, or that we don't appreciate how valuable your contribution is to our practice. You listen to your clients, Olivia, really listen. You empathise with their circum-stances, and somehow you manage to instil in them the belief that their case is your only priority. Indeed, since you joined us, the Family Law department has flourished beyond anything we could have hoped to achieve. Clients, particularly women, have flocked to your office, but the fact that divorce has become so increasingly popular dismays me. Why don't couples stay together nowadays? No, you don't have to answer that!'

Henry settled back into his captain's chair, steepled his fingers and tapped them on his lower lip, eyeing Olivia carefully.

'But I can also see that the pressure of an ever-expanding caseload has sapped your energy and dulled that initial sparkle. And now, it seems, it has destroyed your marriage. Is it contagious, this incessant search for the elusive prize of contentment?'

'I love what I do, Henry …'

'Only too obvious, Olivia my dear, as I understand you already struggle to delegate even the most straightforward of cases to Miles, even though he is a very competent practitioner.'

Olivia clenched her jaw in a futile attempt to prevent Henry from reading the doubt she knew was written boldly across her expression. She had never been first in line when they were handing out acting accolades – learning how to hide her emotions was still a work-in-progress, and it was one of the few essential skills required to be a first-rate lawyer that she had trouble mastering.

'Oh, I know that you and Miles have conflicting views on how you conduct your cases, but I also know that he is eager to prove himself, to carve out his own niche in the department – the law had always possessed a vociferous appetite for the naïve but ambitious young lawyer seeking to make his mark – and I'm not entirely unsympathetic to his desire to change the firm's approach to our matrimonial cases.'

Like many lawyers, Olivia relished sharpening her advocacy and negotiation skills against her legal adversaries, but never to the detriment of her clients' interests. It had always been her aim to assist her clients in a more holistic way, by offering accurate legal advice coupled with a dose of therapy, a cordial attitude to negotiations and a conciliatory approach. Of course, she was going to be better briefed than most on the up-to-date case law in her field because her long-time friend Rachel Denton, who had recently gained a Professorship in Family Law at UCL, made sure of that.

'I can't take a sabbatical, Henry, if that's what you are suggesting. My clients rely on me to be here for them and I can't let them down.'

'They can easily transfer their matters to Miles, and I dare say that Lewis will do his bit.'

Olivia's mind immediately flicked to her fellow partner Lewis Jackson's office, where the windowsill was piled high with carelessly discarded bottles of single malt whisky – gifts from grateful clients as tokens of appreciation for the personal injury compensation he had won on their behalf. Even James Carter, who handled their criminal defence work, had been known to receive a bottle or two of Cognac, although its provenance probably didn't bear close scrutiny. On the other hand, Olivia's office sported a plethora of flower-bedecked cards from clients whose shattered lives she had been a reluctant but necessary part of, and whom could not bring themselves to *thank* her for her involvement in such an interlude of pain.

'Katrina will be a more than competent adviser, too. And what an opportune time to take a break having passed that dubious milestone that I saw reported in December's issue of the *Law Society Gazette.*'

Olivia gulped as her predicament rushed at her like a runaway express train and an involuntary shudder ran the length of her spine as she realised her own marriage would now be joining that running total of five hundred marriage dissolutions. And Henry was wrong – if ever there was a time to take a break from the treadmill of corporate life, this was most certainly *not* it! She needed the distraction.

'But, Henry, I really can't contemplate …'

She heard him inhale a long breath, splaying his liver-spotted hands across his desk blotter, clearly preparing himself for what he had to deliver next and her heart crashed against her ribcage, causing spasms of trepidation to ricochet around her body.

'It's a timely solution, Olivia. This is a difficult subject for me to discuss, but the firm's income has tumbled considerably over the last year or so. All this ruddy uncertainty has bitten us all hard. To be honest, a 50 per cent reduction in your drawings would ease the burden on our Office Account expenditure.'

Olivia didn't know what she had expected Henry to say, but it wasn't that. Trepidation swiftly morphed into full-blown panic – if she'd thought her discussion with Henry about her divorce was going to be difficult, this conversation had climbed to a whole new level and she needed to fight her corner.

'Henry, I realise the way I conduct my cases means there are fewer contested trials, and therefore there are not as many lucrative invoices at the end. But even so, the effects of a countrywide economic downturn can't be laid at my office door!'

'Of course not, and I wasn't implying that, far from it. I'm actually very troubled by the breakdown of your marriage, Olivia, and the fact that your intensive work ethic may have in some way contributed to the sad state of affairs. No more ideal a couple have I come across than you and Nathan, and Jean agrees with me. You are so right for one another. If I'd been a betting man, I would have placed a month's salary on you and Nathan being in the lucky half of the UK marriages that don't end in divorce.'

'Me neither, Henry, but it's happened, and I have to deal with it.'

A surge of sorrow spread through Olivia's chest when she saw the genuine sadness reflected in Henry's eyes, but she also saw a steely determination to deliver his next, much more personal bulletin of truth and she wondered what he would think if she jumped out of her seat and ran back to her office.

'I'm sorry, Ms Hamilton, that cool, calm exterior doesn't fool me. I know you're devastated by this turn of events, and who wouldn't be? You crouch in that chair like a starved waif, with sunken eyes and a blanched complexion, not a highly skilled, respected professional. The law is a demanding mistress; many a lawyer has become addicted to the daily buzz delivered by the joust of advocacy, sucked into the euphoria of winning cases, obsessed with that spurt of adrenaline delivered to their veins as they spar with the likes of Ralph Carlton. They're addicted to arguing the toss with their equally eloquent opponents, then adjourning to the pub to drink themselves delirious in order to douse their rampant stress levels.'

Olivia opened her mouth to argue, to tell Henry he was wrong, but, unusually, words failed her and she was relieved when the next part of his soliloquy was more softly delivered.

'I can't force *you* to invoke the sabbatical clause in our partnership agreement, but *I* fully intend to. I hereby give you notice that from the first of January next year, Jean and I will set sail from Southampton bound for Gibraltar; we will send regular postcards for the office noticeboard to remind everyone that there's a great big world out there waiting to be explored! I truly hope that you'll grasp this opportunity to take stock, Olivia, to answer some of life's questions before you celebrate your fortieth birthday in December, so you *must* act now! If you agree to begin your sabbatical on the first of February, ten months—'

'Ten months!'

'Ten months would bring you back into the Edwards & Co fold on the first of December – two weeks before your milestone celebration – hopefully with a healthier, more balanced view of the world, with lessons learned and a readiness to move forward.'

'No way, I can't do it, Henry! What on earth will I do for ten months?'

The mere thought of spending all that time either holed up in her empty flat, alone, untangling her life from Nathan's whilst he was in Singapore, or meandering aimlessly between her parents in Yorkshire and Hollie's parents down in Cornwall sent shivers of dread through her body. Tears smarted at her eyes, but she gritted her teeth because Henry was continuing to press his case.

'Travel. Reconnect with those neglected friends. Write your

autobiography. Take up ballroom dancing with Rachel. Make a start on that "bucket list" you and Katrina are always talking about. Just take some time out to refocus on *you*.'

'Thanks, Henry, and here was I thinking I was indispensable!'

Acknowledgements

Firstly, I'd like to say a huge thank-you to my wonderful editor Katie Seaman who has helped to make Katie Campbell's story sparkle. Also, I want to thank my family and friends who performed the selfless task of taste-testing the recipes used in Katie's Cornish Kitchen – even the Marmite and peppermint cupcakes! I won't tell you what they thought of those!

Finally, a massive thank-you has to go to you, the readers, for choosing to spend time at Katie's Cornish Kitchen in Perrinby. I hope you've had fun!

Dear Reader,

Thank you so much for taking the time to read this book – we hope you enjoyed it! If you did, we'd be so appreciative if you left a review.

Here at HQ Digital we are dedicated to publishing fiction that will keep you turning the pages into the early hours. We publish a variety of genres, from heartwarming romance, to thrilling crime and sweeping historical fiction.

To find out more about our books, enter competitions and discover exclusive content, please join our community of readers by following us at:

🐦 *@HQDigitalUK*

f *facebook.com/HQDigitalUK*

Are you a budding writer?
We're also looking for authors to join the HQ Digital family!
Please submit your manuscript to:

HQDigital@harpercollins.co.uk.

Hope to hear from you soon!

ONE PLACE. MANY STORIES

If you enjoyed *A Year of Chasing Love*, then why not try another delightfully uplifting romance from HQ Digital?

ONE PLACE. MANY STORIES

Bold, innovative and
empowering publishing.

FOLLOW US ON:

@HQStories